Also by William Eastlake

Go in Beauty
The Bronc People
Portrait of the Artist with Twenty-Six Horses
Castle Keep
The Bamboo Bed

William Eastlake

DANCERS IN THE SCALP HOUSE

A Richard Seaver Book
The Viking Press
New York

To Marilyn

Copyright © 1972, 1973, 1974, 1975 by William Eastlake

All rights reserved
A Richard Seaver Book/The Viking Press
First published in 1975 by The Viking Press, Inc.
625 Madison Avenue, New York, N.Y. 10022
Published simultaneously in Canada by
The Macmillan Company of Canada Limited
Printed in U.S.A.

Library of Congress Cataloging in Publication Data
Eastlake, William.
       Dancers in the scalp house.
       "A Richard Seaver book."
       I. Title.
PZ4.E133Dan [PS3555.A7]   813'.5'4   75-16135
ISBN 0-670-25467-3

1

The eagle Sun was named Sun by the Indians because each day their final eagle, doomed by the dam, circled this part of the Navajo Nation in northern New Mexico like the clock of sun. Sun, a grave and golden eagle-stream of light, sailed without movement, as though propelled by some eternity, to orbit, to circumnavigate, this moon of earth, to relight upon his aerie from which he had risen. And so Sun would sit with the same God dignity and decorous finality with which he had emerged—then once more without seeming volition ride the crest of an updraft above Indian Country on six-foot wings to settle again on his throne-aerie in awful splendor, admonitory, serene—regal and doomed. I have risen.

Sun had risen and surveyed and remarked a land in a beginning flood caused by the dam. A new ocean sea that doomed not only the eagle Sun and the land but a people, a history, a place. A nation—the Checkerboard Clan. A wondrous and wondering place—the Painted Bird, the Portales, and the Wild Horse mesas, all shot with many-colored fire now in the gong of New Mexico sun. Remarked too the hogans, dome beehive-shaped igloos of mud and log houses such as the Learning Hogan, where a white woman dwelt hard by the garden of Sings In Pretty Places, and along the great Chiwilly Arroyo, thick with the green flags of willow and chamisal. The eagle Sun had remarked too the monuments that would not fall to the new ocean sea—the Four Corners Power Plant that would puff poison black on the new shore, and the Playboy sign that would gyrate a naked neon lady sixty feet high, twirling a lasso on the new beach over a new New Mexico, the olden lost and unremarked under the soon-to-be ocean sea.

Soon to be, excepting the devils were out. The cunning savage was concocting a plot against the Great White Father. The ungrateful red man was going to bite the hand that fed the golden ass. The eagle Sun had just, heavy and smooth, glided over the Scalp House, a quiet structure of petrified wood and log and mud belonging to the earth and sometimes occupied by Mary-Forge and always by William William.

William William, who was part Indian, part writer, part rancher, lived on this high cloud-coiffed ranch called the Scalp House, so high you could see all the way to eternity and Old Mexico, and so alone you could hear yourself breathe. The sky a huge gay morning fire, then at the hiatus of noon a distant perfect space, bright and calm and empty. You wait for the implosion of six o'clock when all the gaudy sky, all the greens and yellows and obscene reds, become a yell, a sharp scream of sun before it goes under and out, before the so-damning darkness and before the dazzle of morning, again lighting quiet blue fires in the desert.

But William was thinking and not writing, not yet, thinking about the big white reservation that surrounds the Navajo Nation. "Look and see, look and see, look and see what you are doing to us, building a government dam and burying us under water because we will not flee."

"It seems to me," Mary-Forge said, "you can do all that, you can say 'Look and see, look and see' without quitting life, without..."

"Hurting you?"

"Crippling yourself."

Mary-Forge with that orange hair such as you might see on a fetish stick, hair that frizzled above a scarred but beautiful face. The hair from her progenitors, and the scars within from all. Mary-Forge had quit the States and come back to Indian Country, where the Indians constructed a Learning Hogan to replace the government factory school that taught nothing of life but only of white things.

"You escaped the States, the big white reservation," William said. "Ran..."

"But toward something," she said.

The light shifted, so that in front of the ramada on which Mary-Forge and William sat, the wide blue-green sea calm of desert became red and silhouetted with spiked saguaro and sharp cactus, rife and inimical.

"And so you came to save the world. What's left of it."

"Yes," she said. "What's left of it."

Mary-Forge's parents had left their ranch on the edge of Indian Country several years ago, when Mary-Forge was eighteen. The land would not pay. They both had gotten jobs in a factory in Gallup. Why does the land have to pay? Mary-Forge had known the Indians well when her parents were chasing the cattle, trying to make the land pay. When her parents took off for a factory Mary-Forge had to take off too, then she came back and took over the small bunch of cattle that were left and opened a school that did not pay either. Because this land had shaped Mary-Forge as land will, as Indian Country must, after the battle of the city, which the city won as the city will, "as the city must," she returned to her love and life and fortune of beauty. Because she's queer for the land, the whites said. Indians, they said.

"Beauty," she said. "Survival," she said, "and life." "And you," Mary-Forge said.

"Thank you," he said and kissed her.

"Because," Mary-Forge said, "if I am, if a white woman is, on the land they will not bury us."

"You don't think so."

"No."

William was silent and then he said, "I cannot leave because there is absolutely no place to go. The white people have always made the Indian leave, move on. Now there is no place to go."

"I have come home, too," Mary-Forge said. "We will not leave."

"No, we will never leave," he said. "There is no place to go."

And William thinking there is no place for me to go, but she could go back to the whites from where she came. When they finish the dam and flood the country, she could float a boat on the new sea and catch fish and get drunk while watching the baseball game on television. No, her problem is she wants to save the earth. She wants to save the Indians. To hell with everyone who wants to save the Indians! God damn her! He would tell her to get lost.

"You could get—"

"Keep quiet," she said.

"Did you hear something?"

"I heard you thinking."

"It's not too late for you."

"Yes, it is," she said. "Too damn late. But we're going to make it," she said.

"You could—"

"Damn you, Billy," she said. "We can blow it up."

"The Four Corners Smoke Plant?"

"The dam."

"During the dedication ceremonies?"

"Yes."

"But what are we going to do now?"

"Make love," she said.

And so at the Scalp House they made love on the Navajo bed, big and hot and wild there on the Navajo blanket bed, but then again and after a gentle and sweet resting they were dancing, dancing around and between the giant kachinas and over the myriad Navajo rugs, and beneath the pictures of all the dignity of the Indian nations, not only the faded daguerreotypes of Yellow Knife and Standing Bear, the yellowing and fading history of a world, but the primitive paintings too of George Catlin, the paint thrown on a rough canvas with a spatula and palette knife, so that all the phantom painted people were crude and alive as they danced naked and crude and alive. They danced above the coyotes that crowded beneath the floor and danced around the dull varnished-log living room and petrified-log fireplace, past and over and through the Navajo rugs that were written in the vegetable dyes of beauty from all parts of the Navajo Nation. Around the pots, too, from Zuni and Acoma, and other pots dug up not far from the Scalp House that were made before the Grecian wars by the Indian people, when Sparta and Athens were mere trading posts and before Greek met Greek—danced by the medicine bundles that covered the walls along with the pictures of Chochise, Crazy Horse, Red Cloud, and the Oglala Sioux.

"Come on," she said, "love with me and I will tell you the next exciting adventure of Mary-Forge. More, my love."

"Not now."

"Then write."

"Not now."

"Of course not, Billy. Hold me tight."

And so they went into a very still and deep quietude, enfolded in the bodies of each other and breathing well—consummate, free, and watched down on from the walls by the ancient gods and Cochise, Red Cloud, Crazy Horse, the Oglala Sioux. None disapproved. No one moved. Not a hair. Not a feather. Nothing. Silence.

Between making love they talked about the dam, the Atlas Dam, the great dam the government was building that would back up all that water and bury all the land, a whole country. The Navajo Checkerboard Clan. A nation. A people. Every place and every person a people knew. All buried under the new ocean.

And so between making love they talked about everything but the project, the deadly project. The project was what Thomas Charles—Tom Charlie—the Indian who went to the University of New Mexico, was working on. The project was a secret even among themselves at the time. Still, every other way to destroy the dam had been worked on and there was no solution. Mary-Forge figured it would take 300,000 tons of dynamite to blow up the dam, given the amount of concrete and steel already in place. "That's more dynamite than there is in New Mexico. Texas even."

"I'm not sure about Texas," William said.

When Thomas Charles went to the university they figured it was a waste of time. Now there was the project. What is the project? You wouldn't believe it. People will believe anything about Indians. You will believe anything but this. Was the project a success? We're coming to that. Why didn't you talk about it? We did later. When it was too late? Yes. Too late to stop it? Yes, when a project is started it takes over. It has a life. It is alive. And you say Thomas Charles—Tom Charlie—could carry the device in a suitcase? Not then. Later. And in the meantime you shot down helicopters? Yes, listen. Then after the helicopters what did you do for an encore?

Listen.

But a man came to the door, a Mr. Breckenridge he called himself, and said he had an eviction notice. He said he had "done been deputized and that soon the water from the dam would be up to their ass" and that is what Mary-Forge and William threw him out on, and he hollered back to them, "Listen to that up there. Them is heeleocopters. It's probably Mr. Rhodes from the FB and I, if it ain't Mr. Osmun protecting his goddamn sheep. Listen to me! Get out while you can!"

Listen.

2

And one hour later in the Navajo Learning Hogan the teacher Mary-Forge said above the noise of the helicopter to the Indians sprawled on Navajo rugs: "Man without a sure idea of himself and the purpose of his life cannot live and would sooner destroy himself than remain on earth."

"What does that mean?" Three Shoes said.

"Mary-Forge, I suppose," the Medicine Man said, "is accounting for the high suicide rate among Navajo. Since the white man invaded the Navajo Nation many Navajo see no hope or purpose to life."

"What else is new?" Hosteen Begay said.

"The eagle is being killed off," Mary-Forge said.

"So are we, by the dam that will flood us."

"First things first," Mary-Forge said. "First the sheep ranchers are killing the eagles by shooting them from helicopters."

"We know that. What do we do?"

"We get out of this school and find the people who are killing the eagle."

Mary-Forge was a good surprise to the Indians. A young white woman sure of herself and with a purpose in life, such as Mary-Forge, had been unknown to the Navajo. Mary-Forge had large wide-apart almond-shaped eyes, high full cheekbones, cocky let-us-all-give-thanks tipsy breasts, and good brains. Mary-Forge did not fight for the Indians but alongside the Indians. High on her right cheekbone Mary-Forge had a jagged two-inch scar caused by a stomping she got on the floor of the High Point Bar in Gallup from high-heeled cowboy boots belonging to a sheep rancher from the Twin Slash Heart Ranch.

A helicopter had just flown over. The helicopter came to kill eagles. The only time the Indians ever saw or felt a helicopter on the red reservation was when the white ranchers came to kill eagles. Eagles killed sheep, the ranchers said, and several cases have been known, they said, where white babies have been plucked from playpens and dropped in the ocean. They said.

You could hear plain the whack-whack-whack of the huge rotor blades of the copter in the red schoolhouse. The yellow and blue copter was being flown by a flat-faced, doctor-serious white sheep rancher named Ira Osmun, who believed in conservation through predator control. Eagles were fine birds, but the sheep must be protected. Babies, too.

"Mr. Osmun," Wilson Drago, the shotgun-bearing sado-child-appearing copilot, asked, "have the eagles got any white babies lately?"

"No."

"Then?"

"Because we are exercising predator control."

"When was the last white baby snatched by eagles and dropped into the ocean?"

"Not eagles, Drago, eagle; it only takes one. As long as there is one eagle there is always the possibility of your losing your child."

"I haven't any child."

"If you did."

"But I haven't."

"Someone does."

"No white in the area does."

"If they did, there would be the possibility of their losing them."

"No one can say nay to that," Wilson Drago said. "When was the last time a child was snatched?"

"It must have been a long time ago."

"Before living memory?"

"Yes, even then, Drago, I believe the stories to be apocryphal."

"What's that mean?"

"Lies."

"Then why are we shooting the eagles?"

"Because city people don't care about sheep. City people care about babies. You tell the people in Albuquerque that there's an outside chance, any chance, that their baby will be snatched up and the possibility that it will be dropped in the ocean, kerplunk, and they will let you kill eagles."

"How far is the ocean?"

"People don't care how far the ocean is; they care about their babies."

"True."

"It's that simple."

"When was the last lamb that was snatched up?"

"Yesterday."

"That's serious."

"You better believe it, Drago."

"Why are we hovering over this red hogan?"

"Because before we kill an eagle we got to make sure what Mary-Forge is up to."

"What was she up to last time you heard?"

"Shooting down helicopters."

"All by herself?"

"It only takes one shot."

"You know, I bet that's right."

"You better believe it, Drago."

"Is this where she lives?"

"No—this is the little red schoolhouse she uses to get the Indians to attack the whites."

"What happened to your other copilots?"

"They got scared and quit."

"The last one?"

"Scared and quit."

"Just because of one woman?"

"Yes. You're not scared of a woman, are you, Drago?"

"No, I mean, yes."

"Which is it, yes or no?"

"Yes," Wilson Drago said.

Below, in the red hogan which was shaped like a beehive with a hole on top for the smoke to come out, the Indians and Mary-Forge were getting ready to die on the spot.

"I'm not getting ready to die on the spot," Bull Who Looks Up said.

"You want to save the eagles, don't you?" Mary-Forge said.

"Let me think about that," Hosteen Tzo said.

"Pass me the gun," Mary-Forge said.

Hosteen Tzo allowed his very black hair to hide his wide spatulate face so you could not see him. Kills The Enemy pulled his hair straight back and tied it in a knot, so he defied everyone to look at him, and he looked straight back. Chee Sinoginee always appeared pleased with himself—a man who had just told himself a good story at the expense of no one. More Turquoise had a long, unpronounceable Indian name that came out More Turquoise Than Hope, but he bore up to it well. Hosteen Begay, a pure Navajo, had the round face and eyes and mustache going down the sides of his mouth of an almost-pure Chinese. Tom Yazzie, like his brother (who was called Tom Yazzie's Brother) was tall, very slim, with a strong Mayan face and two braids of coal-black hair that almost touched his ass. His girl friend, Nice Hands' Sister, who looked very nice herself, braided Tom Yazzie's hair, which made him happy. Bull Who Looks Up said he himself looked like the famous Crazy Horse, which was a good strong tough Indian face. The Indian named Looks Important After A Rain also looked important before a rain. He looked important. Lucy-Lucy looked insouciant; her nose turned up a bit and her chin was pointed. The Medicine Man, named When Someone Dies He Is Remembered, had a hacked-out hatchet face that dangled with turquoise, and a neck and chin bangled with bright silver, so that he appeared a dignified walking small fortune. All the other Indians in the smoking hogan could not be seen too well now. Outside in the light of New Mexico, dressed in Levis, they appeared cowboys who were Indians.

Excepting Tom Charlie, whom the other people—the white people—called Thomas Charles. Tom Charlie had lived too many years with the whites, so that he looked like two people. He would not tell the white people who he was. He would not tell the red people who he was. He could not tell himself who he was. He did not know. It showed in his face. The man who did not know who he was. The man who fought with himself.

"I said pass me the gun," Mary-Forge said.

Tom Charlie passed Mary-Forge the gun.

Now from above in the copter the beehive-shaped hogan below looked like a gun turret, a small fort defending the perimeter of Indian Country.

"Someone should ask Mary-Forge," Drago said, " 'What is a nice person like you doing shooting down helicopters?' "

"It's as simple as this, Drago. You are for progress or against progress. Mary-Forge claims that progress is the enemy of progress."

"What's that mean?"

"That gadgets are not progress, that gadgets are only futile and dangerous toys against the anguish and the travail of the human heart."

"What's that mean?"

"I don't know, Drago. I only know that she used that kind of language even before she was put in jail."

"For what?"

"Obstructing justice."

"Is there justice, Mr. Osmun?"

"No. But they put her in jail anyway for lying down in front of a caterpillar tractor on its way to build the dam."

"What if the tractor ran over her?"

"Then we wouldn't be being shot at now, Drago."

"There would be peace on earth."

"Maybe, Drago. Anyway, she tears down big highway signs, talks about blowing up power plants that smoke, and fights progress in general."

"In where?"

"In general, Drago. Progress, she says, is the enemy of progress. But the FBI is wise to her. Stewart Montalban Rhodes is on her tail."

"You mean Stew Rhodes from Socorro? The idiot?"

"If you can't respect the man, Drago, respect the uniform."

"I will try, Mr. Osmun. Will the FBI help us now?"

"No, we are on our own this time, Drago. Mary-Forge is an interesting problem," Ira Osmun said—shouted above the whack-whack-whack of the rotors.

"Every woman is."

"But every woman doesn't end up defending the Indian land and living with the Indians, with the eagles."

"What causes that?"

"We believe the Indians and the eagles become their surrogate children."

"What?"

"That they become a substitute for life."

"Oh? Why do you hate me?"

"What?"

"Why do you use such big words?"

"I'm sorry, Drago. Do you see any eagles?"

"No, but I see a gun."

"Where?"

"Coming out of the top of the hogan."

"Let Mary-Forge fire first."

"Why?"

"To establish a point of law. Then it's not between her eagles and my sheep."

"It becomes your ass or hers."

"Yes."

"But it could be my life."

"I've considered that, Drago."

"Thank you," Wilson Drago said. "Thank you very much."

Sun, the golden eagle that was very carefully watching the two white people who lived in the giant bird that went whack-whack-whack, was ready.

Today would be the day of death for Sun. His mate had been killed two days before. Without her the eaglets in the woven-of-yucca high basket nest would die. Today would be the day of death for Sun because, without a sure idea of himself, without purpose in life, an eagle would sooner destroy himself than remain on earth. The last day of Sun.

"Because," Mary-Forge said, taking the weapon and jerking in a shell, "because I know, even though the Indians and we and the eagle, even though we have no chance ever, we can go through the motions of courage, compassion, and concern. Because we are Sun and alive too. Because, although the present doesn't like us

14

much, the future will honor us and give us credit for our failures. Hello, Sun."

"Stop talking and aim carefully," the Medicine Man said.

"Did I say something?"

"You made a speech."

"I'm sorry," Mary-Forge said.

"Aim carefully."

Mary-Forge was standing on the wide shoulders of the Indian named Looks Important After A Rain. All the other Indians who belonged in the Learning Hogan stood around and below her in the dim and alive dust, watching Mary-Forge revolve like a gun turret with her lever-operated Marlin 30-30 pointing out of the smoke hatch high up on the slow-turning and hard shoulders of Looks Important After A Rain.

"Why don't you shoot?" Hosteen Tzo said. He almost whispered it, as though the great noise of the copter did not exist.

"The thing keeps bobbling," Mary-Forge shouted down to the Indians.

Looking through the gun sights, she had to go up and down, up and down, to try to get a shot. She did not want to hit the cowboys. It would be good enough to hit the engine or the rotor blades. Why not hit the cowboys? Because there are always more cowboys. There are not many eagles left on the planet earth, there are several million cowboys. There are more cowboys than there are Indians. That's for sure. But what is important now is that if we give one eagle for one cowboy, soon all the eagles will have disappeared from the earth and cowboys will be standing in your bed. No, the helicopter is scarce. They will not give one helicopter for one eagle. A helicopter costs too much money. How much? A quarter of a million dollars, I bet. Hit them where their heart is. Hit them right in their helicopter.

But it danced. Now Mary-Forge noticed that, although it was dancing, it was going up and down with a rhythm. The thing to do is wait until it hits bottom and then follow it up. She did and fired off a shot.

"Good girl," the Medicine Man said.

"That was close," Ira Osmun said to his shotgun, Wilson Drago. "Now that we know where Mary-Forge is, we can chase the eagle."

"I hear," Drago said, "that William William is behind this."

"William William is behind everything, Drago. He writes."

"Why?"

"We don't know."

"Does the FBI know this?"

"Yes."

"What are they doing about it?"

"Nothing. Not now. Tomorrow you wait and see."

"Does the FBI know that their Stewart Montalban Rhodes is Stew Rhodes?"

"I believe so, Drago. Drago, if you can't respect the uniform, look for the man."

Ira Osmun allowed the chopper to spurt up and away, to tilt off at a weird angle, so that it clawed its way sideways like a crab that flew, a piece of junk, of tin and chrome and gaudy paint, alien and obscene in the perfect pure blue New Mexican sky, an intruder in the path of sun. Now the chopper clawed its way to the aerie of Sun.

The eagle had watched it all happen. Sun had watched it happen many times now. Two days ago when they killed his mate was the last time. Sun looked down at his golden-eagle chicks. The eaglets were absolute white—they would remain white and vulnerable for several months until the new feathers. But there was no more time. Sun watched the huge man junk bird clawing its way down the long valley that led to Mount Taylor. His home; his home, and above all the homes of the Indians.

Like the Indians, the ancestors of Sun had one time roamed a virgin continent abloom with the glory of life, alive with fresh flashing streams, a smogless sky, all the world a sweet poem of life where all was beginning. Nothing ever ended. Now it was all ending. The eagle, Sun, did not prepare to defend himself. He would not defend himself. There was nothing now to defend. The last hour of Sun.

"Catch me," Mary-Forge shouted from the top of the hogan, and jumped. When she was caught by More Turquoise she continued to shout, as the noise of the chopper was still there. "They've taken off for Mount Taylor to kill Sun. We've got to get on our horses and get our asses over there."

"Why?"

"To save Sun," Mary-Forge shouted. "Sun is the last eagle left in the county."

"But this is not a movie," the Medicine Man said. "We don't have to get on horses and gallop across the prairie. We can get in my pickup and drive there—quietly."

"On the road it will take two hours," Mary-Forge said. "And we'll need horses when we get there, to follow the chopper."

Outside they slammed the saddles on the amazed Indian ponies, then threw themselves on and fled down the canyon, a stream of dust and light, a commingling of vivid flash and twirl, so when the horses disappeared into the cottonwoods you held your breath until the phantoms, the abrupt magic of motion, appeared again on the Cabrillo draw.

"Come on now, baby," Mary-Forge whispered to her horse, Poco Mas. "Come on now, baby, move good. Be good to me, baby, move good. Move good, baby. Move good. You can take that fence, baby. Take it! Good boy, baby. Good boy, Poco. Good boy. Tom Charlie understands. He has taken a day off from the project. Look at him go. He's pulling ahead of us; are you going to let him get away with that, Poco?" Poco did not let the horse of Tom Charlie stay ahead but passed him quickly, with Mary-

Forge swinging her gun high and Tom Charlie gesturing with his gun at the tin bird that crabbed across the sky.

"You see, Drago," Ira Osmun shouted to Wilson Drago, "we are the villains of the piece."

"What?"

"The bad guys."

"It's pretty hard to think of yourself as the bad guy, Mr. Osmun."

"Well, we are."

"Who are the good guys?"

"Mary-Forge."

"Screw me."

"No, Mary-Forge wouldn't do that because you're a bad guy. Because you kill eagles. People who never saw an eagle, never will see an eagle, never want to see an eagle, want eagles all over the place. Except the poor. The poor want sheep to eat. Did you ever hear of a poor person complaining about the lack of eagles? Did you ever hear a poor person complain about a dam that brings them money money money? There is an outfit of rich gentlemen called the Sierra Club. They egg on Indian-lovers like Mary-Forge to kill ranchers and blow up dams."

"Why?"

"Because the Sierra Club ladies and gentlemen have nothing else to do."

"You think Mary-Forge actually has sex with the Indians?"

"Why else would she be on the reservation?"

"I never thought about that."

"Think about it."

"I guess you're right."

"Drago, what do you think about?"

"I don't think about eagles."

"What do you think about?"

"Ordinarily?"

"Yes."

"Like when I'm drinking?"

"Yes."

"Religion."

"Good, Drago, I like to hear you say that. Good. What religion?"

"They are all good. I guess Billy Graham is the best."

"Yes, if you're stupid."

"What?"

"Nothing, Drago. Keep your eye peeled for the eagle."

"You said I was stupid."

"I may have said the Sierra Club was stupid."

"Did you?"

"No, how could you be stupid and be that rich?"

"Why are they queer for eagles then?"

"The Sierra Club is for anything that is getting scarce. Land buried by dams. Indians, eagles, anything. Mary-Forge is against natural evolution, too."

"What's natural evolution mean?"

"When something is finished it's finished, forget it. We got a new evolution, the machine, this copter, a new bird."

"That makes sense."

"Remember, we don't want to kill eagles."

"We have to."

"That's right."

The eagle that had to be killed, Sun, perched like an eagle on his aerie-throne. A king, a keeper of one hundred square miles of Indian Country, an arbiter, a jury and judge, a shadow clock that had measured time for two thousand years in slow shadow-circle, and so now the earth, the Indians, the place, this astonishing land soon beneath a new dead sea, would be without reckoning, certainly without the serene majesty of Sun, without, and this is what is our epitaph and harbinger, without the gold of silence, the long lonely shadow beneath silent wing replaced soon by dead sea, now by the whack-whack-whack of tin, proceeding with crablike crippled crawl—the sweet song of man in awkward crazy metallic and cockeyed pounce, approached Sun.

Sun looked down on the eaglets in the nest. The thing to do would be to glide away from the whack-bird, away from the nest. To fight it out somewhere else. If he could tangle himself in the wings of the whack-bird, that would be the end of the whack-bird and the end of Sun. Sun jumped off his aerie without movement, not abrupt or even peremptory, but as though the reel of film had cut and then proceeded to a different scene. The bird Sun, the eagle, the great golden glider moving across the wilds of purple mesa in air-fed steady no-beat, in hushed deadly amaze, seemed in funereal stateliness mounting upward on invisible winds toward the other sun.

"If he climbs we will climb with him, Drago. He is bound to run out of updrafts."

Wilson Drago slid open the door on his side and shifted the Harrington and Richardson pump gun into the ready position.

"How high will this thing climb, sir?"

"Ten thousand feet."

"The bird can climb higher than that."

"Yet he has to come down, Drago."

"How much fuel we got?"

"Fifty gallons."

"What are we consuming?"

"A gallon a minute."

"Shall I try a shot?"

"Yes."

Sun was spiraling upward in tight circles, on a good rising

current of air, when the pellets of lead hit him. They hit like a gentle rain that gave him a quick lift. Sun was out of range. Both the copter and Sun were spiraling upward. The copter was gaining.

"Shall I try another shot?"

"Yes."

This time the lead pellets slammed into Sun like a hard hail and moved him upward and crazy-tilted him, as a great ship will yaw in a sudden gust. Sun was still out of range.

Now the upward current of air ceased, collapsed under Sun abruptly, and the copter closed the distance until Ira Osmun and Wilson Drago were alongside and looking into small yellow eyes, as the great sailing ship of Sun coasted downward into bluing and deep sky.

"Shall I try another shot?"

"Yes."

Wilson Drago raised the Harrington and Richardson shotgun and pumped in a shell with a solid slam. He could almost touch Sun with the muzzle. The swift vessel of Sun sailed on, as though expecting to take the broadside from the 12-gauge gun that would send him to the bottom—to the floor of earth.

"Now, Drago!"

But the gliding ship of bird had already disappeared—folded its huge wing of sail and shot downward, down down down downward, until just before earth it unleashed its enormous sail of wing and glided over the surface of earth—Indian Country.

Down came the copter in quick chase.

There stood the Indians all in a row.

"Don't fire, men," Mary-Forge shouted, "until Sun has passed."

As Sun sailed toward the Indians, the shadow of Sun came first, shading each Indian separately. Now came the swifting Sun, and each mounted Indian raised his gun in salute. Again separately and in the order in which Sun arrived and passed, now the Indians leveled their guns to kill the whack-bird.

"Oh, this is great, Drago," Ira Osmun shouted, "the Indians want to fight!"

"What's great about that?"

"It's natural to fight Indians."

"It is?"

"Yes."

"Well, I'll be!"

"My grandfather would be proud of us now."

"Did he fight Indians?"

"He sure did. It's only a small part of the time the whites have been here that they haven't fought Indians."

"Fighting has been hard on the Indians."

"That may well be, Drago, but it's natural."

"Why?"

"Because people naturally have a fear of strangers. It's called xenophobia. When you don't go along with nature you get into trouble. You suppress your natural instincts, and that is dangerous. That's what's wrong with this country."

"It is? I wondered about that."

"There's nothing wrong with shooting Indians."

"I wondered about that."

"It's natural."

"No, Mr. Osmun, there is something wrong."

"What's that?"

"Look. The Indians are shooting back."

Ira Osmun twisted the copter up and away. "Get out the rifle. We'll take care of the Indians."

"What about the eagle?"

"We've first got to take care of the Indians who are shooting at us, and that girl who is shooting at us."

"Is she crazy?"

"Why else would she have intercourse with the Indians?"

"You mean screwing them?"

"Yes."

"She could have all sorts of reasons. We don't even know that she is screwing them. Maybe we are screwing the Indians."

"Drago, we discussed this before and decided that Mary-Forge was."

"What if she is?"

"Drago, you can't make up your mind about anything. You're being neurotic. When you don't understand why you do something you're being neurotic."

"I am?"

"Yes, get out the rifle."

"I still think it's her business if she is queer for Indians and eagles, against dams—anything."

"But not if she shoots at us when she's doing it. That's neurotic."

"You're right there, Mr. Osmun."

"Get the rifle."

"Okay."

"You know, Drago, people, particularly people who love the Indians, are suppressing a need to kill them. It's called a love-hate relationship."

"It is? You can stop talking now, Mr. Osmun. I said I'd get the rifle."

Below the helicopter that circled in the brilliant, eye-hurting New Mexican day, Mary-Forge told the Indians that the copter would be back, that the ranchers would not fight the eagle while being fired on by Indians. "The ranchers will not make the same mistake Custer did."

"What was that?"

"Fight on two fronts. Custer attacked the Sioux before he finished off Sitting Bull. We are the Sioux."

"We are? That's nice," the Navajo Bull Who Looks Up said. "When do we get out of this class?"

"We never do," Lucy-Lucy said.

"Get your ass behind the rocks!" Mary-Forge shouted. "Here they come!"

The copter flew over and sprayed the rocks with M16 automatic-rifle fire.

"That should teach the teacher that we outgun them, Drago," Ira Osmun said. "Now we can get the eagle!"

The golden eagle called Sun spiraled upward again, its wings steady, wild, sure in the glorious and rapt quietude of the blue blue blue New Mexico morning, a golden eagle against the blue, a kind of heliograph, and a flashing jewel in the perfect and New Mexico sea of sky. The golden eagle, recapitulent, lost then found as it twirled steady and upward in the shattered light, pretentious and fine, followed by the tin bird.

Sun knew that he must gain height. All the power of maneuver lay in getting above the tin bird. He knew too and from experience that the tin bird could go only a certain height. He knew too and from experience that the air current he rode up could collapse at once and without warning. He knew too and from the experience of several battles now with the bird of tin that the enemy was quick and could spit things out that could pain, then kill. All this he knew from experience. But the tin bird was learning too.

The tin bird jerked upward after the golden eagle. The golden eagle, Sun, wandered upward, as though searching and lost. A last and final tryst, because now, always until now, until now no one killed everything that moved. You always had a chance. Now there was no chance. Soon there would be no Sun.

"Remember, Drago, I've got to stay away from him or above him—he can take us with him. The last time, when we got his mate, he almost took us with him. I just barely got away when he attacked the rotors—when the rotor goes we go, Drago—we fall like a rock, smash like a glass. They will pick you up with a dustpan."

"Who?"

"Those Indians down there."

"Mr. Osmun, I don't want to play this game."

"You want to save the sheep, don't you?"

"No."

"Why not?"

"I don't have any sheep to save."

"You don't have any sheep, you don't have any children. But you have pride."

"I don't know."

"Then fire when I tell you to and you'll get some."

"I don't know."

"Do you want eagles to take over the country?"

"I don't know."

"Eagles and Indians at one time controlled this whole country, Drago; you couldn't put out a baby or a lamb in my grandfather's time without an Indian or an eagle would grab it. Now we got progress. Civilization. That means a man is free to go about his business. Build a dam in Indian Country. Motorboats. Varoom varoom varoom! That's the music of progress, Drago."

"It is?"

"The only Indian from this part of the reservation that got a real education was Thomas Charles. He will be a credit to his race and to his country."

"He will?"

"Yes, now that we got the Indians on the ropes we can't let them go, Drago."

"We can't?"

"No, that would be letting civilized people down. It would be letting my grandfather down. What would I say to him?"

"Are you going to see your grandfather?"

"No, he's dead. We'll be dead too, Drago, if you don't shoot. That eagle will put us down there so those Indians will pick us up with a dustpan. You don't want that, do you?"

"I don't know."

"You better find out right smart, or I'll throw you out of this whack-bird myself."

"Would you?"

"Someone's got to live, Drago. The eagle doesn't want to live."

"Why do you say that?"

"This eagle knew we were after him. He knew we would get him; he could have left the country. The eagle could have flown north to Canada. He would be protected there."

"Maybe the eagle thinks this is his country."

"No, this is a civilized country. Will you shoot the eagle?"

"No."

"I like the eagle and the Indians as well as the next man, Drago, but a sheep rancher has to take sides. It's either my sheep or the eagles and the Indians. Whose side are you on, Drago?"

"I guess I'm on theirs."

The helicopter was much lighter now without Drago in it. The copter handled much better and was able to gain on the eagle.

Ira Osmun continued to talk to Wilson Drago as though he were still there. Wilson Drago was one of Ira Osmun's sheep-herders and should have taken a more active interest in sheep.

"The way I see it, Drago, if you wouldn't defend me, the eagle would have brought us both down. It was only a small push I gave you, almost a touch as you were leaning out. By lightening the plane you made a small contribution to my sheep. To civilization. We all do what we can, Drago, and you have contributed your bit. If there is anything I can't stand it's an enemy among my sheep."

The copter continued to follow the eagle up, but now more lightsome and quick, with more alacrity and interest in the chase.

The Indians on the ground were amazed to see the white man come down. Another dropout. "Poor old Wilson Drago. We knew him well. Another man who couldn't take progress, dams—civilization. Many times has Drago shot at us while we were stealing his sheep. We thought anyone might be a dropout, but not Wilson Drago. It shows you how tough it's getting on the white reservation. They're killing each other. Soon there will be nothing left but Indians."

"Good morning, Indian."

"Good morning, Indian."

"Isn't it a beautiful day. Do you notice there is nothing left but us Indians?"

"And one eagle."

The Indians were making all these strange observations over what remained of the body of the world's leading sheepherder, Wilson Drago.

"He created quite a splash," Tzo said.

"And I never thought he would make it," Hosteen Begay said.

"The last time I saw him drunk in Gallup I thought he was coming apart, but this is a surprise," More Turquoise said.

"I knew he had it in him, but I never expected it to come out all at once," Chee Sinoginee said.

"I can't find his scalp. What do you suppose he did with it? Did he hide it?" Kills The Enemy said.

"The other white man got it," Nice Hands' Sister said.

"I bet he did," Lucy-Lucy said.

"They don't care about Indians any more."

"No, when they drop in on you they don't bring their scalp."

"It's as if they don't trust an Indian any more," Tom Charlie said.

"Please, please," Mary-Forge said. "The man is dead."

"Man? Man? I don't seen any man, just a lot of blood and shit."

"Well, there is a man. Or was a man."

"Well there's nothing now," Tzo said, "not even a goddamn scalp."

"Well, Drago's in the white man's heaven," Hosteen Begay said. "On streets of gold tending his flock."

"And shooting eagles."

"Drago's going higher and higher to white man's heaven, much higher than his what do you call it? . . ."

"Helicopter."

". . . can go," Lucy-Lucy said.

"I don't like all this sacrilege," Mary-Forge said. "Remember I am a Christian."

"What?"

"I was brought up in the Christian tradition."

"Now you're hedging," Hosteen Begay said.

Ah, these Indians, Mary-Forge thought, how did I get involved? And she said aloud, "Once upon a time I was young and innocent."

"Print that!" Bull Who Looks Up said.

"We better get higher up the mountain," Mary-Forge shouted at the Indians, "so when Osmun closes on the eagle we can get a better shot."

"Okay, teacher."

"There's only one white guy left," she said.

"I find that encouraging, if true," Sinoginee said.

"Load your rifles and pull your horses after you," Mary-Forge said.

"My Country 'Tis of Thee," Ira Osmun hummed as he swirled the copter in pursuit of the eagle. "You didn't die in vain, Drago. That is, you were not vain, you were a very modest chap. We can climb much higher without you, Drago. I am going to get the last eagle this time, Drago. I think he's reached the top of his climb."

Sun watched the tin whack-bird come up. The tin bird came up whack-whack-whack, its wings never flapping, just turning in a big circle. What did it eat? How did it mate? Where did it come from? From across the huge water on a strong wind. The evil wind. Sun circled, seeing that he must get higher; the tin bird was coming up quicker today. Sun could see the people he always saw below. The people who lived in his country, filing up the mountain. They seemed to be wanting to get closer to him now.

Now Ira Osmun felt then saw all the Indians in the world firing at him from below. "How are you going to knock down an eagle when all the Indians in the world are firing at you from Mount Taylor? It was Mary-Forge who put them up to it, for sure. An Indian would not have the nerve to shoot at a white man. You don't have to drop down and kill all the Indians. They—the people in the East—who have no sheep would call that a massacre. Indians are very popular at the moment. If you simply knock off Mary-Forge, that would do the trick. Women are not very popular at the moment. Why? Because they have a conspiracy against men. You didn't know that? It's true, Drago. It's a sign, Drago, it's a sign. We better take the hint. When women are girls they are a delight, but when they become women they become the enemy. Why, Drago? Did you say something, Drago? I thought I heard someone say something. I must have been hit. My mind must be wandering. What was I saying? It's part of the conspiracy. I heard a rumor that the Indians have got a gift. What's that mean? Something. I must have been hit. What was I doing? Oh, yes, I was going to get Mary-Forge—the girl who is against dams and queer for Indians and eagles. The eagle can wait."

And Ira Osmun put the copter in full throttle, then cradled the M16 automatic rifle in his left arm with the muzzle pointing out the door. With his right hand he placed the copter in a swift power glide down.

Sun saw the obscene tin bird go into its dive down. Now would be a chance to get it while the tin bird was busy hunting its prey on the ground. Sun took one more final look over the aerie nest to check the birds. The eaglets were doing fine. Drawing the enemy away from the nest had been successful. The eaglets craned their necks at the familiar shape before Sun folded his great span of wings and shot down on top of the tin bird.

Mary-Forge, mounted on Poco Mas, saw the tin bird coming, the M16 quicking out nicks of flame. She could not get the Indians to take cover. The Indians had placed their horses behind the protection of the boulders and were all standing out in the open and were blasting away at the zooming-in copter. Mary-Forge was still shouting at the Indians, but they would not take cover. They have seen too many goddamn movies, Mary-Forge thought, they have read too many books. They are stupid stupid stupid dumb dumb dumb Indians. How stupid and how dumb can you get? They want to save the eagle. Standing exposed naked to the machine gun. The stupid Indians. Mary-Forge raised her rifle at the zooming-in copter in a follow-me gesture, then took off in a straight line, the horse pounding, and the flame-nicking copter followed; so did Sun. So now there were three.

The tin bird was alive in flame all at once. Something had hit the fuel tank and all of everything exploded in fire; the rotors of the tin bird were still turning and fanning the flame, so that it was not only a streaking meteor across Indian Country, but at once a boil of fire that shot downward from the terrific draft, laying a torch of flame across the desert, so that the mesquite and sagebrush became a steady line of flame, ending where the tin whack-bird hit into the rocks and went silent in a grand tower of fire.

"It was Sun that did it," Tom Yazzie said.

The death of Sun.

All of the Indians and Mary-Forge were standing around the dying fire of the big whack-bird in the smoke that shrouded the death of Sun.

"When an eagle," the Medicine Man said, "when a true bird has no hope . . ."

"Yes?"

"When the eagle is no more . . ." the Medicine Man said.

"Yes?"

"When the water covers our land . . ."

"Yes?"

"Then we are no more."

"True," every person shrouded in smoke said.

Kills The Enemy said, "Before the whites bury us we should give them Tom Charlie's gift. Or are we going to have a wet Wounded Knee here?"

The Indians remained silent in the smoke.

3

An eagle the Indians named Star sailed in one beginning night to reclaim the country of Sun. Now Star's wide shadow passed over the great white dam, then the big eagle Star settled on the old high rock throne-aerie in awful and mimic splendor, and again admonitory, serene—regal and doomed.

Thomas Charles in his near hogan worked quietly and alone.

Mary-Forge and William sat watching but saying nothing at all on the long wide ramada of the Scalp House that overlooked the wild silent country, so hushed that you expected something huge to happen. And it did. The sun exploded on the edge of the Sangre de Cristos and then went under.

"I was thinking that I've been back nine months now," Mary-Forge said. "Long enough to have had a child," she said. "A child that would be half writer and half red and half white and half unacceptable because the world out there where the sun went is very real and the world of us is—where did I put my purse?"

" 'Romantic.' Is that the word you wanted?"

"No, the purse. That is the word I wanted. Billy Boy is the word I wanted."

"Thank you," he said. "And saddlebag is the other word you wanted."

She did not have a purse. She had ridden up on a horse with only a saddlebag, ridden around the sign, around the rose garden, around the sign that says "Sings In Pretty Places."

That is what the sign says—"Sings In Pretty Places"—and any horse too is always careful not to touch it.

The sign was put up about the time the others first went to the moon, or more important (to the Navajo) about the time the water from the dam began to back up at the base of Lost Horse Mesa. They didn't know how long the moon madness lasted on the outside, but in the Navajo Nation it was over soon. It was like Mary-Forge's mother, who got involved in a fad religion and twirled like a top. Then just stopped. That's the way it was with the interest in man on the moon in the Navajo Nation. Interest quit. And the moon returned to its old romantic self, on which Indian poets sometimes dwell and to which pregnant women turn their bellies, and once again the moon came up and waxed and waned without the others crawling all over it and getting it dirty and treating the moon as though it were not a sacred object placed there to awe and delight the Indians in the night. But although the interest in the moon quit, the water from the dam continued to back up. And as though to defy the flood and as though to challenge the water, to challenge the dam builders, Mary-Forge planted a rose garden. It would be a sudden magic of roses in Indian Country, and she wanted to grow the red-white-and-bluest and biggest-on-earth Herbert Hoover rose.

"Are Herbert Hoover roses red, white, and blue?"

"Yes."

"Why?"

Mary-Forge wanted not only Herbert Hoover roses but Luther Burbank and a Calvin Coolidge, too.

"Calvin Coolidge said that unemployment adds to the people out of work," Bull Who Looks Up said.

Mary-Forge felt her rose garden was a gesture against the water, that no one should act as though the dam builders were going to triumph, that no one should make preparations for the death of the land. The rose garden would be a signal, a gay flag of continued and continuous life.

But they thought the rose garden must be some expression too of defeat. Some sign that the inner life of Mary-Forge had failed. Some protest against the desert in her heart. Why does a young woman start a school for Indians in nowhere? Because that's where the Indians live. But no one ever gave the Indians a rose garden. But Mary-Forge had given one Indian a rose. It was an Apache Indian from Dulce who was truly responsible for the rose garden. An Apache Indian from the Jicarilla Apache Nation. Apaches are rich. Oil money. Unlike among the Navajos, the oil money is not put into a common fund for the Apache Nation but given to all equally regardless of race, creed, or ethnic background—if they are Apache. The rich Apaches drift south in the winter into Navajo Country to become richer. That is, they adopt Navajo children, which makes the children Apaches, which gives the family more prestige and more money, for, Bull Who Looks Up said, as the size of the family increases so do its numbers, or the size of the family increases in direct proportion to its numbers.

The Apache poet Sings In Pretty Places didn't have a dime. No Navajo had ever met a poor Apache before. I'm not talking about the Mescaleros or White Mountain Apaches. They are poor as kiva mice, but the Jicarilla Apaches are rich enough to drink an imported California wine called Thunderbird. Some live in Lincoln Continentals and drive Caddies.

"Apaches that rich?"

"Yes."

"Whatever happened, to Sings In Pretty Places then? Why wasn't he rich?"

"Did you ever hear of a poor Jew?"

"No."

"Well, there are millions. That's the way it is with the Apaches. The facts don't support the legend. It was a good year for oil but not for a poet."

"I like that line."

The Apache Sings In Pretty Places drifted south that year, so poor he could be mistaken for a Navajo, writing what he called the poetic history of the Indians. He got as far as the White Horse Post before he was killed.

"Killed?"

"Yes."

"Who by?"

"We didn't know then. Poetry lovers? No one knew."

"Was his poetry any good?"

"Yes."

"Can you read one?"

"Yes.

> You can see why Indians
> Have grave
> Reservations
> About
> Reservations.
> Why
> The Indian
> Has not seen
> The light, still
> Trusts
> His medicine bundle,
> Keeps his arrows

Dry.
Why
The Indian watches the
Hills to see the
Latest
White man smoke signals
Of the mind.
What
Hath God,
The white man's God,
Wrought now?
To make the Indian wish
Columbus
Sank
Or had worshiped some God less
Strange."

"He was a cheerful cuss. Why was he killed?"

"Mary-Forge."

"Mary-Forge?"

"Yes. Mary-Forge runs this Learning Hogan for Navajos, and of course he would come there, being a poet."

"Being a poet?"

"Yes. She encouraged that kind of thing. Women do."

"Yes."

"Well, Sings In Pretty Places arrived hungry, as poets will."

"Yes."

"And she was alone, cleaning up the place, stoking up the fire, tidying things as women will, and he just stood there on the sheepskin. No one had seen him come in. He said he had a secret message."

"What?" Mary-Forge said. "Stand in the light. Is it something about the flood? Something about the project? Tom Charlie?"

He moved and stood under the hogan vent hole, where the light fell on him. "A message from the grave," he said.

He looked like a poet, and that is maybe his flaw, the teacher in the teacher thought; he should look like a football player or a lumberjack, now that the people in these professions have taken to looking like poets. He had the long face, the drooping mustache that goes with poets, and the dark liquid eyes that became all alight when a discovery was made, and wore loose blue jeans and jacket that hung in absolute poverty, and he stood and moved in the style of convict or poet without destination or hope or maybe even relations to planet or star—this planet—any star.

"Message from the grave?" Mary-Forge said.

"Yes. What did I say?"

"It doesn't matter," Mary-Forge said. "Nothing matters. Your being a convict or a poet. Nothing matters. Poet?"

"Yes."

"Name?"

"Sings In Pretty Places."

"That's too bad," Mary-Forge said. "But we can change that. Did anyone see you come here?"

"No."

"Then we still have some kind of a chance. I know all about you, Sings In Pretty Places. I wonder that you're still alive. What made you call yourself a poet?"

"Because that's what I am."

"But that's what everyone is," Mary-Forge said. "But we hide it. Or we hole up in Santa Fe or Taos. We don't walk around the reservation in broad daylight."

"Do whites know you're a poet?"

"Of course not," Mary-Forge said. "But I burn everything I write. And I'm surrounded by friends, by Indians. But that won't save you. Do you have it bad?"

"Yes."

"How much do you write?"

"I have to write every day now. I used to be able to go three days without writing."

"Have you tried quitting?"

"Yes."

"The Medicine Man says no one is cured until he has stopped writing poems for two years. I don't know whether it's safe for me to be around you."

"It's not catching."

"Yes, it is," Mary-Forge said. "And you have a bad case. But I don't give a damn. You stay here until you're rested up, and then you can make a run for it."

"Where to?"

"Some city. A poet can always get lost in a city."

"I don't like cities."

"Poets can't be choosers," Mary-Forge said. "Sit down and eat. What would you like? Milk and honey? Nectar and ambrosia? What do poets eat lately?"

"I'm tired."

"Just relax. I'll fix you something."

The Apache poet Sings In Pretty Places stayed there three weeks before the roof fell in. They wanted him for contributing to the delinquency of a minor. A young girl named Story Smith he had met near Aztec. But they had other charges, too. Contemplated dam busting, several others.

"What I want you to do," Mary-Forge told the wild Indian, told the poet, told whatever the youth of the world is called now. "What I want you to try to do is act normal. Did you ever try smoking a cigar? Did you ever think of going to the trading post and watching television? Don't you know what softball is? Find out who's leading the American League in runs batted in. Pray together. Paul Newman. Burt Lancaster. Debbie Reynolds."

"Debbie Reynolds?"

"I'm sure there must be a name like that in the movies."

"Yes," Sings In Pretty Places said, "I would think so."

"What else can you do?"

"I'm sure you'll think of something even more exciting," he said, "for your next episode of Mary-Forge helps the Indians."

"If I can't help you, then maybe we can work it out together. Who was the girl?"

"A white girl."

"Do we all look alike? White girls?"

"Yes."

"Oh, come on."

"Her name was Story Smith and she had that long straw-colored hair hiding a blue-eyed and red-apple child blank face. She said she ran away from home and wanted to meet an Indian."

"Or a black?"

"Anything. Maybe anything her parents are not. I liked her. I liked her very much."

"Her red-apple child blank face?"

"Yes."

"What other crimes did you commit?"

"What other crimes have you white people got?"

"Contemplated dam busting."

"But what charge can the whites arrest me on?"

"Contributing to the delinquency of a minor."

"What's that mean?"

"You taught the young something. Story Smith?"

"Is that against the law?"

"Yes."

"Then why haven't they closed your Learning Hogan? Contemplated dam busting and contributing to the delinquency of all the Indians."

"They have," Mary-Forge said. "The Bureau of Indian Affairs put a padlock on the front door. You came through the window."

"I did?"

"Everyone does," Mary-Forge said.

"I am too hassled to live much longer," the Indian poet said. "I will be lucky to make it through the night."

"I will see that you make it through the night," Mary-Forge said.

And she did, not only that night but that week, almost that month. It was the time of the cactus fruit harvest, when the Indians gather tunas, red-ripe berries, fruit from the cow's tongue cactus and the beaver tail. It is the time, too, in the Lower Sonoran, when they gather the pitahaya fruit from the saguaro and the organ pipe. It is also the time when they gather wild piñon nuts in the high country. The Navajo Nation covers a whole world of food without planting. The Indian reaps but he does not sow. The Indian religion does not encourage work. The Indian religion is not against work, but the Indian religion is not against anything. The Indian belief completes a circle, and life comes back on itself, so that there is a continuity in time and place and person. The Indian belief is a circle that contains all the rhythms of the poetry of life. Tomorrow is yesterday. The future is now and the past is present. I will go down to the well last week and come back yesterday.

"You will, will you?" Mary-Forge said.

But Sings In Pretty Places was gone, and she was still all alone and thinking to herself. Thinking: He's got to learn. He's got to learn that you can't go around the white man's world writing poetry without a permit, without some kind of certification or job to prove that it's only some kind of hobby, a temporary aberration or ploy to gain time against the inspection of the books, or such as the work of a Sunday landscape painter, work that is done without purpose and apology. But the arrogance of an unemployed poet wandering Indian Country must be some grand deceit, something more heinous than the crime already committed with the blue-eyed child blank face. Look, she told herself,

he's probably not even being pursued. He's only chasing himself; what we imagined to be the enemy is ourselves. When a
poet fails to get an audience he creates one. Defeat must have a
cause and the cause is never ourselves. Yes, she told herself. Yes,
Mary-Forge thought, Sings In Pretty Places is something I have
invented, something any woman would invent to bring some
romance, some poetry, to a lonely hogan on the far side of the
reservation. A demon poet seeking succor from the mob is
sheltered by Mary-Forge and brought back to health. Mary-Forge
Saves Poet. Posterity Grateful. Poet returns to kiss Mary-Forge's
toes. Remembers dark days before fame when Mary-Forge sacri-
ficed all for art. Yes. Get hold of yourself, Mary-Forge told herself.
There never was, never will be, never could be a man named Sings
In Pretty Places.

Story Smith, the child white girl who had met up with Sings
In Pretty Places, was young, beautiful, and good. They all are.
She had run away from her parents, who were old, ugly, and
bad. They all are. But parents are getting younger now and
children are getting older. The parents are running away from
the children. Parents run faster. They are difficult to spot because
they stay at home. The girl child left her parents in Garden City,
Long Island, after her parents had run away. She had come to
Indian Country because it is the most beautiful place in the world
and the Indians are kind. When she was arrested for being alone
she was found to have books in her possession, and Story Smith
was shot.

"Where?"

"All over."

"Where?"

"On the plaza in Santa Fe across from the Palace of the
Governors. The tourists were asked to leave."

"I still find it difficult to believe they shot her."

"No one knows."

"What else is new?"

"Story Smith was last seen rocking on the porch in the state mental institution at Las Vegas, New Mexico."

"But she believes she was executed?"

"Yes."

"Then nothing else matters."

"No, nothing else matters now."

"He's dead."

"Who's dead?"

"Sings In Pretty Places."

"Say that again."

It was More Turquoise. He stood there on one foot alongside the tall window, in an attitude of resignation and disbelief.

"He hung himself on the sign."

"What sign?"

"The big highway neon Coke sign outside San Ysidro."

"Then I failed," Mary-Forge said.

"He left the Learning Hogan this poem."

"Then I failed," Mary-Forge said. And she read:

> "He went to school
> Once in a while
> Because he was an Indian.
> He figured that he was not important,
> Because he was an Indian.
> He figured in America
> His death was not important,
> So he died.
> You can do it with booze,
> A white man's war,
> You can do it
> When

There is nothing but neon
Flashing."

"Then I failed, William," Mary-Forge said. She was standing
in the darkness of the Scalp House tack room. He moved toward
the looping light, hoping she would move too, but she preferred
the dark. "I failed, Billy," she said.

"No," he said. "It's us, every one of us that has failed. But not
you." He hung up the bridle and stumbled on. "Not you, because
you tried. Not you, because he left you the poem, the poetry. Not
you because . . ." He put up the trail rope. "Not you because . . .
what did he call it?"

"The youth of the world."

"Yes. Trusted you. Came to you after he knew it was too
late. Too late to be saved. Too late to save himself. So he wasn't
asking you for that. Not to do that, not save him, but something
else."

"What else?"

He hitched the saddle up on the rack.

"You mean his poems?" she said. "He wanted me to save
those?"

"Not the poems maybe. He knew it was too late for even that,
but something bigger."

"Bigger?"

"Something he knew about, had always known about, being
an Indian, he must have known, must have recognized you when
he first saw you, knew you were the person. Knew you were
the man—"

"The man?"

"The woman, to carry on."

"What on?"

"The poetry of life. I believe he thought it was that simple.
We all do."

"Do you?"

"Yes," he said.

And so as men will, and women accomplish, she built a rose garden in the desert. Unlike the sphinx for dead kings it bloomed and again unlike a desert monument to dead kings the garden remarks a future instead of a past. The sudden magic of roses is by the Nile of the Chiwilly Wash, the temple of the Learning Hogan alongside the pyramid shadow of the Portales Mesa. And it bright blooms—and the delight of roses is for all who need to walk and sing in pretty places. And that's what the sign says, and any horse is always careful not to touch it.

"But Tom Charlie did. He let his horse go right through the rose garden."

"Why?"

"He must have been thinking about the gift."

"The gift?"

"The project."

"Is that good?"

"No, it is not," the Medicine Man said.

4

You would have thought the death would be an ending, that Sings In Pretty Places would take his place in the legend and the myth, along with Crazy Horse and Rain In The Face, that Sings In Pretty Places would if not become inviolate in death, then along with the Coke sign on which he hung become some kind of announcement, a silent and cryptic advertisement of pause, re-freshment, and death.

"Because," Mary-Forge said, "because we buried Sings In Pretty Places does not mean we got shut of him, does not mean that six feet of dirt can hush a death style, can—"

"What?"

"Death style."

"All right."

"Cannot forever, it can't, and maybe that's the secret of the Indian, certainly of the poet in the Indian."

"Will you repeat that?" the Medicine Man said.

"The poet in the Indian," Mary-Forge said.

"I wanted that again," the Medicine Man said, "because I believe you are trying to say the Indian nation will live."

"But she believes it," Lucy-Lucy said.

"That," the Medicine Man said, "that the extermination of the Indian has failed, that the dam will disappear because the spirit and the curse of the land . . ."

"Lives on."

"Yes."

"But she believes it," Lucy-Lucy said.

"No, it's not that bad," Sinoginee said. "I believe they are only two hundred dollars apart."

"Two hundred dollars apart, but we can live with it," was a quote from the used-car dealers in Gallup, whose occupation was swindling the Indians.

Mary-Forge and the Indians did not long remain two hundred dollars apart. They finally agreed that the life and death of Sings In Pretty Places should not go unremarked, that the rose garden was not enough.

"But," Bull Who Looks Up said, "we can't dedicate an aircraft carrier to Sings In Pretty Places because the Indians don't have an aircraft carrier."

"The white people have many aircraft carriers."

"What for?"

"They bomb each other."

"What for?"

Everyone looked at the Medicine Man.

"We don't know," the Medicine Man said. "Insanity."

"You mean white people are crazy?"

"Yes."

"All of them?"

"Yes."

"You mean every white nation has an aircraft carrier?"

"No, some are still saving up for one."

"What has this got to do with Sings In Pretty Places, who

killed himself by hanging himself from the neon Coke sign on Route Sixty-six, where all could see?" Mary-Forge said.

"Plenty."

"Explain."

"How can white people be concerned with a dead Indian poet when the payments are due on an aircraft carrier?"

"And that reminds me," the Medicine Man said, staring at Thomas Charles. "How can an Indian be any better who is working on what do you call it?"

"The gift, I guess."

"Yes," the Medicine Man said, "how can an Indian be any better?"

Thomas Charles said nothing.

"That reminds me too," Hosteen Begay said to Tom Yazzie, wanting to change the subject. "I co-signed a note for you for Honest Joe Stapleton. Did you pay?"

"For the Packard?"

"Yes."

"I traded it in on a Nash."

"The problem is getting Indian cars out of Gallup," Hosteen Begay said.

"I got the Nash as far as Star Lake," Tom Yazzie said.

"Did you report it to Honest Joe Stapleton?"

"Yes, he said it was a record."

"Have we finished with aircraft carriers and with Tom Charlie?"

"Yes."

"Then let's get back to Sings In Pretty Places."

They never got around to him, not then, because Tom Yazzie got back to the collapse of his Packard and the death of his Nash, but the next day they got back to Sings In Pretty Places when Sings In Pretty Places' girl arrived, the girl with the child blank face.

Story Smith said she had fled the coop.

The insane asylum.

Story Smith said she wanted to be with those who had loved her lover. She said we were all she had in the world. Now that her mother and father had run away from home.

Tom Yazzie, Tom Yazzie's Brother, and Hosteen Begay had picked Story Smith up in the Nash near Tinian, near the damn dam that was growing, found her on her way to the Learning Hogan and placed her in the rumble seat. The Nash got them almost as far as the White Horse Trading Post before it died of a broken heart.

"Who?"

"The Nash. That's what she said, the girl with the child blank face. Her name is Story Smith. And she said the Nash died sick at heart."

"Story Smith also said," Hosteen Begay said, "that she has penis envy. What's that?"

"It doesn't make any difference what it is," Mary-Forge said. "Penis envy is out."

"You sure she still couldn't have penis envy?"

"Yes," Mary-Forge said.

They all looked at Tom Charlie, who had gone to the University of New Mexico.

"It's highly improbable," Thomas Charles said. "The last paper on it came out of the Mayo Clinic."

"Isn't that where Ernest Hemingway died?" William William said.

"No, that's where Hemingway was treated," Thomas Charles said.

"What for?"

"Writing."

"Where did he die?"

"Idaho."

"What from?"

"Writing."

"Can you catch that from a toilet seat?"

"You sure can," Mary-Forge said.

Outside, Story Smith wandered through the rose garden, which was hard by the Learning Hogan and beneath the slick red rock and black shadow of the Portales Mesa, the mesa adamant and huge. Story Smith watched up at it in breathful amaze, then back to the familiar rose. Story Smith was dressed in the style and decorous manner of university youth. She wore a no-bra and a no-panties and a no-midriff that allowed her belly button to pop at the rose. And what she called with the abruptness and flash of university youth her ass, was tight bound with the rag of Levis, the flag of wealth and discontent and some outrage at life and J. C. Penney, too, because it is the costume, sold or given or thrown at you in Free Stores, with a red heart and orange arrow pointing up the anus, but all hidden now by the flowing somber grandma dress, which is yet another flash badge in which youth assumes the decorum of old age as her elders in minidress at once mimic the child.

Outside, Story Smith wandered through the rose garden and thought. And told herself. And smelled the roses. And thought— I have come back to Jesus. I have found myself through Jesus. How can I help these people who killed my lover? Jesus—oh, Jesus—Jesus Christ!

"Why have you come here?" Mary-Forge asked Story Smith.

They both stared at each other tentatively. Mary-Forge was surrounded by red Indians. Story Smith by white roses.

"I've come because I have found . . ."

"What have you found?"

"Jesus."

Oh, Mary-Forge the teacher to the Indians thought, and she

said, "Oh." And then said, "Oh, but this is Indian Country and—"

"I know, but I don't want to take anything from the Indians —I want to give them something."

"What?"

"Jesus."

"Are you being followed?"

"Yes."

"Then, you escaped?"

"Yes."

"From the insane asylum?"

"Yes."

"And you expect me to hide you?"

"Yes."

"Is that the reputation I have?"

"Yes."

"Why don't you go back? Weren't you happy at the institution?"

"No," Story Smith said, "but there's Indian Country"—and she stared around in wild surmise and looked up high at the eagle Star that floated by and felt the long knife she carried in a leather case alongside the granny dress.

The two keepers from the mental institution who were chasing Story Smith in a yellow Ford Pinto were insane.

"Oh, that's so old," Doctor Rollo Nye said.

"What's so old?" Spanky Talley said.

"I was thinking about people who go in for role reversal."

"What's that?"

"Inability to distinguish between sanity and insanity. There's a London doctor named R. D. Laing who goes around the States saying everyone is crazy but himself."

"Has he ever met himself?"

"I don't think so."

"If he had he wouldn't say things like that."

"Yes."

"Have you ever met yourself?"

"Me?"

"Yes."

"No."

"Would you like to?"

"I would like to have any experience that would help me become a better psychiatrist."

"What's wrong with Story Smith?"

"She has what we call the sanity syndrome."

"All kidding aside, what's wrong with Story Smith?"

"Have you seen her file?"

"No."

"She killed three people."

"Indians?"

"No, she hasn't killed an Indian yet."

"What I would like to do," Story Smith said to Mary-Forge, "is kill an Indian."

"You mean symbolically."

"Yes."

"Wash them in the blood of the Lamb?"

"Yes."

"Have them reborn again."

"Yes."

"I'm sorry," Mary-Forge said. "The Indians have a religion and I believe it would be rude to try and sell them another."

"Then you won't let me talk to your class?"

"No."

"But if an Indian and I want to walk together alone, you cannot stop us."

"No. Why do you carry that knife?"

"For protection." The long knife hung down from her belt in a leather sheath. "For protection," Story Smith said. "I hitchhike," Story Smith said. "Some men want to rape you. Other men do not. I am more interested in the men who do not."

"But for those who do, the knife is for your protection?"

"You can say that," Story Smith said. "Let me show you how sharp this knife is." And she moved toward Mary-Forge through the white roses.

Spanky Talley and Doctor Rollo Nye, the two gentlemen pursuing Story Smith in the Pinto, drove into the Two Point Bar between the Painted Bird Mesa and the White Horse Trading Post, because this would be the last chance to get a drink before they hit the reservation. The reservation is dry.

Doctor Rollo Nye and Spanky Talley were not the movie version of bad guys who work in an institution. They were quiet, unassuming, and a bit withdrawn.

Rollo Nye asked for a martoony.

"What?"

"Martini, then."

"No mixed drinks."

"Vodka on the rocks."

"You?"

"Same."

"How did you get the name 'Spanky,' Spanky?" the doctor said.

"I don't know whether I got the name from my deviation or my name gave me the inclination for the deviation."

"Perversion."

"A perversion is what the people who live across the street do instead of watching television."

"Yes."

"Do you plan a paper on it?"

"No."

"This girl ..."

"Story Smith."

"Yes. Why does she come to Indian Country?"

"There's a girl out here, Mary-Forge, who runs a free school for the Indians—orange hair. She seems to attract the disturbed."

"Why?"

"Because she lives out here at the end of the world. It's where you jump off."

Doctor Rollo Nye and Spanky Talley stared out the door at the blue space at the end of the world, silent, immense, and awful, and at once a shattering violence of color that went on into an infinity of still mesa, unmoving cloud, New Mexican day without limit or time, even place, on the planet earth, fantastical, gaudy, surreal—silent.

"You say it's where you go to ..."

"Jump off."

"You said orange hair?"

"And a scar on the left cheekbone—Mary-Forge."

"And she teaches the Indians?"

"Yes."

"What?"

"Something." Doctor Nye moved his drink. "Love of place."

"So they won't jump off?"

"Yes."

"Would you say we are the Medicine Men of the white reservation?"

"I would say we need another drink," Doctor Nye said.

"Yes, we should give Mary-Forge a bit more time to try her rose garden. It's a tranquilizer garden."

"Or a death garden," Rollo Nye said. "She calls it 'Sings In Pretty Places,' after the Apache poet she knew who hung himself on a sign. His name was Sings In Pretty Places."

"I like that."

"I can see Mary-Forge now," Rollo Nye said, "the blood running down that scar beneath the orange hair—"

"I can't."

"—among the white roses."

"Let me show you," Story Smith said—Story Smith was the bloom and the imprint, the talisman of all youth, of life without scar, excepting the covert and slash to the mind. The invisible and secret mourn of time and death and grandma dress she moved not with the quick of the very young but with the sad quick of Story Smith—youth without the ballet, without the grace of the human heart—adumbrated, jerky, arcane and removed—"this knife."

Eight Indians came out of the Learning Hogan.

"Loco."

"Man."

"Loco," Hosteen Tzo said.

"Let me," Story Smith said, "show you how the knife works." She was standing in the roses and leaning toward Mary-Forge. "You see I don't want to hurt you, I only want to show you the problem."

"Problem?"

"Yes, look." The knife touched Mary-Forge. "The problem is that people have no faith—they follow tracks in the mud they no longer believe in. As God said, 'Let there be light.' He was asking for something, I don't think we ever got it. Imagine having to fire God. Someone is going to have to dismiss Him—look at the mess He's made. I said to Jesus yesterday, 'Hello, Jesus.' Does this hurt?"

"Yes."

Story Smith eased the pressure. "Is that better?"

"Yes."

"I said to Jesus, 'People are without power unless they have a gun or a knife or a howl of the wild.' What are you doing out here living with the Indians? Would you ball an Indian? Allow one to marry your sister? Brother? Aunt? Don't know? I don't like standing here in the desert holding a knife on you, but I must know. Did you love him?"

"Who?"

"Sings In Pretty Places."

"I cared for him."

"Tell those Indians to go back in the hogan." She paused, and then she said, "If you cared for Sings In Pretty Places then you will want to join him."

"Sings In Pretty Places is dead."

"I know," Story Smith said. "Let us take a walk. It is too crowded in this rose garden."

She will accomplish in some other way, Mary-Forge thought. Women will not kill. But you cannot say women because each woman is separate and unique.

"Insane," Story Smith said.

"What?"

"Keep walking. The establishment has forced us into this. Without a gun or a knife or a howl in the wild, where else can a sister go?"

"Home."

"My parents ran away. They got through all the road blocks. They are living in a commune called a country club that keeps out Jews."

"But your parents come home at night."

"Yes. Keep walking. Keeps out blacks and children and the poor. Oh, Jesus."

"Why?"

"Oh, Jesus."

"Why do you want to hurt me?"

"Because you stole Sings In Pretty Places."

"I cared."

"Then you will join him in that Happy Hunting Ground. Do you believe in a death after life? Oh, Jesus, I have work to do. But you can keep him happy. The doctor at the institution, Doctor Rollo, said, 'Story Smith, give me that knife.'" She paused and said, "I think my father went to the showers, where he hides from me in his nakedness. Tell me about yourself. I don't want to hurt you, but I feel responsible for your death."

"I'm still alive," Mary-Forge said.

"But not for long," Story Smith said.

And Story Smith pressed the knife into and above the Levis of Mary-Forge where there was a white flesh gap between rump and shoulders where the denim brassiere tied in back.

"Listen," Story Smith said, "I don't believe there was ever an Indian named Sings In Pretty Places. I think I made it all up. Do you think people made up Jesus, too? Don't try to think of what I want you to say, don't be like Spanky. Do you believe with Doctor Rollo that religion is an insanity that is permitted? If you do, then all I can say is—but not for long." And she pressed the knife into Mary-Forge so that Mary-Forge had to hurry up the trail or bleed. And she did both. And the blood soaked into her Levis until it hid the name of the maker of the pants—Levi Strauss.

"I don't like to come out here and cut you," Story Smith said from Mary-Forge's rear, "but someone has to come out here and teach teachers not to have sex with Indians now that love is dead. Now that the religion of sanity has become acceptable. You probably share the particular thought that people in the institution are mad. That's not true. We are different. Yes. Mad, no. Ask Spanky."

Mary-Forge said nothing.

"Why do you say nothing when I am sticking a knife in you? You are just like Doctor Rollo. Move faster. Now stop and tell those Indians to stop following us."

"Stop following us," Mary-Forge hollered without stopping.

"I don't have eyes in my ass," Story Smith said, "but in an institution you develop hindsight. What Doctor Rollo calls a dangerous look backward. What Spanky calls ass sight. Call off your Indians."

"Get lost!" Mary-Forge hollered.

The Indians that were following on the flanks and the coyotes at the rear stopped and signaled from group to group in pantomime. Tom Yazzie signaled that the girl was crazy, which is the same gesture in any sign language, and then said in another gesture that they must proceed slowly, and in another that if they did not their teacher Mary-Forge would be dead. The Medicine Man agreed and when his head moved you could see his dangling turquoise earrings hit into the wild New Mexican sun. Now the Indians followed as in a Western movie, in a stutter motion and then time for a silent confabulation before following the splattered sign of obscene blood, brilliant and fresh and death-red and natural, too, and you wondered how much more blood there was before you came upon the body in the rocks, the white girl, red. All red.

Now all movement of the Indians ceased and Hosteen Begay signaled the Indians to sit. There is a myth among whites that Indians imitating the whites used officers that always led. No, each battle was led by the most competent. The Indians do not believe in continuing with an elitist unfit. Today the most competent was Hosteen Begay. He told them to sit. The Indians sat. Tomorrow it might be Tzo, the next day More Turquoise or Tom Yazzie. No, never Tom Yazzie, but certainly Tom Yazzie's Brother. Women never led a war party, never butchered other human beings. Then what was happening up ahead? That was a woman with the knife. But a white woman. The other people. The Navajos on the Checkerboard do not believe the others have souls. They have money, which may be a form of soul, but the Indians who supported this were losing their case. Mary-Forge, their white teacher, had a soul because she gave love of place, and that is the only signal of a soul the Indians knew. Now she was being bled away on the rocks and soon she would disappear. The sign of her blood was becoming erratic and faint. They could rush the scene, but then a lover would be dead. The only lover who was white who had not betrayed the cause.

Hosteen Begay had stopped the Indians because something was happening up ahead.

"Do you believe in sisterhood?" Story Smith asked.

"I believe in your knife," Mary-Forge said.

"Why did you steal my lover, Sings In Pretty Places?"

"You said before that Sings In Pretty Places did not exist."

"Now I believe he did," Story Smith said.

"What was Sings In Pretty Places like?"

"You know what he was like."

"Did he sing?" Mary-Forge said, and then in a still louder voice, "Did he sing?"

"Yes," Story Smith said, "he sang in pretty places. But now he is dead and I must kill you." Story Smith's knife held Mary-Forge against a cliff of yellowing sandstone near Route 44 that ran to Shiprock or Gallup or Albuquerque or the institution, depending on which way you wanted to go.

Story Smith, with her wrist and elbow rigid, leaned her weight very slowly forward, increasing the pressure on the twelve-inch knife.

"Listen!" Mary-Forge said.

"To what?"

"Sings In Pretty Places."

"I don't hear anything."

"Yes, you do."

"Yes, I do."

"It's Sings In Pretty Places."

"Then, he's alive?"

"Yes."

The pressure on the knife eased.

They listened.

The Indians were at once all magically there.

"May I borrow your knife?" the Medicine Man said.

"Yes. Listen to Sings In Pretty Places," Story Smith said.

Hosteen Begay was sitting in the rose garden singing. Singing and enshrouded in the bower of rose on rose on rose, so that his face was symbiotic, belonging to and part of a bouquet and more without becoming an anomaly, a strangeness in the New Mexican desert, they became—the roses and Hosteen Begay—an Indian and rose extravaganza of delight and sound, not alien but a blaze of eloquence and Indian damn foolishness and guile, merging and never quite disparate from the desert cactus and mesquite—became sweet.

"That's not the word I would use to describe Story Smith," Doctor Rollo Nye said. "Sweet."

They had stopped the Ford Pinto because they had seen some Indians on the side of the road, Route 44, up ahead.

"I wasn't thinking about Story Smith," Spanky said, "but that singing."

"Is that Story up ahead?"

"Yes, it is," Spanky said.

"It is going to be all right, doctor," Story Smith said as he came up. "Spanky, it's going to be all right," she said. "Sings In Pretty Places is alive."

"Yes, from that singing, Sings In Pretty Places must be alive and well in Indian Country," Doctor Rollo said. "That's nice. Do you want to come along with us now? We're going to have a party. Come along."

"Before we knock your teeth out," Spanky said.

"If you only cared that much," Story said.

"But I will give you a spanking."

"If you only cared that much," Story said.

"Has the bleeding stopped?" Doctor Rollo said.

"Yes, Mary-Forge is going to make it all right," the Medicine Man said.

"Jesus Saves," Story Smith said, going back with Doctor Rollo and Spanky in the Pinto. "Yes, Jesus saves."

"I hope so," Spanky said. "What with high taxes and all."

"Oh, Jesus," Story Smith said, "oh, God, help him, Jesus."

"This here old Indian fellow," Spanky said, "goes up to Jesus Christ when he's being nailed to that cross and he says, 'Does it hurt?' and Jesus says, 'Only when I laugh.'"

"I think we've had enough of that," Doctor Rollo said.

"I hear tell," Spanky said, "they arrested that preacher Oral Roberts in Alabama just because of his name."

"I said that was enough," Doctor Rollo said.

"Oh, God, help us, oh, Jesus," Story Smith said. "Please, Jesus."

The Indians laid the teacher Mary-Forge down tenderly in the Learning Hogan.

It was not so much the cut in the back that Mary-Forge felt now, not entirely, or the dam that would flood the beloved country, or the asphalt going nowhere, not entirely, or the jet plane screaming now over silent Indian Country, or Tom Charlie's project, the gift, but all joining together and entirely when she said, "It's not the insane, those like Story Smith, we have to worry about, but the sane. The moral insanity of the sane."

"Would you repeat that?" Thomas Charles said.

"She does not have to repeat anything to an Indian who has the sickness of the others," the Medicine Man said.

"But I will repeat it," Mary-Forge said, and she did, and the Indians saw in her paling face not the scar, the wound, the loss of blood, but the loss of humankind slipping and dripping away as though all life were Sings In Pretty Places and, along with the neon sign on which he hung, again became some kind of announcement, again a silent and cryptic announcement of pause, refreshment, and death.

"We shall," Chee Sinoginee said, "retire to the drawing room."

"The Indians," Mary-Forge said, "on the wild side, will save us yet."

"Lest we forget."

"Lest we forget," Thomas Charles said.

5

From way up here the eagle Star had seen yesterday way down there the Indian dangling from the Coca-Cola sign, and saw today the naked neon girl just erected on Route 44 advertising the Playboy Club; he could see now to the man beneath the naked neon sign playing with his naked self, and see too the water that rose behind the dam on this thirteenth day before the dam dedication and the flood. Now the eagle Star curved downward and out, a meteor, a portent of the omen coming on, a death and resurrection, Star, a sweeping and non-neon signature in the sky—diaphanous and swift.

"You can see the Medicine Man and Mary-Forge are not buying the project," Chee Sinoginee said to Tom Charlie.

"They must."

"Because the project, our gift, is the only drummer the whites, the others, will listen to?"

"Yes," Thomas Charles said.

"You are an Indian and you are an other. Which drummer do you hear?"

"Both," he said.

"That can fuck up your head."

"Yes," he said.

And Thomas Charles thought, Yes, it's enough to make any Indian crazy being two people, but because I have the project I am three people. I am red, I am white, and I am God. That is, I can blow everything up, or like Sings In Pretty Places I can blow myself up. That would solve the problem. No it would not. Yes it would. No it would not. But first I must complete the gift. I have the training and all the components for it. I know how to assemble them perfectly. Then I will decide whether to give this gift to the white man at the dam dedication. It would be in gratitude for all that the American people have done for the Indian. I could be a white-giver. I could take it back. No I couldn't. Yes I could. It's too late. No it isn't. Yes it is. . . .

And so, while the water rose behind the dam and the project went on well too, in another part of the reservation a man named Stewart Montalban Rhodes was watching the naked neon girl and waiting for the Indians to do something. In still another piece of Indian Country Mary-Forge today wore her orange-colored hair like an Indian, and when she moved, it swung like a bell. Mary-Forge called the school the open-air school for Indians. The school was held in a Learning Hogan, but she called it an open-air school anyway because she could think of no other name. Only the brave came. She charged the Indians work. They had to feed the coyotes, clean the hogan, and make the fire and keep the fire going.

Now Mary-Forge looked out at the wide serrated shock of Indian Country that undulated, rose, and fell in a quiet riot and gentle swirl of fabulous, then muted-serene colors to the border of Mexico. And this is what she thought.

She would tell the class about the symptoms of progress and how the disease grew until it clouded the human heart and covered the earth with signs and hid all of the beauty therein. And that is the lesson for today. Without books? Yes, because that is how she got them, got the Indians. Because their minds had been battered with books. White books. Books that made no sense to an Indian. Printed historical lies that had nothing to do with Indian lives. Men from the moon teaching earth people. No, men from factories tumbling steel and iron, people with plastic looks, people with plastic books, with plastic words like Sin, and Thou Shalt Not, to people of earth and quiet dignity. And that is how she got the covey of Indians, because the BIA Federal Torreon school in its wisdom had eschewed the Indians, then repudiated them and cast them out. "Indians are stupid. Not stupid exactly, but congenitally lazy and suffer from a nonverbal syndrome. Stubborn." That is how Mary-Forge got a group of Indians.

"When are you coming up for air, Mary-Forge?" the missionary said.

"I was just thinking," she said, "we should tear down those highway signs. Those ugly highway signs that hide our world."

"You've got to think," the missionary said. "You've got to consider the students."

"That's what I'm thinking of," she said. "Tearing down the highway signs is the best education I can give them. And it would reveal Painted Bird Mesa again."

"I don't know," he said.

The missionary doesn't seem to know anything now, Mary-Forge thought. He used to be Four Square until the Indians converted him away from it. But he's still a missionary. He is still selling something. His problem is he does not know what he has for sale now. But he's selling it.

"I will ask the Indians to help me pull down that big Playboy Club sign," Mary-Forge said.

The problem of getting together a task force of cowboys and Indians to do the job was easy. If you do not believe this, look at the distance between Albuquerque and Santa Fe and see if you see any signs. See if you see any sign of signs. The only sign you will see is cut posts in the air that once held signs. However, the distance between Albuquerque and Cuba, Route 44, is the space of beauty the sign company was polluting now. The new sign advertised a Playboy Club, and on the top of the sign and thirty feet high was a blue-neon naked girl swinging a red-neon lasso.

"They've built a big electric tease there."

"Where?"

"At the Jemez turnoff," Mary-Forge said.

They rode there on horseback. When they got to the Painted Bird Mesa they watched with amaze at what had gone up. The sign was as big as a mountain. One of the horses was mounted by a chain saw. Packing a chain saw. A horse packing a chain saw to cut down a sign big as a mountain. They watched the sign and wondered, silently. One of the horses now snorted and pawed the Painted Bird Mesa.

Way down at the sign a man who was disguised as a hard hat looked up and saw the cowboys and Indians on the Painted Bird Mesa. He was an FBI man, and he was here to protect the sign. Not that the FBI's job is to protect signs, but a man who will destroy a sign will destroy his country, and an FBI man's job is to save his country from radicals. The FBI man's real name, and FBI men do have names, was Stewart Montalban Rhodes, born in Socorro, New Mexico, in June 1925 and now at the Jemez turnoff in New Mexico in January 1974.

Oh, it's good to look up and see cowboys and Indians coming over the horizon, he thought. What is more American than cowboys and Indians?

Apple pie, horse shit, and huge electric signs, Mary-Forge thought as they rode in from the mesa toward the sign. Mary-Forge thought again and looked hard again and realized that all the planning had come to nothing, that they had brought the chain saw for naught, that the sign and all the posts were made of steel.

As they rode up to the sign, the FBI man, Stewart Montalban Rhodes, said, "Hello. It's good to see some real Americans in a real American setting. Look at this country."

"We're trying; we've come to tear your sign down," Mary-Forge said.

"I wish you hadn't said that."

"Why?"

"I'm going to have to arrest you."

"You don't have to do anything in this world you don't want to do."

"The teacher's right," Bull Who Looks Up said.

"You bet your ass I'm right," Mary-Forge said.

"Do teachers talk like that?"

"This one does."

"Stop her," the FBI man said.

"Don't talk rude," Coyotes Love Me said to the FBI man.

"She was being obscene."

"One man's obscenity is another man's lyric," Coyotes Love Me said.

"What the Indians were trying to say was mind your own business," Mary-Forge said.

"I'm arresting you for something else."

"What else?"

"Tearing down the sign."

"We didn't tear down the sign."

"You're planning to. That's just as bad."

"You can't arrest people for thinking about tearing down a sign."

"You have the stuff to do it."

"A chain saw for steel?"

"Well, you thought the sign was made of wood."

"You can't arrest people for thinking something is made of wood," Hosteen Begay said.

"I guess not," the FBI man said. "You're a pretty smart Indian."

"He is the best pupil I've got," Mary-Forge said. "If he can manage to stay out of college I think he's got it licked."

"You mean you are a teacher who doesn't believe in school?"

"Yes."

"What do you believe in?"

"Indians."

"What else?"

"Indians, some young people. They are our link with the future."

"Listen," the FBI man said, "I only try to do a job. I am helping my country. Trying to do my best. Is there something wrong with fighting obscenity?"

"This sign is an obscenity."

"That's just an opinion. This is private property."

"We are private property. That's all the private property there is," Mary-Forge said. "Come, students, we will get the proper tools to tear this thing down."

At the Scalp House William gave the cause of Mary-Forge some hacksaws but told her it would take days to saw through steel that thick, that she could get an acetylene torch at Slaughter's Garage.

"Very well," Mary-Forge said.

While the FBI man waited at the Playboy Club sign on Route 44 below Painted Bird Mesa for Mary-Forge to make another assault, he mused about his career. His grandfather had worked for the Secret Service and told without humor that one of his early missions had been to tap the telephone of Alexander Graham Bell. His grandfather went west with the telephone, tapping it as it went along. He died in Albuquerque tapping a conversation between Shirley Temple and Pancho Villa.

"Is that you, Pancho?"

"No."

"Do you still like me?"

"No."

"How are my pictures going there?"

"No."

"Do you speak English?"

"No."

Rhodes's father followed in his father's footsteps until he was caught at it and killed by friendly Indians.

Now Stewart Montalban Rhodes looked up at the electric twinkling purple tits of the Playboy ad and said aloud, which made the huge sign now audio as well as video, "I know that Thomas Charles, called Tom Charlie, got a job at the Los Alamos atomic laboratory, and what would you do with what you learned if you were an Indian?"

"Tell me," Mary-Forge said to her classroom full, her Learning Hogan full, of Indians, "what would make you happy? Would it make you happy to blow up the white man's signs?"

"Yes!"

"Would it still make you happy that the stockholders in that sign company, some of them widows and orphans, but no Indians, might lose their shirts?"

"Yes!"

"You Indians are still as cruel as ever," Mary-Forge said. "Still bloodthirsty, still savages. Will I have to call the white cavalry to rescue me again today?"

"Yes!"

"I want to find out whether you're against signs or against shirts."

"Yes!"

"I want to find out who watered my cattle today, who led them beside the still waters?"

"I did," Three Shoes said.

"Good. You're a straight arrow, Three Shoes."

The pupil, Three Shoes, was fifty-three years old. Most were young, but some were older than Three Shoes. Everyone came to the free school when they were free. The old slid down in their seats to look small, the small stood up to look big. All the Indians had a ball at the Learning Hogan. The Indians studied hard, things of interest, how to blow up dams and bridges and oil wells and missionaries and power plants to feed Los Angeles. How to raid wagon trains of tourists and succor their young.

"What does that mean, succor the young?" Kills The Enemy wanted to know.

"It's simple, Kills The Enemy," Three Shoes said. "You don't kill women and children."

"Why not? They're white, aren't they?"

"You could have been born a white person."

"Oh God, don't say that, please don't say that."

"Well, I said it. And we spare the women and children. Everyone could have been born a white person."

"No."

"Why not?"

"I refuse to believe it."

"You can't say that."

"Okay. Let them go."

"That's white of you, Kills The Enemy."

"I told you this would happen if we let them go," Kills The Enemy said. "And if we let the white women and children go they will breed."

"But if we've killed off all of the other white people they will have nobody to breed with."

"Well, I guess they'll breed with me."

"That is awfully red of you, Kills The Enemy."

"What I want to know is, while we're talking about killing off wagon trains of tourists we don't do anything to the white people right here." He looked at Mary-Forge. "She looks to this Indian whiter than a snowman. Snowperson."

"*Et tu*, Brutus," Mary-Forge said to Kills The Enemy.

"We can't kill her because she never stops talking."

"I haven't said anything," Mary-Forge said.

"Yes, you have," Three Shoes said. "You've said enough to bring us all together. You have rescued us from the white schools. You have made our small ones stand tall, and for this your name, Mary-Forge, will be truly blessed among all Indians forever."

"And ever," More Turquoise said.

"Let us sing. We have captured you, Mary-Forge, and we don't intend to let you go."

"Let's hear it for Mary-Forge!"

The applause was ear hurting and the missionary Welling Bramberg, passing by, wondered what all the shouting was about.

If the Indians be Indians, Stewart Montalban Rhodes thought, sitting under the obscene Playboy sign, if the Indians object to this insult to nature, all they have to do is get a law passed against it. Indians don't believe in private property. Well, all they have to do is get a law passed against it. No. Private property is sacred. They will never get a law passed against it. Indians will never become civilized, the FBI man thought, watching the girl's neon rear end swing as she swung the neon loop over the great Playboy sign that hid the Painted Bird Mesa, and he thought about Tom Charlie.

While Stewart Montalban Rhodes was watching the naked

neon girl, waiting for the Indians to attack, he had a further thought on what was wrong with the country. Pornography. Most of his spare time was spent at the Stag pornographic movie in Albuquerque, because the magazines in America and the book publishers in America have been pretty much taken over by the Tom Charlies. Educating the Indians can be a dangerous thing, agreed?

When William William gave Mary-Forge the hacksaw for the sign, he was thinking of the secret. Not the secret of Thomas Charles—the project, the gift—but the other secret of the Indians—which is nothing more than anything. After the chores of the workaday world that Indians do—which is nothing more than anything, but Indians do it well. The great Indian secret. Nothing. William wrote about the secret nothing in this fashion: Nothing. It is the delight of cold morning sunrise. It is the ecstasy and somber fulfillment of the human spirit in watching the sun come down red red redding all in magnificent effulgent blaze from in back of the Sangre de Cristo Mountains. The snow-drenched mountains. Nothing is the gamboling of the sheep. Nothing is the myriad dancings of the yebechais of Blessing Way, of Healing Way. Nothing is the crisp mornings and the piñon smoke and the brother, sister, and peoplehood of all Indians on a July day. Nothing is all the sweetness of infant Navajo babes in cradle boards and the way a coyote looks at you when you talk at him. Nothing is love and compassion and an inkling into the sufferings of others and the smack of lightning and the tintinnabulation of a small rain on the hogan roof, and the joy in the feeling for life. Not the complications of and dismay at life's problems, but the ease and wonderment at life's mysteries. Nothing is quiet courage and resistance to the white man's way. Nothing is watching a dam grow to flood our country, a dam the white man does not need. And nothing is an Indian watching a white man selling him a God in which the white man does not believe.

"Yes, take the hacksaw," he said.

Mary-Forge said to the Indians, "What do you want to do?"

"Tear down a sign."

"Great," Mary-Forge said. "Because an Indian will never follow an idea that is not his own. Let's do this thing you so cleverly and wickedly thought of with the guile of an Indian. Those books the white man writes about the Indians. You can't trust the savages."

"Oh, how true," Tzo said.

"Do you know what?" the Medicine Man said. "Did you ever see the paintings in the Yuribi Caves? The Indian is the only man who could paint the Indian. The whites Russell and Remington painted romantic realism, fake illustrations for fake books. Realism is the last refuge of a man who can't paint. Art is the art of the impossible. Why don't we get a decent museum in Albuquerque?"

"That's no way for an Indian to talk," Mary-Forge said. "You're supposed to grunt in clichés. Haven't you read any books?"

"I have traveled all over the country," the Medicine Man said, "studying the white man's medicine. It amounts to selling herbs under different names and charging a fortune. White men's medicine is not a profession, it's a conspiracy. I've come back now to the Indian way. Medicine is the art of allowing the people to die without charging them. When do we tear the sign down?"

"Whenever you say the word," Mary-Forge said.

"I say the word now," the Medicine Man said.

The Medicine Man in Indian Country is popular again. He has not been so popular since the Great Depression. "It's not that I'm complaining," When Someone Dies He Is Remembered said. That's what our Medicine Man's Indian name is. His white name is something stupid like Winthrop C. Hopgood.

"Where did you get a stupid name like Winthrop C. Hopgood, When Someone Dies He Is Remembered?" More Turquoise Than Hope asked.

"I reached the end of my rope in Madison, Wisconsin, and bought it from a Chinese man. Girls get perturbed making love to When Someone Dies He Is Remembered."

"But not to Winthrop C. Hopgood?"

"Not Chinese women," the Medicine Man said.

"What about the sign?"

"What sign?"

"The Playboy sign."

"What about it?"

"Are we going to tear it down?"

"Yes, but let me finish the lecture. Medicine is morality."

"It's your charm and your wit and your good looks."

"That's only part of it," the Medicine Man said.

"What's the latest cure?"

"Tearing down signs," the Medicine Man said. "It makes you feel like a new rain. Let's go."

Stewart Montalban Rhodes finished what he was doing, zipped up his pants, then removed his gun from his shoulder holster, pointed it at his temple, and pulled the trigger. There was nothing but a click.

I guess, the FBI man thought, somebody upstairs doesn't want me to die.

Now the FBI man aimed the gun up at the gyrating rear end of the neon girl and pulled the trigger and the gun went off and she lost a piece of her red behind.

I guess someone upstairs doesn't like her, the FBI man thought. Who do I shoot next?

"Me."

"Who are you?"

"The Medicine Man."

"Indian?"

"Yes."

"You've come to take down the sign?"

"Yes."

"Well, I'm doing it for you."

"Why?"

"Because I've sinned."

"There is no sin."

"I've sinned right under this sign."

"No."

"You don't know what I did."

"Yes, I do."

"And you forgive me?"

"Yes."

"Well, I don't forgive myself. I'm going to shoot up everything."

"Shoot me."

"You're a tough Indian. I respect that. I'm a weak person."

"No, you're not. What you did under that sign was the only thing to do under that sign."

"I do it other places."

"Where?"

"Everywhere."

"Where is everywhere?"

"The Stag Theater."

"That's all right."

"Watching TV."

"That's all right."

"When I caught myself doing it under this sign I said that's the last straw."

"How did you catch yourself? You've been trained by the FBI, I suppose."

"Yes. That's what I'd done with my whole life."

"What have you done with your whole life?"

"You know."

"No, I don't."

"I'm unpatriotic."

"No."

"What you're saying is that I can do anything I like."

"Yes."

"You're nice. Or crazy. Or something."

"I'm a Medicine Man."

"Let me think about that," Stewart Montalban Rhodes said.

"You need a rest, a vacation. You've stalked too many people."

"I'm going to shoot the place up," the FBI man said, raising the gun at everything, including himself.

"Shoot me."

"Here is the gun. You got more nerve than anyone I ever met." Rhodes handed over the gun. "I guess I'm going crazy. I shouldn't have a gun—I'm un-American."

"Shooting the rear end of the go-go girl that hides the Painted Bird Mesa is the most American act I ever heard of."

"You're nice. What do we do next?"

"Remove the sign in an orderly fashion."

The teacher and Indians rode up. They were happy that the FBI man had given up without a fight. They were happy that the Medicine Man had insisted on going into the valley and the shadow to talk first. They unpacked the hacksaw and the acetylene torch from the pack horses, and high and quickly the sparks flew as the torch melted through the steel girders that held up the sign that was eighty-five feet high and was the glory of all the world, and some of the Indians hated to see it go, but it went and there was Painted Bird Mesa again. And the Lord said it was good, and it came to pass that the Indians said it was okay, and going back through Rough Rock and down Lost Canyon, they could all still see the terrific explosion in the dark of the mind's eye as the neon go-go girl, with the neon rope throwing a loop fifty yards wide, standing on a purple mountain surrounded by an orange city and sixty girls, sixty, pointing their purple breasts upward, fell in flames and with a roar that could be heard in Albuquerque.

"Will we dance to celebrate when we get back to the reservation?"

"Yes."

And they danced. In sin, the white man believes himself part of the problem. In life, the Indian believes himself part of the solution. And they danced, to the big boom drum and the loud yawp of the Medicine Man, all hitting back off the cliff of Painted Bird Mesa, which you can see now as clear as a New Mexican day.

All danced. Everyone.

Excepting Thomas Charles

Because

Tom Charlie was thinking.

An Indian thinking can be dangerous.

6

From way up here the eagle Star could see the explosion way down there of the naked neon sign, then hear the drums way down there of the dancing. From the Indians, from the Scalp House. And Star could see too from his forensic and ubiquitous view and on the eleventh day before the flood no ark but a freak and flash sign, BACK TO GOD REAL ESTATE, JUNIUS DORTORT THE THIRD, DEVELOPER, to which the graffiti had been added by a wayward Indian, JUNIUS DORTORT THE THIRD AND SEVEN-EIGHTHS. Star swept outward and away until he, Star, became a mere pictograph against the orange then reddening Indian sky—Star evolving, then fading, becoming distant, spectral, and faint.

William William watched the eagle fade and then wrote this:

And so later and together and naked and still dancing as though we had something to dance past, so we were putting something behind us by the very act of movement, as though it, the dance, were an act of grace that by this incantation, this ritual, this ballet of silent and mimic pantomime we abjured all the dead ends of thought, all the words that led only to more words and mere words, all the logic that ended in consternation and repudiation of the very good smell and

sweat of earth and sex, not again to dissolve in some logic of nothing, some soft music of ending where it began in a fake sophistica-
tion of bald and trite metaphor while we are all sentient and alive
and can dance. Dancing, moving in the Scalp House, while out
there a world is come alive. A reborning and a repulse of strangers
in our country. Strangers who have gathered from all over the world
to commence a civilization, end a beauty. Build a dam and sell the
remaining Indian land back to the Indians.

"I can't concentrate," William William said.

"You mean," Kills The Enemy said, listening to the advertising on the small Japanese battery radio in the Learning Hogan,
"they are selling us back Indian land?"

"Yes," Mary-Forge said.

"They're fucking us," Hosteen Tzo said.

"Can I say something here?" the teacher, Mary-Forge, said.
"That word," she said, "is not a dirty word. I don't like our using
that word in that way. It's a beautiful word and we should
always use it as a good word. Using it as an ugly word is a
misuse you picked up from us whites."

"No," Lucy-Lucy said, "the Indians were here long before the
others. We always did it. I believe. How did I get here? Who
am I?"

"You're an Indian. You got here through the great spirit,"
Hosteen Begay said. "Are there any more questions? If not we
will repair to the great desert and buy a lot."

"A lot of what?"

"Land," Bull Who Looks Up said.

"So ass forward," Mary-Forge said.

So. Mary-Forge not only had orange hair but the temperament
that went with it. The admonitions and explications that went
with the hair and were learned through punching cattle, which
she did on the side. Or did she teach on the side? The Little Red
Schoolhouse, the Learning Hogan—they called it both—was located on the edge of Indian Country in northern New Mexico

hard by the white ranches, so the Indians suffered the worst of both worlds. All Indians are forced to live in two worlds since they were invaded by the whites. So. They drink a lot. They are forced to go to schools run by whites where they are taught the Elizabethan Drama, *Ivanhoe,* and Ping-Pong. So they started a school of their own with Mary-Forge, who is white but has orange hair, a good tight belly, solid breasts, and a sense of humor—Indian humor. And a sense of outrage—moral outrage caused now by the whites, who stole most of the Indian nation and are now gaily engaged in stealing it all. You don't believe it? That is because you went to a little white schoolhouse.

"And were told little white lies," Coyotes Love Me said.

"Let's not be bitter, men," Kills The Enemy said. "Get these men on out of the sun and feed them. We'll kill off the rest of the Indians and sign the treaty in the morning. You're looking well, Custer, but what happened to your scalp?"

Such is history in the Little Red Schoolhouse as told from the point of view of God and thirteen Indians and the teacher in the orange hair. Who used no books. A book is a white man's threat to us Indians, a dangerous weapon. Propaganda. Dropped on the Indians just before the battle, mother.

"Would you like a nice piece of real estate?"

"Would you like to start life all over again on the Indian reservation?"

"Do you complain of a nagging back? Heartburn? Take two Indians and a glass of water. Come to Indian Country. It's the only place left. Send for your free copy of the treaty with the Indians. We got it for nothing, too."

"You can bet your ass they did."

"We can't bet our ass, we lost that a long time ago."

"Let's get this show on the road," Bull Who Looks Up said. "Mary-Forge is going to take us back to our Happy Hunting Ground. Leading us with her flag of orange hair."

"This way, men."

"Which way?"

"This."

"Mary-Forge will personally shoot down the first Indian who turns tail."

"What about the second?"

"She will marry him and raise enough children with God's help for another assault."

"That will take time."

"Time is all the Indian has got left."

"Is time on our side?"

"Not any more."

"But *Newsweek* gave us a good write-up."

"Oh, Jesus," Mary-Forge said, "get your asses moving."

So. The Indian land the whites were selling was called Back To God. The real-estate company started by putting all the possible names for the development on a blackboard so the stockholders could "shoot holes in them." HIAWATHA HEAVEN was shot down first by a Boston gentleman, in a blue tweed with one leather elbow patch, with one thousand shares. Then the LAST HAPPY HUNTING GROUND was shot down by the same man.

"Who's that guy?"

"Six thousand shares."

"Who?"

"The genius."

Then LET ME CALL YOU INDIAN, BIDE A WEE TIME RESERVATION, SOMEWHERE AN INDIAN IS CALLING, and A LOVE THAT WILL NEVER DIE were shot down in that order by everyone. Then the genius wrote on the blackboard, BACK TO GOD. There was an awful silence. Then all of the stockholders clapped. Clap. Clap. Clap. Clap. The stock was floated on the big board by Merrill Lynch, Pierce, Fenner & Smith, and then and on the first day and before profit-taking it came to pass that the stock was up one-eighth. Then it came to pass that the genius, Mr. Dortort The Third, whom they called behind his back Mr. Dortort The Third And Seven-Eighths, did something and the stock rose fifteen and seven-eighths. Then he did something else and it fell nineteen and seven-eighths. That nineteen and seven-eighths looked awful big. Then the genius Mr. Dortort The Third And Seven-Eighths stepped in, and the stock rose accordingly. It is now way up there.

"Where?" Nice Hands' Sister said.

The deed for the Indian land is held by a holding company called GAK. General Activities Korporation. It was formed by a group of Boston gentlemen and incorporated in the Panama Canal Zone.

"Wait," Bull Who Looks Up said, "you got these people pegged as bad guys, but nobody is going all the way to the Panama Canal Zone to screw the Indians."

"Wait and see," Nice Hands' Sister said.

"The thing is, if you incorporate in the Canal Zone and are involved in fraud, they can arrest you only when you're passing through the canal and then legally only on the fifth Thursday of every month."

"Let us have no more nonsense," Mary-Forge said. "Let us go and let us see."

"Let us behold," Hosteen Tzo said.

They all got in Mary-Forge's Ford pickup with I-beam front suspension and went to Santa Fe to La Fonda Hotel, where the radio had said that white people would pick them up in a limousine and take them to the land development—free. But first there would be a free meal in the Granada Room of La Fonda. Mary-Forge and the Indians went through the fake Indian lobby of La Fonda, past the fake cowboys and the fake Indians, without attracting too much attention. Then they went up to the desk to register.

"Do you have a reservation?"

"Yes. But it will soon be under water."

"I can't play games," the desk clerk said. "Do you have luggage? I can't register you without luggage."

"Afraid we'll skip?" Kills The Enemy said.

"I don't own this place," the desk clerk said. "I don't make the rules. It's owned by a trust."

"Then they should trust us."

"Indians? I have nothing against Indians, but you don't have a reservation and you don't have luggage. Most Indians stay at the bridge."

"Where's that?"

"Just this side of the airport."

"Can we get a bath there?"

"People piss off the bridge, yes."

"You mean you want us to sleep under the Arroyo Seco Bridge."

"I did, as a young man."

"Until you pulled yourself up by your own bootstraps. No welfare checks. What this country needs today is more bridges. Well, let me tell you, young man," Kills The Enemy said, "we have a piece of luggage that will astonish you."

"Where?"

"Coming," Kills The Enemy said.

"Tom Yazzie and Tom Charlie came in carrying the project on their shoulders. They set it down gently between two fake Santa Fe cowboys and a local Indian with blanket and feathers.

"That's a suitcase?" the clerk said. The clerk and two female bookkeepers came out from behind the desk to have a look.

"Well, I can only let one Indian in with one suitcase. The rest of you will have to stay at the bridge."

"We will all stay at the bridge," Mary-Forge said. And then she said quietly to Thomas Charles, "Why in the hell did you bring the gift with you?"

"Because it was not safe to leave it in the hogan."

"It won't be safe at Back To God, either," Mary-Forge said. "Let's eat."

When they went into the Granada Room and sat at the free table all hell broke loose.

"Look," a white man said to them, "we are selling the land. We are not giving it back to the Indians."

"Listen," Mary-Forge said, "the radio said come one, come all."

"Look," the man said, "that didn't mean Indians. It stands to reason. Unless you're the Indians that are going to do the war dance?"

"No."

"I know you are not the Indian that's going up in the balloon. There's only one and I've already fed him in the kitchen."

"His last meal on earth."

"We send an Indian up in a balloon every Sunday."

"How many Indians have you gotten rid of that way?"

"We have only lost three so far."

"Out of how many?"

"Four."

"No more jokes," Mary-Forge said. "Let's eat."

"I'm sorry," the man said. "I'll have to consult with Mr. Dortort."

"I'm sorry," Mr. Dortort The Third And Seven-Eighths said, coming up with a pink face, "there has been some misunderstanding. Harry Krapp is a local man who only understands local customs. We welcome Indians. Harry Krapp recruits only Indians for the balloon. We welcome outside Indians regardless of race, creed, color, or place of national origin."

"Then let's eat," Mary-Forge said.

"And enjoy," Mr. Dortort said, moving away.

Mary-Forge and the Indians did not realize they had been talking to the genius, Mr. Dortort himself, who with the pink pink face and white Levis and the one leather shoulder patch on his left elbow had inspired the development. He had bought two hundred thousand acres of Indian Country. Bought? Well, he got it. The genius divided the two hundred thousand acres into "one-acre ranches," but that only made a profit of a few hundred thousand, so he cut the lots down to one-half acres and called them ranchos, then to one-quarter acres and called them ranchitos, then because they were going like hot Indians he sold them as fifty-foot "estates." Which is a bargain any way you look at it. It is an irresistible bargain. It is an impossible bargain to resist when the gang of the genius has got you committed to a free meal at La Fonda.

Mary-Forge and the Indians hadn't eaten a square meal for a week, so they put it away nicely and looked around for more.

"That's all," Harry Krapp said. "You've cleaned us out."

Actually, La Fonda is loaded with grub, but Harry Krapp put a cut-off point on the kitchen.

"And all the while," More Turquoise said, "we could be oil-rich Indians eager to make our fortune in land speculation. The genius knows this. But Harry Krapp is a small man. He is willing to risk the disaster of this whole enterprise for a couple of extra plates of egg foo yung. He cut us off in the kitchen. Harry Krapp is a small man."

"Right this way to the bus," Harry Krapp said, "the next stop is Back To God."

"Back to who?"

"God," Harry Krapp said.

The black driver of the bus in an Uncle Tom chauffeur's cap said, "You all," in a Texas accent, "in the right bus?"

"Yes," Mary-Forge said.

"You all going Back To God?"

"Yes."

"Then please move to the rear," the black bus driver said, "so the other peoples can sit."

"We're happy where we are," Mary-Forge said.

"What's that you're putting on top of the bus?" the black Texas driver asked.

"A suitcase."

"Why? No one sleeps yet at Back To God. I don't even think they'll sell Indians an estate. I don't even know whether I want to live next to Indians."

"Maybe the suitcase will convince you."

"No."

"What's inside will convince you."

"What's inside?" The black Texan put the gear shift in low and looked at them.

"A gift."

"It's going to take a lot more than a gift to get you into Back To God."

The bus jerked off, with the project on top. The bus moved fast, as though the whole kit and caboodle, the bus load and the swaying thing on top, were in a big rush to get Back To God.

"The black gentleman must be in cahoots with Harry Krapp," Looks Important After A Rain said. "Harry Krapp is not aware that an Indian can get tired fighting the whites, and before he goes to that happy Happy Hunting Ground he might want to try living on an estate. Back To God is as good as anywhere."

"But not Back To God," the black driver said, "I know the policy. No Indians. I don't want to see you get hurt, I know the policy, I don't want to see you all get hurt."

"We all won't get hurt," Bull Who Looks Up said, "but you all might. Why do you hate Indians?"

"I don't hate Indians."

"Why do you hate Indians?" Mary-Forge said.

"Indians drink too much."

"Where did Back To God find you?"

"El Paso."

"Do you have an estate?"

"Everyone who works for GAK has to buy an estate."

"Do you have a little one?"

"No, I have one of the big fifty-foot ones."

"Is it off to the side?"

"A little off to the side."

"Is it under water?"

"A little under water."

"That way you can drink with the Indians," Nice Hands' Sister said.

So. The road to Back To God for the first part ran through the picturesque ruins of Santa Fe: an abandoned Dairy Queen, three competing foot-long-hot-dog stands, and long rows of imported Indians selling each other fake jewelry. The outskirts of Santa Fe were devoted to mobile homes piled on top of each other. Most of Santa Fe is devoted to a water shortage, but they didn't see that part. Past the outskirts they beheld an outdoor opera house devoted to deficit spending and stuff sung in German and Italian. The Japanese conductor was standing outside as though he had just escaped.

"Santa Fe," the black driver said, "is the cultural capital of the Southwest."

"That I believe," Lucy-Lucy said.

"If William William writes up this trip in his book he won't sell any books in Santa Fe," Coyotes Love Me said to Mary-Forge.

"I don't think he intends to write about this."

"We must be prepared for every eventuality," Bull Who Looks Up said.

"He might do something on Back To God," Mary-Forge said.

"If we get out alive," Lucy-Lucy said.

And so the Indians with the thing on top were going down the last hill before Back To God.

"You just don't take a counterculture and fight it," Harry Krapp said. "That's what we in the corporation believe." They had arrived at the Back To God Estates and were let out by the black Texan at the Back To God Lodge and were greeted by Harry Krapp who said, "That's what we in GAK believe."

Outside and through the window they could see the Indian about to go up in the balloon.

"What kind of an Indian is he?" More Turquoise said.

"I don't think he is a real Indian," Harry Krapp said, "I think he's an Eskimo."

"Eskimos are Indians," Mary-Forge said. "Where did you find an Eskimo?"

"He found us. There is a government Indian sanitation health school in Algodones. They bring Indians in from all over the world."

"The world?"

"I think so," Harry Krapp said.

"Haven't we got American Eskimos?"

"I think so," Harry Krapp said.

"Then why don't you use them?"

"We should," Harry Krapp said.

"How much do you pay?"

"Fifty dollars."

"When they come down?"

"Yes."

"Why don't you pay before they go up?"

"We should," Harry Krapp said.

"What's the attraction?"

"People like to see a man disappear in a balloon, then they buy an estate. The balloon ascension is one of the attractions that gets them out here. It's funny, but seeing a man disappear in a balloon seems to make a person want to buy a piece of land. It was Mr. Dortort's idea."

"Where do the people come from?"

"New York."

"Why?"

"Because last Sunday we took a half page in *The New York Times*."

"What did it say?"

"Back To God."

They were all, the teacher Mary-Forge and all the Indians, seated in the Cochise Saloon with Harry Krapp, in front of a huge window that overlooked Indian Country, being served cocktails by the Texas black. He had exchanged his Tom chauffeur's cap for a Tom white jacket, but he still resented the Indians. Like his cap the jacket had written in gold flourish, "Back To God."

"Mr. Dortort feels," Harry Krapp said, "that we in GAK, we in Back To God, should not discriminate against the Indian. Mr. Dortort has long felt that you should not start a community without a plan, without a ghetto. You should not let a ghetto develop haphazardly but should start a community with a ghetto. And a slum."

"What?"

"Mr. Dortort studied city planning at CCNY."

"Where?"

"That's a university."

"What's the difference between a ghetto and a slum?"

"Listen to how he answers this," the teacher Mary-Forge said.

There was a silence as they all looked out through the huge window at Indian Country.

"Plenty," Harry Krapp said.

There was more silence and then Lucy-Lucy said, "Well, we listened, teacher."

"Mr. Dortort believes," Harry Krapp said, "that a ghetto should be set aside for an ethnic group, say the Indian."

"Yes."

"While the slum should be open to all."

"That sounds fair."

"You mean the slum is open to all, regardless of race, creed, or place of national origin?"

"Yes."

"Could an Indian buy into the slum?"

"No."

"Why?"

"Mr. Dortort has set aside the ghetto for the Indian."

"I can't believe," Mary-Forge said, "that you're serious."

"You'd be surprised," Harry Krapp said. "People like to know where they stand."

"How do people know they're in the slum?"

"The garbage is not collected there."

"Is it collected in the ghetto?"

"We don't know that yet."

"I still can't believe you're serious."

"Why do you think Mr. Dortort is called a genius?"

"I give up," Tzo said.

"Well, I haven't given up," Harry Krapp said. "Shall we look at the estates?"

"I think we could look better if we had another drink under our belts," Coyotes Love Me said.

"The black Texan has gone to pick up another load at La Fonda," Harry Krapp said.

Then Thomas Charles remembered that the gift was still on top of the bus. The gift would have to go back to Santa Fe and then come Back To God. What would happen to all the mud houses in Santa Fe if there was an accident? Thomas Charles tried to stop thinking about this and tried to think about the estates.

Outside in the hot, dry, and rising quickly New Mexican sun and among the cholla and beaver tail and Johnny-jump-ups, the balloon was being inflated by the sun and two tanks of laughing gas. The Eskimo stood alongside the balloon basket on one leg, guarded by two hippie types in bib overalls.

"Do they ever escape?"

"No. And don't worry about the balloon going up without us. It won't go up until at least another load gets here. First of all," Harry Krapp said, "we will look at the higher estates."

"You mean view-wise or price-wise?"

"High-wise."

"Do they cost more?"

"Everything costs more," Harry Krapp said.

"If a person is so dishonest," Mary-Forge thought aloud, "how can they fail?"

"They try harder," Tom Yazzie said. "That's how they fail. They couldn't even sell me a lot on the beach."

"What beach?"

"The one Mr. Dortort has in mind."

"We built a development in Phoenix with real waves," Harry Krapp said.

"You're not just saying this because we are Indians?"

"Our competition built another development in Arizona and brought over the London Bridge. Yes," Krapp said, "they brought the London Bridge over to Arizona stone by stone. We have a plan to bring the Caspian Sea over to New Mexico bucket by bucket. The Russians don't want it any more."

"Do the Russians own it?"

"I think they do."

"It's not the London Bridge."

"But we try harder," Harry Krapp said.

"We have got to be leaving," Mary-Forge said.

"You have just arrived."

"I would like to get back to the Caspian," More Turquoise said. "Did the Russians get tired of it?"

"Probably."

"They've had it a long time."

"Yes."

"Then people drown in it."

"And ships from time to time go down."

"With all hands," Lucy-Lucy said.

"That raises the insurance."

"People have to pay for other people's mistakes."

"I think we'd better get going," Mary-Forge said.

"We haven't seen the ocean yet, not even the Pacific," Coyotes Love Me said.

"We're not guaranteeing the Pacific," Harry Krapp said.

"But you haven't lied to us yet. We'd better get going," Mary-Forge said.

"Mr. Dortort once thought, and hasn't abandoned the idea yet, that if the Russian Caspian Sea thing falls through he's thinking of digging a small canal and draining part of the Pacific up this way. The problem is when it backs up, Albuquerque will have to be abandoned."

"That is no problem at all," Coyotes Love Me said. "Just post a notice."

"I will tell Mr. Dortort that. It will fill in a gap in his thinking. It's surprising what you can learn if you listen to the Indian."

"The voice of the Indian."

"What's your name?"

"Coyotes Love Me."

"We could change our lake's name to Coyotes Love Me."

"From what?"

"The Pacific Ocean," Mr. Dortort said, coming up. He looked out in the direction of the Pacific as Cortez had done. "It's not a bad idea at all. Coyotes Love Me," he said. "Fabulous," he said.

The Texas black driver came up now and said that he had brought another load of customers and would the Indians please take the gift off the top.

Going home, they passed the place where the balloon was going up and it was gone. The New York people were busy buying fifty-foot estates on the Coyotes Love Me. Everyone at Back To God seemed very happy for now.

7

When they got the gift back to the hogan, Thomas Charles wanted to take it out again.

"Why?"

"To test security."

"What's that mean?"

"To see if we can get the suitcase past security guards. The dam dedication will have security guards. This will be a test."

"Where?"

"The smoke factory."

"What's that?"

"The Four Corners Power Plant."

The huge and very tall smokestack that supplied power to California and a black spread of gloom to Indian Country was going full steam today. The Four Corners Power Plant was—is—so named because it is located where the states of Arizona, Utah, Colorado, New Mexico—every state but California—touch each other. California placed the smoke plant as far from California as the transmission lines would stretch. Ideally the Californians wanted the smoke plant in Denmark, but then there were the Danes. That was a problem. In Indian Country there were nothing but Indians. There was no problem.

"Blow it up," Kills The Enemy said.

"The California legislature has taken the problem, the Indian complaint, under advisement. The governor has formed a committee...."

"Whatever that means," Lucy-Lucy said. "I guess it means the white people will continue to keep to shit on us...."

"Yes."

"We will blow it up," Kills The Enemy said.

Ah, but how? It is all well and good and a big emotional charge to go out and blow things up, to think about blowing up, dwell on blowing up, even plan on blowing up, but how do you do it? Actually do it? You begin by beginning. You ride over to the great smoke plant on horses. You survey the scene, you case the place, you talk to the plant's public-relations man. To find out how the smoke thing works? Where is its weakest link? Its exposed place? Its black Achilles' heel?

Thomas Charles brought the gift, the project, out to the smoke plant on the buckboard, a one-horse wagon, so that by all using horses they could cut the time in half by taking the shortcut and giving innocence to the project—no one is arriving excepting cowboys and Indians.

"You can't bring that thing in here," the guard said to Tom Charlie.

"It's a body," Tom Charlie said.

"The body of whom?" the guard said, "or is it who?"

"Whom," Thomas Charles said.

The guard got on the gate telephone and said, "An Indian out here has the body of Whom." There was a pause and then he said to Tom Charlie, "The public-relations man wants to know whether you Indians want to be taken seriously or comically; that is, is this a comedy or a tragedy?"

"Tragedy."

"Then what's with this 'the whom'?"

"You started it."

"I was only trying to find the correct English."

"Whom."

The guard hung up the phone and said to Tom Charlie, "Open it up."

"You already let all the other Indians in without inspection."

"They were on horseback."

The manager came out now and said to the guard, "Can't you see it's an Indian?"

"Yes."

"That it's not an ecology person?"

"Yes."

"Well, let him in. You know the dangerous profile of an ecology person. Intelligent. Humanitarian type. Reflective. Concerned. Dedicated. Inadequate father image."

"How can you tell whether a person has an inadequate father image?"

"That's what the book says. You are on your own, Marty," he said to the guard.

"Go ahead in," the guard said to Tom Charlie.

"It is not necessary to add the word 'in,'" Thomas Charles said. "You have added a dangling preposition. 'Go ahead' is sufficient. 'In' is redundant," the Indian said.

The guard started to draw out his .45-caliber pistol, but the manager of the smoke plant made a mollifying gesture and the guard put the gun back and Tom Charlie and the horse pulling the load with Whom got past security. And so Thomas Charles thought aloud as he drove the project through the gate, "It's got four names now—the project, the thing, the gift, and Whom.

Countries have always had this problem with the beast. Naming the creature. Now the Indians have the problem."

"If you were going to blow this place up, how would you go about it?" Hosteen Begay asked the public-relations man.

"I don't know."

"What's a public-relations man for?"

"I don't know. Yes, I do."

"Make up your mind."

"I am supposed to sell the plant."

"How much are you asking?"

"I sell it in a figurative sense."

"How much?"

"Actually in terms of getting along with the Indians."

"Did you ever see an Indian?" Bull Who Looks Up said.

"Yes."

"Touch one?"

"Not in terms of touching an Indian, no."

"Want to?"

"I want to touch them in a figurative sense. Are you Indians?"

"Yes."

"The girl there with the orange hair, is she an Indian?"

"In terms of a figurative sense, yes, she is," Bull Who Looks Up said.

"I never saw an Indian before with orange hair," the public-relations man said.

"Tomorrow we're going to charge fifty cents to see her. You're the last one to see her free."

"I would like you to show us," Mary-Forge said, "how this electrical-generating plant works."

"It's not an electrical-generating plant, it's a smoke-generating plant," the public-relations man said. "Oh, I suppose it generates some electricity, but mostly it generates smoke."

"And you do a good job," Mary-Forge said.

"Thank you," the public-relations man said.

"Where do you sell the smoke?"

"That's not my end of the business."

"What is your end of the business?"

"Public relations," the public-relations man said.

"And you do a damn good job," Mary-Forge said.

"Thank you. I try to be honest."

The public-relations man's plastic office in the Four Corners Power Building overlooked a plastic lawn beneath a plastic sky—that is, there was a plastic patio outside the plastic window that re-created Indian Country as it was before white men came.

The public-relations man wore a blue-plastic hat above a red-plastic tie. Between was a wide, you'll-never-know-dear-how-much-I-love-you-please-don't-take-my-sunshine-away cherubic face.

"What are you doing here?" the public-relations man said.

"We just thought we'd come and have a look-see."

"No, you came to blow the place up. Why can't you be honest?" the public-relations man said. "I never met a man yet who didn't want to blow this place up. I've thought about it myself." And the public-relations man looked out over the blue-plastic sky from beneath his blue-plastic cowboy hat.

"Even the company that built it," he said, "would like to blow it up, but no one has figured out a way to do it."

"Dynamite."

"No, it's insured. The insurance company would rebuild it."

"Blow up the insurance company."

"No, they're insured too."

"Drop the insurance."

"There's a law against that."

"Cut the power line."

"There's not much power that goes over the power line."

"Where does the power go?"

"Smoke," the public-relations man said.

"I never met an honest white man before," Coyotes Love Me said.

"I want to warn you Indians," the public-relations man said, "that honesty is the last weapon of a desperate man."

"Are the whites that desperate? That they will even use honesty?"

"Yes."

"Wasn't honesty outlawed by the Geneva Convention or the Red Cross or something?"

"No. They forgot about honesty."

"Jesus, you are desperate," Bull Who Looks Up said. "Poison gas we could put up with, but an honest white man—what do you do? There's no book on that."

"Come on, show us the plant," Mary-Forge said.

Everyone rose.

"You're crying," Mary-Forge said to the public-relations man.

"Am I?"

"It must be the smoke."

"No, the office is air-conditioned. We bring the air in from Canada."

"Then you're crying."

"I guess so," the public-relations man said.

"Buck up," Mary-Forge said. "Someone has to generate electricity."

"Why?" the public-relations man said.

The public-relations man showed Mary-Forge and the Indians all through the smoke plant. He particularly showed them where the smoke was purified before it went out the smokestack.

"Then where does the smoke out there come from?"

"Smoke? They've formed a committee to solve that problem," the public-relations man said.

"Buck up," Mary-Forge said. "Someone has to make progress."

"Why?" the public-relations man said.

"Because," Tom Yazzie said, "the country must go forward."

"Must it?"

"Yes," More Turquoise said. "What would a white woman do without an electric shaver to shave her legs?"

"Do white women use an electric shaver to shave their legs?" Nice Hands' Sister said.

"If they feel like it."

"If we feel like it, could we blow this place up?"

"Yes," Thomas Charles said.

"Where is the gift?"

"The plant security guard is watching it," Tom Charlie said.

"Would anyone," the public-relations man said, "like a shot of Canadian air?"

They went into the room now where the coal was turned into dust before it was spat into the furnace.

"We scrape this coal," the public-relations man said, "off the top of Indian Country, the Fruitland and the Mesa Verde formations. The company figures there's enough coal overlaying Navajo Country to last the southern-California people a hundred years."

"What will they do when the hundred years are up?"

"We don't know."

"They could always grind up us Navajos that are left into dust," Bull Who Looks Up said, "and squirt us into the furnace."

"Oddly enough," the public-relations man said, "California Electric and Gas had the Rand Corporation do a study on that. They found there would be a public outcry."

"Why public outcry?" Coyotes Love Me said. "Why all of a sudden?"

"People are funny."

"That funny?"

"This is all in a hundred years."

"People won't become that funny in a hundred years."

"People could get into Indians in a hundred years."

"They're into Indians already," Hosteen Begay said, "that's the problem."

"Can I say something?" Mary-Forge said.

"Speak, O orange-headed white teacher of the red man, oh, speak," Nice Hands' Sister said.

"We came here to figure how to blow this place up, and you sit around talking like a bunch of Indians."

"We can always figure how to blow it up in the morning," Hosteen Begay said. "Let's have a shot of Canadian air."

They were all quiet in the vast cathedral-high room that made jet-plane sounds when the coal was being crunched up to be made into smoke. In the next room were the electric generators that hardly made any noise at all. They only made a gentle hum and huddled in a corner as though apologizing for being there at all. The public-relations man opened the door, and they could all see the generators sleeping in a row. One big one, which called itself Made In Japan, made an abrupt oriental snoring noise as though having a bad dream. The other generators just slept quietly, occasionally talking in their sleep with small click noises as their breaker points snapped on, but they refused to start up until the Japanese generator stopped snoring. The Made By Volkswagen generator was going great guns, but it was small and high-strung. It even ran when it was turned off.

"It's a persistent son of a bitch," the public-relations man mused. "We had a German once who understood it. He used to beat it every night. But we've got them licked now," he added abstractedly, as though talking about a different world.

"Who?"

"The people who cut the transmission lines."

"Who?"

"They call themselves The Committee To Save What's Left. They see all that smoke; they have spotters in the mountains.

They see all that smoke and cut the transmission lines. That's fooling them. There's nothing in the lines. Just this smoke here."

"Just smoke."

"We expect to have all the generators on steam in a couple of months."

"That soon?"

"Yes."

"Even the Made In America ones?"

"Maybe."

"You could always get the German back."

"Yes."

The public-relations man was talking absently, as though thinking about something else. Now he said definitely, "You know, we're not a bunch of clowns here. There are always start-up problems in a big plant like this. Soon we will get the bugs out and we can get cracking."

"What are the bugs?"

"People like yourself who try to shut us down. We feel you out, try to get to know your tricks. We figure it's best not to start up and then get blown up."

"That's bad public relations."

"Yes."

"Meanwhile, what do people in California do for electricity?"

"They make do. You Indians haven't had electricity for two thousand years."

"Did we have electricity before that?"

"You must have had something," the public-relations man said.

"Why can't we," Mary-Forge said—the teacher in the teacher said—"why can't we stick to a conversation that makes sense?"

"Smoke?"

"Yes," Mary-Forge said. "If this plant only makes smoke, what does California do for electricity?"

"Japan."

"You mean California brings their electricity from Japan?"

"Maybe."

"You mean the Japanese make better electricity than we do?"

"Cheaper," the public-relations man said. "But there's talk of switching to Great Arab Lighting."

Outside, the Indians and Mary-Forge were moving away on their myriad-colored horses, beneath the canopy of smoke, and Mary-Forge thought: But today was not defeat, no, not that. It was a kind of dream, a white nightmare, a phantasmagoric and contemporary white frolic and farce in which the Indian is victim and buffoon to the white man, but played out on the real Indian land, not stage, of Indian heritage and hope.

Lucy-Lucy drove her piebald alongside Mary-Forge's bay. "This today mean the white people going to keep to shit on us? And then drown us?"

"Yes," Mary-Forge said, "yes." And the Indians remembered and Mary-Forge dreamed of how it was before the others came.

It was very cold and Thomas Charles was very late getting back with the buckboard to the hogan.

"Come on ahead in," Hosteen Tzo said.

Tom Charlie came into the hogan without any nonsense.

"How is the gift?" Tzo said.

"You mean Whom?"

"No, I mean how."

"It's got enough names already," Tom Charlie said. "Now the gift is sleeping."

"Good," Tzo said. "Don't wake it till the dam dedication. Are you going to invite your friends from Los Alamos?"

"No, I hadn't thought about it."

"They would be pleased to discover how well you're doing," Tzo said.

8

The Star view on the eighth day before the flood was black-shrouded by the plume from the tall chimney penis in the sky, the Four Corners Power Plant, which joined four states in writing a message to the birds and to the beasts and to the eagle in this new man-made cloud of prosperity and happiness to all and to all a good night. A message to the eagle Star was also writ below in the tracing of the bulldozers removing the mesa to get the coal to feed the plant to bring instant happiness and to all a good day. Star stood alongside his aerie as this eighth day came to pass before the flood, and made quiet witness.

Every Indian had an idea of how to get rid of the dam, but they were all too impractical and lunatic, and it gave everyone in the clan some comfort to know that an Indian was no longer a victim and impotent, dependent on a Washington caprice that would bury the clan. That Tom Charlie could say no. That Tom Charlie could make the dam disappear. Magic. Like the coal company that was making the Painted Bird Mesa disappear. Magic again. No, this time it was real. But we would stop them. Myth. No one can stop them. So when you are impotent you make myths to achieve. You develop power through the fantasy of myth. This was the myth of the clan. It may be told a thousand years from now. This is how it was told now by William. Not a bad teller for a half Indian. But first there was the person who came to the Scalp House with an eviction notice.

William William and Mary-Forge had just finished making love in the Scalp House on the Navajo rugs beneath the Acoma pots, beneath the stern picture eyes of Cochise, Crazy Horse, Red Shirt, and the eviction deputy, Mr. Breckenridge, was reporting back to his wife.

"So when I came into the room they was fornicating on the floor. All of them!"

"All?"

"This William William and this Mary-Forge were not going at it like normal people will, but all of them. I mean their whole bodies—all of everything."

"You mean like in a doctor book?"

"No, like in them hard-core movies."

"Do you aspire to that, Mr. Breckenridge?"

"I only wanted to serve them with a writ of eviction."

"But you was embarrassed."

"I did not know what to do. You see, the door was open and I heard this banging and this screaming and this moaning, so I drew my gun and went in this place they call the Scalp House and they was only the two of them naked as snakes."

"You done seen those hard and core movies, Mr. Breckenridge?"

"No," the process server said to his wife. "I never."

"I hear tell they're an education."

"I never," he said. And then he said wondrously, "I never will need to now, never."

"And then you just quit," she said, "without serving no eviction papers for the dam?"

"Yes," he said, "they was naked as snakes."

"When the dam is filled they is all ready to swim."

"Not swim," he said. "Christ almighty you should have seen them going at it. The fur was flying."

"Like in a hard and core movie?"

"Them has never been my purview."

"But that's the idea."

"Yes, that's the idea," he said. "I never did get no chanct to serve them."

"They also serve who only stand and wait."

"But the government don't pay for that," he said. "I will wait for the day when they has quieted down."

"That will be the day."

"I reckon it will be a bit," he said.

"Damn it, Billy, someone was just in here."

"While we were dancing?" William said.

"Yes, you can see these cowboy-boot tracks."

"Why, do you suppose?"

"He left? Because we hadn't any clothes on. Get dressed and I will tell you a good story."

"Tell me this way. What's the story about?"

"These coal people who are skimming the last piece of ass off this mesa before the flood."

"I know that."

"But you don't know this," she said.

"Let me tell it."

"All right, you're the storyteller, but make it a good myth."

"Yes," William said.

"Go ahead," she said. "Am I in it?"

"You're in it."

"Go ahead," she said.

"The story is called 'Even When the Coyote Asks, It Is Surely Rude to Show the Coyote the Way Out of the Coyote Burrow.' "

"Pour me a drink."

She took it to a Two Gray Hills Navajo rug, sat, crossed her legs and tucked them in, and stared at the picture of Cochise.

Once upon a time the earth was round, then the strip miners came and scraped away the Painted Bird Mesa for the coal . . .

"Is there any intelligent life among the whites?" the Navajo Coyotes Love Me asked.

"We do not know," the Medicine Man said.

"When all the mesas are gone from their strip mining and Indian Country is as flat as the earth before it became round—"

"What do you mean, before the earth became round?"

"When you could slide off the edge."

"Did you ever see anyone slide off the earth?"

"Yes, the beaver off the beaver dam on the Sangre de Cristo. The beavers do not know the world is round."

"Do the coyotes know?"

"The coyotes on the Painted Bird will find out when the bulldozers reach down into their homes."

The coyotes beneath the Painted Bird were not speculating whether the earth was round or flat; they were, however, impressed that it was getting noisy. Each day the others, the whites, would shovel with their great machine, and the earth would get noisier and flatter. So the people who discovered the earth was round were making it flat. Columbus was right only temporarily. "When the others finish, the world will be as flat as a pancake."

"And people with it."

"You observed that?"

"Yes."

"You don't believe the others might suddenly suffer temporary sanity and keep the world round?" Coyotes Love Me said.

"No," the Medicine Man said. "I go along with the flat-as-a-pancake theory."

The coyotes beneath the Painted Bird Mesa were no worse off than the Indians on top. The Indians on top were scraped off and the coyotes were dug up. But the Beebody Coal Company had to make a living. Beebody was said to belong to the Klean-Ko Copper

Corporation. No one was certain, Klean-Ko or Beebody. The white people called Klean-Ko a conglomerate corporation, which means if it's in trouble nobody owns it. The Klean-Ko executives were in jail and the Beebody president was being held for scraping off all of western West Virginia—by mistake. When western West Virginia disappeared, Beebody came to Indian Country. Beebody still referred to the people of western West Virginia as Gooks. People who did not appreciate what Beebody had done for them. Beebody had given western West Virginians full employment to scrape themselves off. When they had no place to live, Beebody, without pressure from the government but with pressure from the heart, distributed C rations to all regardless of color—most of them were black from the coal now—and then finally set up refugee camps outside of Johnstown until the refugees were moved by a godsend of a flood, when the Beebody dam broke.

The Beebody executives, to maintain secrecy, spoke to each other only by pay telephone and referred to each other only as Lardy Dardy. They put a pay telephone on top of the Painted Bird. When it rang and you answered it, the other end would say, "This is the other end. Is Mr. Lardy or Mr. Dardy there?" When you said, "Speaking," the other end would say, "Hey, you Lardy Dardy," and hang up. After that, another part of the mesa would disappear.

The government sent out a team of men with a game plan to help the Indians, but they only had time to bug the Medicine Man's hogan and hold up the local liquor store, where they left a printed message: "For national security so keep it secret. Hey, you Lardy Dardy."

"But Beebody did put a pay phone on the Painted Bird."

"You mean everything else is not true?"

"The part about bugging the Medicine Man's psychiatrist is not true."

"I didn't hear that part."

"Then read tomorrow morning's newspaper," Kills The Enemy said. "Every crime the white man forgot to commit today he will commit tomorrow."

"You sound bitter."

"I am watching," Kills The Enemy said. "I am feeling the Painted Bird Mesa disappear."

The Beebody people had their workmen, their Tom Swift and his electric-shovel operators, dressed as Indians. The workmen were refugees from western West Virginia. They were very convincing Indians. Their Indian costumes were loaned to them by the Central Intelligence Agency through the Committee to Re-elect the Mayor of Gallup. The reason for this is perfectly clear: it is best to nip a conspiracy in the bud. Custer tried to do this at the Rosebud and failed—this is our second chance. This is what a government is for. If you don't believe in the government, why don't you leave America and go back where you came from?

"That's a thought."

"Where would you go?" the Navajo Looks Important After A Rain said.

"After I'm scraped off?"

"Yes."

"Back where I came from."

"Where did you come from?"

"Here."

"After tomorrow here will not exist."

"That's not a thought."

"What is it?"

"The real thing," the Medicine Man said.

They all watched the Painted Bird disappear.

The Painted Bird disappeared at the rate of one square mile per day. That was the schedule to remove the overburden, the earth above the Mesa Verde formation where the coal lay. The coal was then mixed with Navajo water and the black slurry piped to the Four Corners Power Plant, where it was separated from the water and then turned into smoke to shroud Navajo Country. The Painted Bird hid excellent coal according to Beebody; it was running ninety-nine-point-oh-five sulfur, which made deadly green smoke guaranteed to kill anything on two legs trying to start trouble. Did you ever ask yourself why anyone like Mary-Forge would be in Indian Country if they weren't trying to start trouble? When they could live in Miami, say, or Palm Springs?

"I lived in Pittsburgh once," More Turquoise said, "on the government program to relocate the Indians."

"What do people do in Pittsburgh for a living?"

"They die."

"That's nice."

"Why doesn't our beloved white teacher, Mary-Forge, have a

plan to save the Painted Bird? Some plan to keep the world round."

"I will speak to them," Mary-Forge said.

"To whom will you speak?"

"The Beebody people. I will ask them why they want the world flat."

"And when you speak to them," the Medicine Man said, "remember the legends and the myths. Make it a good story."

"And don't kick them in the balls," Lucy-Lucy said.

When Mary-Forge asked this question, "Why do you want the world flat?" the nice hard hat demurred. He was sitting in his air-conditioned office in the electric shovel, surrounded by his instruments.

When he had demurred a while longer, the hard hat said, "Coal. Money." Then he paused and said, "Because I am fed up with women taking over."

"What has that got to do with removing the Painted Bird?"

"Everything."

"Do you want to tell me more? Feel free to talk."

"Beebody has been good to me," the hard hat nonsequitured.

"The Painted Bird means a great deal in the spiritual life of the Indians, and you are destroying the home of the coyotes."

Then the hard hat pressed a button that increased the speed of the great machine that removed fifty tons of the mesa with each scoop and repeated, "Beebody's been good to me."

Mary-Forge wrote out a note and placed it in front of the hard hat. The note said, "Are we being bugged by Beebody?" The hard hat took his pencil and wrote, "Yes." Then Mary-Forge wrote, "Where can we go to escape the bug?"

Hard hat wrote, "Everywhere is bugged."

She wrote, "Outside, too?"

He wrote, "Yes."

"How?"

"The bugs are bugged. If you see a large bug crawling or flying, it's probably not a bug but a bug."

"Can a Beebody bug crawl?"

"Yes, and a Beebody bug can fly, too."

"Can you leave the shovel?" she wrote.

"Yes."

"Who will run the shovel?"

"The shovel runs itself," the hard hat wrote.

"Sure?"

"Sure."

"Then what are you doing here?"

"Beebody demands that someone be with the shovel at all times."

"To keep the shovel company?"

"Yes."

"What if it eats its way through a city?"

"That's the city's problem."

"Is there coal under Albuquerque?"

"Yes."

"Tomorrow the world?"

"Yes."

"Follow me," Mary-Forge wrote, and the hard hat did, Mary-Forge writing as they went and the hard hat writing back.

"It's beautiful out."

"Yes."

"Is that bird bugged?"

"Yes."

"How can you tell?"

"It's been trained to fly close to me."

"That flower?"

"No."

"How can you tell?"

"I watched it grow and tagged it," he wrote.

Mary-Forge led the hard hat down a slope the shovel had caused and then into a hole the huge electric shovel had not reached. The hard hat followed Mary-Forge into the hole, and the coyotes in the hole fled way to the back of the den. The coyotes knew Mary-Forge and did not panic, but they did not know the hard hat.

"We can sit up here," Mary-Forge said when they came to a widening in the tunnel. "We can talk here," Mary-Forge said, "away from the bug and safe with the coyotes."

"This is better," he said.

"How can we turn the machine off?" she said.

"No way," he said.

"There must be some way."

"No way," he said.

"If it was started it can be stopped."

"That, I'm afraid, is female logic," he said. "Male logic has discovered the law that once something is started it cannot be stopped. The males have been proven correct. Take the women's liberation movement. You don't realize it here in Indian Country, but in the city women have got something started that no one can stop."

"Won't it stop when women get what they want?"

"When women get what they want, then there are their desires."

The coyotes were listening to all this and not making any sense of it.

"I have never gone into women's desires with a hard hat before," Mary-Forge said, "but I have got a proposition that I think would save the Painted Bird."

"Shoot," he said.

That word frightened the coyotes. They had heard "shoot" many times before and had felt the result of that word.

It did not frighten Mary-Forge because the word was being used metaphorically.

The word "metaphorically" meant nothing to the coyotes and they let it pass.

"My proposition is this," Mary-Forge said. "First, tell me your name. I don't think it's fair to call any man who works a hard hat."

"Sandia," he said.

"I had a dog once by that name."

"I don't think it was me," he said. "I don't believe much in reincarnation."

"No, my dog didn't look like you at all," Mary-Forge said.

The coyotes began muttering among themselves and looking at each other. They had never been visited with such a strange conversation. Coyotes do not understand in detail any human language. Coyotes who have been around humans get the import of what is being said, but this conversation made no sense to them, and they all swore it could make no sense to human beings, either.

"What I don't understand is," Mary-Forge said, "when your machine approaches a city there must be some system. . . ."

"Yes, there is a self-destruct system built in."

"You mean your machine destroys itself."

"No," he said, "the city destroys itself."

"I still don't understand why you can't stop the machine," Mary-Forge said.

"Because it's got a back-up system, it would continue to run anyway."

"I have the answer," Mary-Forge said. "Will you listen to my proposition?"

"Yes."

"Lie to the machine."

"It only takes orders from Mr. Lardy or Mr. Dardy."

"Are you certain you are not Mr. Lardy or Mr. Dardy?"

"I am Sandia."

"That would be an excellent ploy," Mary-Forge said, "to cook up the story you cooked up to fool the Indians so you could go on destroying the coyotes and Painted Bird to get your coal for God knows why."

The man who called himself Sandia looked up at the tunnel ceiling and said, "Watch out, the roof is cracking, the shovel is scraping close." And then he said as the tunnel collapsed near the opening, "It's too late." And then he removed a two-way radio gadget from his coat and said into it, "This is Lardy Dardy calling Shovel Number One," and the gadget said back, "This is a recording. You have dialed the wrong number. Will you please hang up and try again."

He tried again.

"This is Lardy Dardy calling Shovel Number One."

The gadget answered, "This is Shovel Number One. When you hear the click, will you speak your piece and then shut up."

"Shovel Number One, this is Lardy Dardy. Shut yourself off."

"This is a recording. How do I know this is Lardy Dardy speaking?"

"Believe me, this is Lardy Dardy."

"I never believed you, Lardy Dardy. Why should I believe you now?" the machine said.

"Because you are about to scrape me off the earth," the hard hat said.

"When you hear the click, Lardy Dardy, I'm coming to get you. When I make my next pass with the shovel, it will be all over for you."

The hard hat who called himself Sandia and Lardy Dardy looked over at Mary-Forge and said, "We programmed all that into the shovel so that if someone called to stop the shovel when I was out, he would be foiled."

"And now you've foiled yourself."

"Yes."

Now he grabbed the gadget again and said into it quietly, "This is Lardy Dardy, Shovel Number One. How can I make it up to you?"

It was all too late. The shovel was making another pass, and the hard hat who called himself Sandia or Mr. Lardy or Mr. Dardy ran for the blocked exit and tried to claw his way out, and he was scooped up in the shovel and processed into coal slurry and piped to the Four Corners Power Plant, where he added to civilization by contributing four-point-two kilowatts of power.

Mary-Forge and the coyotes were as safe and sound as a Bee-body bug in a rug. They maintained their cool and did not rush to the blocked exit because they knew every coyote den has three tunnel exits to foil the beings that say the earth is flat, say "Hey, you Lardy Dardy!"

The Medicine Man did not believe one word of my story. He said it is the stuff that legends, myths, totems, and taboos are made of. But he said we live by legends, myths, totems, and taboos. He said all power to the myth. He said when he saw Mary-Forge going down the Portales ridge, spectral against the New Mexico fire of October—he yelled—"Hey, you Lardy Dardy!" And then he said quietly and almost to himself, "We should try our very best to keep our earth round."

"I like your story," Mary-Forge said to William. "Are you going to put that in the book?"

"It's the kind of a story an editor would want out."

"Why would he want it out, William?"

"Extraneous."

"Life is extraneous."

"That is a very profound remark, Mary-Forge. The Indians will give you a medal."

"What will you give me?"

"This," he said, "and this and this and this," and the Scalp House shook and she said, "My God, Billy, let's close the door."

9

Historically no one is certain who started actual scalping first, the red or the white. It may be only that the whites made the mistake of writing it down. Rewards for Indian scalps. The Puritans. The Pilgrims. Advertisements in the newspapers. Rewards for the top of another person's head. Indians.

We do not know who, the Indian or the others, started scalping first, but we do know that Tom Charlie did not create the monster first. It was conceived just over the hill at Los Alamos and born just across the desert at Alamogordo. As children, the Indians heard it go off and saw across the big desert distance the cloud that was more like a black picture sound, leaving something white, something new, as at Plymouth Rock when those distant Indians saw the first sail, something white, something new. A portent not of the Indians' Tom Charlie but of the others' Thomas Charles.

The coyote Sister Courage was not given her appellation by some trader, Indian, or other innocent, but got her name by having her leg gnawed off by herself to escape a sheep rancher's trap; and Sister Courage still led the pack; not only led and dominated the band that was becoming a mere bunch, a mere seven. And so under the white man's need for the coal under the rock of Painted Bird Mesa, the mesa along with the seven coyotes was dissolving in hurt. And they would all vanish unremarked because soon there would be no signature or sign that the Painted Bird or coyote was once fantastical and real, soon buried beneath the water, and the Indian, the Checkerboard Clan, unremarked too.

Everyone had gathered in the Learning Hogan to save the last of the coyotes in the Checkerboard area.

"Are you feeling yourself a coyote today?"

"Yes," Mary-Forge said.

And Mary-Forge did. That was the strangeness in Mary-Forge, the strangeness of Indians. The Indian believes that every being that is sentient and alive is a sister or a brother being. There is no distinction between a coyote being and a human being. All have a soul or none has a soul.

"We must," Mary-Forge said, "do something right away. Today is the day. The Albuquerque Gun Club has declared the Checkerboard a free-fire zone. Which means the Gun Club and Junior Jaycees will have a Coyote Shoot here this afternoon. They said this is their last chance before the flood."

"There's nobody here but us Indians."

"That's right," Mary-Forge said. "Now what we will do," Mary-Forge said, "is put up signs along the highway with an arrow pointing, saying 'This Way to the Coyote Shoot.'"

"Where will the signs lead to?" Tom Yazzie asked.

"Over a cliff."

"Which one?"

"The Painted Bird Mesa."

The Junior Jaycees were happy to see the signs that the Albuquerque Gun Club had put up. The Gun Club was happy to see the signs the Jaycees had put up. The Indians were happy about the signs they had put up. The Indians were happiest about the sign they had put up fifty yards before the brink of the Painted Bird Mesa which said, "You may increase speed to 70 miles an hour."

The Indians erected a grandstand of rocks fifteen yards from the brink, where they could wave to the coyote killers. The coyote killers were happy about just having their speed increased, and they waved to the Indians just before they shot off the cliff. The Indians had erected a sign two miles back, "Fasten your seat belts." Which the coyote killers must have obediently done, because no bodies flew out when they hit the bottom below the Painted Bird, only guns.

The Indians had also built a grandstand of rocks below, where the cars landed. Some of the Indians chose to watch the coyote shooters take off and others chose to see them land.

Judy Rhodes and her husband, the intrepid FBI man Stewart Montalban Rhodes, were driving in a Winnebago expandable American Motor Home on his weekend off, and he was now acting in his capacity as the Acting Past President of the Junior Jaycees and Acting Chairperson of the Ad Hoc Committee for the Indian Country Coyote Shoot. His 30-30 Marlin rifle with German scope hung over the motor-home fireplace beneath the picture of himself. A plastic Christmas tree was still up in the living room of the motor home and the six darling Rhodes children still gamboled beneath it, playing with their presents—seven miniature M60 machine guns and fourteen M23 model Sherman tanks with 90-degree revolving cannon turrets, two Barbie Dolls with built-in flamethrowers, a lead battalion of Green Berets led by a Hollywood actor, a small black box labeled "atomic bomb," and under the branches of the plastic tree a snow scene showing Our Saviour raising some people from the dead in color or black and white, depending on which button you pressed.

It was a good Christmas setting, particularly touching in that Christmas had carried over into Easter and along with the children had been brought along for the Coyote Shoot.

Judy had just emerged from the library with the latest Book of the Day Club selection, a best-seller humdinger that she carried reverently through the atrium of pool and rubber plants into the TV room, where Clark Gable, Jeannette MacDonald, Spencer Tracy, and King Vidor had gotten together a humdinger. Judy, who looked like the dear-departed Hollywood Judy and was named after her, adjusted the air conditioner for Indian Country. It had special filters to keep out the outside and a switch that added perfume. It used to work fine but now it did not work. When she turned on the perfume she got the smell of her children. She looked out the window to the motor-home patio. The dogs were all grouped around the small swimming pool. Because of size limitations, when the motor home was moving it was impossible to have a full-size swimming pool and an aviary, too, and Stewart did not want to give up his collection of Cambodian birds when they moved from their house into their home.

When the motor home stopped for the Coyote Shoot, they would press a button and the motor home would accordion out to four times its traveling size. The swimming pool would expand to four times its traveling size, but more water would have to be added to the pool. In contradistinction to swimming pools, Stewart noted, water will not expand.

Judy decided to take her dive now rather than wait for the expanded swimming pool to fill with water when they stopped for the Coyote Shoot.

Stewart Montalban Rhodes, who drove the American Home, drew attention to himself by not wearing his hair like a girl, which was the fashion, but short like the German officers in World War I. He also affected for the Coyote Shoot a German cross over his left breast, carried a silver dirk on his belt and an American flag in his lapel. His face was covered with huge chrome-trimmed dark glasses over a Dutch Masters' cigar.

"We have been ordered to increase our speed," he said over the intercom, reading the Indian sign.

Judy Rhodes heard her husband in the Cambodian aviary. She was on her way through the gymnasium to the outside-swimming-pool diving board to take her dive when she heard this announcement and noted that her husband was always being ordered to do something. Stewart had been ordered to Asia and Washington to do things, and when things went wrong it was not his fault because he had been ordered to do things.

"We are now passing a section of cheering waving Indians. Wave back," Stewart Montalban Rhodes announced. Judy waved from the aviary midst the fluttering bright Cambodian birds. Then she moved out naked to the swimming pool patio onto the diving board and poised for a swan dive.

"Have a good day," she called to the Indians.

"Right on!" the Indians hollered back.

The American Motor Home was preceded in the Coyote Shoot by a yellow-with-red-stripe Japanese Toyota Celica sports car. Before the edge of the Painted Bird Mesa there was a rise in the terrain, so that it worked as a ski jump for the Toyota, so that Stewart saw the Japanese Junior Jaycee rising through the air without any visible means of support—without any road beneath the Japanese Junior Jaycee at all.

But Stewart Rhodes did as he was ordered, as the Indians knew he would, and increased his speed. The yellow Japanese thing made the biggest leap so far, just short of two hundred meters. The Indians scattered, then watched the motor home fly.

"He's going to make it," Mary-Forge said.

"I never saw so much moxie," Lucy-Lucy said, "and a white man, too."

"Look what's coming out of the home in the clouds," Mary-Forge said.

All the American Motor Home was coming apart and down.

Birds and dogs, all the *Reader's Digest* since it was born, a string quartet, *The Encyclopaedia Britannica* in forty-eight volumes and *The Decline and Fall* in two. The largest record collection in motor-home recorded history sailed into the next county, and the Cambodian birds headed east. Judy came down naked in a beautiful swan dive.

"Isn't that sweet," Lucy-Lucy said.

"When is that house coming down?" Mary-Forge said.

"The motor home?"

It came down with a bang.

"But we have still another bigger bang," Kills The Enemy said.

This was the end of the Coyote Shoot. Stewart and Judy, carrying the gun from over the motor-home fireplace, had crawled to a ledge on the Painted Bird Mesa to await orders that would never come. They were covered with their own blood, and it was difficult to see because of the red in their eyes, but on the plain below at the end of all the junked cars they could easily see the Indian sign, "Welcome to the Coyote Shoot."

And now the far voice of a coyote, Sister Courage, came on emergent as a distant white sail, and soon the big stage of all the world was filled with the howling music, rising as in a hymn, baleful and sad and at once joyful.

"We got the bomb," Kills The Enemy said.

"Not true," the Medicine Man said. "Maybe it's that we only have an educated Indian marching around with a giant suitcase."

"No, we have the bomb," the Indian Kills The Enemy said. "The Indians have the bomb."

10

And man said let there be a flood.

And on the seventh day before the flood, man said let the earth be flat and man said it was good, and on the sixth day man said let man leap off the mesas of the earth in their machines into the canyons and there was great rejoicing and then it came to pass—and at a great distance below the eagle Star—there came unto New Mexico a movie corporation with great signs saying EUGENE GENOVESE PRODUCTIONS, and the peole of the earth did bow down to this sign and there was much sinning and much iniquity in Gallup, nakedness and fornication, unnatural acts and unspeakable sex, and man said this was good and Eugene Genovese Productions said it would gross one million dollars in Pittsburgh, Pennsylvania, alone. The eagle Star beheld aloft from the heavens this caravan crossing to the caravansary, Gallup, New Mexico, in this land of Canaan. Star watched the camels and asses and all manner of beasts of burden come to film in 3D and CinemaScope this Indian earth before the final flood and man

said it was good and Eugene Genovese said it was fab, fabulous—
socko—and the eagle Star folded its wings and shuttered its eyes
against the dividing of the Red Sea, as it must part for the god
of American film directors, Eugene Genovese.

Before the movie caravan arrived, when William saw Mary-
Forge come riding up to the Scalp House on that paint horse and
not her Appaloosa, he knew he would have to tell her, tell her
that he could not stand to have his mind screwed over any more
by the gift, by Whom, by the thing or whatever it was called
how, "or by that damn paint horse."

"What has the paint horse got to do with it?"

"Because no one should ride that paint horse," he said. "Tom
Yazzie turned that horse out because it's not a horse but a killer,
something that should be used as a catapult or a slingshot, but
not for you to come riding up here on, casually as though on a
Sunday outing, and making every white man and Indian in the
Checkerboard feel like a Girl Scout."

"It's green broke," she said, and got down from the paint, and
she stared into the young paint's mismatched eyes and said,
"There is no such thing as a bad horse or a bad boy. Put that
cliché into your book, Billy."

"I appreciate the fact that you can ride that paint," he said.

"Not on your sweet ass you don't, Billy, and neither do I, but
it's the only horse in town. A movie company has rented all the
rest from Tom Yazzie's Brother."

"Tom Yazzie's Brother doesn't own all the Indian horses."

"Tell that to Tom Yazzie's Brother," she said.

"You are not a cowboy, you are a cowperson. Right?" the
Indian Tom Yazzie said to the horse-riding white teacher Mary-
Forge.

"Ignore him," Tom Yazzie's Sister said as they stepped inside the Learning Hogan.

"Are you going to Gallup to watch them make the picture show?"

Mary-Forge ignored him. She was thinking this, that even here in the Learning Hogan in northern New Mexico you cannot ignore all the white reservation. But you can ignore the white fads that press in on Indian Country, the froufrous and the baubles and the words that substitute for the act; an Indian can even ignore the wars that the whites come up with every ten years by giving the United States Army draft people three different names, all legal, and three different addresses, all valid: the winter hogan, the summer wickiup, and the bar in Gallup. The names would be your Anglo name, your Indian name, and your relocation name; the relocation name is your benign-neglect name. That is the name under which they throw the Indian in a concentration camp called the ghetto of the city of Chicago and even ignore the Navajo's scream for help as he sinks down down down, and the only weapon an Indian has got is a sense of humor but now he has got another weapon—Thomas Charles.

And then inside the hogan Tom Charlie was saying, "Then there is the threat which has been bruited about the reservation since Custer. It is always freighted with some ominous word: relocation, termination, or independence for the Indian, which gives the others the legal right to swindle the Indian out of Indian land or to bury it under water."

"I thought this was going to be a sex seminar," Hosteen Begay said. "How did 'bruited about' and 'freighted' with what was it get into it?"

"Everything doesn't have to be sex," Lucy-Lucy said.

"But a sex seminar should touch on sex."

"Not necessarily," Lucy-Lucy said. "Take the case of The Last Tango in Gallup."

"You mean The Last Tango in Paris or someplace."

"No, I've never been to Paris or someplace," Lucy-Lucy said. "Nothing is relevant outside the Indian experience. If we haven't learned that, we have wasted our youth chasing a white man's dream. When I say Gallup I don't mean Albuquerque or someplace. I mean the nuclear-proliferation experience of Gallup."

"What does 'nuclear proliferation' mean?"

"Sex," Lucy-Lucy said.

"I thought it meant something else."

"Then you have never been to Gallup," Lucy-Lucy said.

In Gallup the bartender at the Bullet Proof Bar and Grill said, "Before the movie people arrive I should like on this occasion to defend nuclear proliferation against some charges that have been brought against it."

"Can I ask something?" Stewart Rhodes, the FBI man, said.

"Not now," the bartender said. "We have some serious business."

The FBI man moved away and sat in a quiet corner all by himself as two Indians walked up to the bar. Stewart Rhodes was still battered from the Coyote Shoot and he seemed subdued.

"Two Coors, please."

"How old are you?" the bartender said to the young Indians.

"Seventy-three."

"And you?"

"Seventy-four."

"Can I see your ID?"

"No."

There was a silence, with the bartender still holding on to the two cans of Coors.

"Why?"

"Because we don't recognize the United States," Tom Yazzie said.

"Why not?"

"Eye trouble."

"I took this job," the bartender said, "to improve my mind, to philosophize, and instead I meet Indians with eye trouble. Would you recognize the United States if it behaved itself?"

"No, an Indian would never recognize it then."

"You don't look seventy-three."

"An Indian will fool you," Hosteen Begay said.

"I'm going to give you the beer anyway," the bartender said, pushing forward the two Coors.

"Thank you," Hosteen Begay said, "because we're fresh out of money."

"I meant 'give' in the figurative sense, not in the literal sense," the bartender said.

"In any sense we appreciate it," Tom Yazzie said. "Here's looking at you," and Tom Yazzie and Hosteen Begay drank the Coors.

"How is the FBI doing today?" Bull Who Looks Up asked.

"This is our charming young white teacher from our Learning Hogan," Tom Yazzie said to the bartender as Mary-Forge came up. "We were just discussing nuclear proliferation with the bartender here," Tom Yazzie said to Mary-Forge.

"Did you find out what it means?"

"Free beer," Hosteen Begay said.

"Who's that?" the bartender asked.

"Tom Charlie. He always sits by himself and thinks."

"Does he have any money?"

"No, the project got it all."

"What's the project?"

" 'No One Knows My Name.' "

"How is the FBI doing today?" Bull Who Looks Up asked.

"Can I change the subject?" the bartender said.

"Yes."

"What do you think of Tolstoy?"

"He's okay."

"Chekhov?"

"Check-Off?"

"Chekhov."

"He's okay."

"Senzaki and McCandless?"

"Two are always better than one," Tom Yazzie said.

"I am McCandless," the bartender said. "Senzaki works in the rear. We're doing a book."

"We'll have a drink on that," Bull Who Looks Up said.

And so the problem with Indian Country is that the Indians have a sense of humor about themselves, and another problem is, Mary-Forge thought, everyone is writing a book about the Indians. Everyone is writing a book about the Indians but the Indians. Except William my love who is half Indian. Even McCandless and Senzaki got an advance from a New York publisher on their Indian book, *Some Indians I Have Known,* just by thinking about some Indians they had known. Senzaki, while he worked in the rear, wrote a chapter, then McCandless would go in the rear and write a chapter based on his experiences up front. The book had a first printing of fifty thousand copies before it was written.

"How can a book," Nice Hands' Sister said, "have a first printing of fifty thousand copies before it is written?"

"Computers."

"Do you want to enlarge on that?"

"No."

"Do you want to expand on that?"

"Yes, computers send a man to the moon, don't they? How do you think they re-elect the Mayor of Gallup? Computers."

"But McCandless and Senzaki will still have to write the book?"

"Only to fulfill a symbolic obligation. The publishers really don't want the book written."

"Now that it's printed?"

"Yes."

"That's interesting," Nice Hands' Sister said. "I think I'll have another beer."

The bartender opened another can of Coors.

"You're still going to write it?"

"Only as an afterthought," the bartender said. "But what interests me at the moment is who is going to pay for the beer."

"Computers," Hosteen Tzo said.

But all this is small talk compared to the big event of the evening. The arrival of The Genius, film director Eugene Genovese, who looked like a French onion with its hat on backward. He wanted to make a final picture on the Navajo Checkerboard location before it disappeared. Each year a major motion-picture company makes a major motion picture in Gallup. The definitive picture on the American Indian. Extras make twenty-eight dollars a day. Indians would like that money. They make the pictures in Gallup because of the availability of Indians. They don't hire Indians.

The problem was put sensibly by The Genius. "Indians don't look like Indians. We have tried all kinds of make-up, but we still can't get them to look like Indians. The American public has an idea of what an Indian looks like, and I'll be goddamned if an Indian is going to change it."

"Then why do you make your major motion pictures in Gallup?"

"Realism," The Genius said. "Now Dustin—"

"Dustin who?"

"Dustin Hoffman looks like an Indian," the Director said. "The American public makes these decisions. Marlon looks like an Indian."

"He does?" Bull Who Looks Up said. "Marlon who?"

"Brando, yes," The Genius said.

"Interesting."

"You might say these things are out of our hands," the Director said. "God, there's nothing better I'd like than to use Indians as Indians. But we can use some of your people to clean up. I want your people, the Indians, to have a hand in the picture."

"We appreciate that, Mr. . . . ."

"Genovese," The Genius said. "Eugene Genovese. Do you have something I can sign?"

"Sign this," Bull Who Looks Up said.

The Genius gave his autograph and said, "What was that?"

"The bar bill," Nice Hands' Sister said.

The Genius, Eugene Genovese, had gotten his reputation by making the first major American-Indian film for a major studio for under ten million. For being the first major director to see the potential in the adult youth market, and for being the first major oil company to raise the price of regular gas.

"You're losing me," Bull Who Looks Up said.

"Mr. Genovese," McCandless said, "was the first major Hollywood personality to discover oil under a major studio lot when family entertainment went out the window. The American family is not interested in seeing real Indians or seeing real anything. When a white man comes home from a hard day's work and he's tired, he just want to see somebody killed."

"I'll buy that," Lucy-Lucy said.

"The industry has been good to me," Mr. Genovese said.

"You have been good to it, sir."

A tear formed in the corner of Mr. Genovese's eye. "Everything I learned about film I learned from Father Duffy."

"The radical priest?"

"Yes."

The tear splashed on the table.

"Don't you see," McCandless said, "he doesn't want to talk about it."

"I want to talk about youth," Mr. Genovese said. "I am into youth."

"Oh, God," Lucy-Lucy said.

"Nothing else is relevant," The Genius said carefully. "It's all covered in Transactional Analysis."

"Fill us in."

"The Child, the Adult, and the Parent. It will all be in the picture," The Genius said. "The film will touch on lesbianism, transvestism, oral sex—all in a family way, of course."

"Are you okay, Mr. Genovese?"

"Yes, I'm okay. Are you okay?"

"We're all okay, Mr. Genovese, but we thought the picture was about Indians."

"It is, but it's an Art picture."

"Oh?"

"Yes, the youth are into Art. I don't know why it is, but I just can't seem to make a bad picture. I need a bad picture to give me a sense of humility. Father Duffy always said that."

"He did?"

"Yes."

There were no more tears forming in Mr. Genovese's eyes. He seemed to be feeling more at home among the Indians.

"The way I see it," The Genius said, "is the facts. As long as we're negotiating with the Soviet Union we've got to have the biggest bang in the world, second to none. Without that, you saw what happened to Custer, didn't you? When I make a picture I consider everything. I never made a picture that didn't get at least two Academy Awards."

"That shows you what the picture industry thinks of Art," Mr. McCandless said.

There was a silence in the Bullet Proof Bar and Grill, and then The Genius said, "Did you mean that facetiously, Mr. Mc-Candless?"

"No."

"Does anyone have a picture option on your *Some Indians I Have Known*?"

"No."

"I'll take it," Mr. Genovese said.

"How did you learn about it? *Some Indians I Have Known* is not written yet."

"It's the talk of the trades," The Genius said flatly.

"What are the trades?" Hosteen Begay said.

"They are winds that blow from east to west," Kills The Enemy said. "The teacher Mary-Forge said Columbus got here pushed by the trades. If it weren't for the trades, the Indians wouldn't be here now. We would never have been discovered."

"Do you mean that facetiously?"

"Yes," Kills The Enemy said.

"You can see why we can't make a picture about real Indians."

"Yes," Kills The Enemy said.

Mr. Genovese was quiet and then he said in a steady voice, "Nevertheless my last picture was socko. Look what it did in Freeport, Pennsylvania." He tossed a copy of the *Hollywood Reporter* on the table.

"Are you okay, Mr. Genovese?"

"Yes, I'm okay. Are you okay?"

"Yes, we are all okay, Mr. Genovese."

The next day bloomed high and bright and early in Indian Country. It was the start of the picture show. All the Indians were there; Mr. Genovese was there. Mr. Genovese showed up without a script. He said that De Sica, Bertolucci, and Fellini never used a script.

"Who are they?"

"The best Italian restaurant in Albuquerque," Lucy-Lucy said, "and they don't have a menu."

Mr. Genovese called everyone together for a pep talk before the shooting started.

"If there's going to be shooting we better get out of here quick," Three Shoes said.

Mary-Forge was there. She had closed the Learning Hogan because she wanted everyone to see, hear, and feel what it was like to see, hear, and feel people from another planet acting out what they figured was life on earth as creatures from the planet Hollywood know it.

"I don't think," the Medicine Man said, "we should indict the people from another planet until we see what they do. They may have an interesting concept of life on earth. We Indians tend to patronize, to feel superior. We should look and listen."

The Medicine Man was accoutered in all his regalia of precious blue-green turquoise and silver amulets, so that he was a walking dignified treasure house. His hatchet, hacked-out face was scarred in the manner of topographical maps or the farms of the Navajo Nation plowed, furrowed, and harrowed, then spike-toothed before it was dragged with the wisdom of time, the nobility and consternation at God's joke and of time.

Everyone was standing in front of the Gallup Chamber of Commerce for the movie show send-off sponsored by the Junior Jaycees and the Committtee to Re-Elect the Mayor of Gallup. Someone from the Committee to Re-Elect had stolen the sound equipment so the Mayor had to holler so that none of the Indians in the rear could hear—it was like a silent movie.

"Louder," Mary-Forge said.

"We can hear enough," the Medicine Man said.

The Mayor said, "Someone from the Committee to Re-Elect has stolen the sound equipment, but I was elected to do a job and I intend to do it. I will not resign. Mr. Genovese has indicated to me that Genovese Productions intends to spend two million here." He turned to Mr. Genovese. "You indicated this, but what did you say?"

"Three," Mr. Genovese whispered.

"Cash?"

"Do you want it in cash?"

"Yes."

"Okay."

"Are you sure you're okay?"

"Yes, I'm okay. Are you okay?"

"Yes, I'm okay."

"Three million," the Mayor hollered.

"Three million what?" Kills The Enemy whispered to the others in the rear.

"Navajos," Hosteen Begay said. "That's how many Indians the Seventh Cavalry is going to kill."

"Why?"

"Because more Indians than that will put them over the budget."

"Will the people in the rear kindly talk louder, so we can't hear the Mayor."

"I think," Mary-Forge said, "that now they are going to give the Hollywood people the keys to the Navajo Nation."

The Mayor stepped forward with a gold and velvet box, looked in, and then whispered to The Genius, "Someone has stolen the key to the country."

"Why would anyone want to do that?" Mr. Genovese said.

"Why don't I just hand you the box?" the Mayor said.

"I don't know why you don't. You can answer that question better than I can. Why don't you? Is there money in the box?"

"No."

"Incriminating documents?"

"No. My idea is to hand you the box and give the Indians the impression that you received the key."

"We can't hear you back here!"

"Why don't you," Mr. Genovese whispered to the Mayor, "make a clean breast of the whole thing?"

"I have a policy against that," the Mayor said. "I suppose I'm old-fashioned."

"Did I ever tell you the joke about the Hollywood starlet who—"

"We can't hear you back here!"

Mr. Genovese took the box, thanked the Mayor, and then announced, "We're going to hire real-live Indians."

"We can't hear you back here!"

"Anyone who wants an acting job report to my tent at oh-three hundred."

"Three o'clock," the Assistant Director said.

None of the Indians from the Checkerboard wanted a job on the movie excepting Kills The Enemy.

Mary-Forge thought all Indians might take a job, that it might be educational, but she left it to the Medicine Man.

"I don't think so," the Medicine Man said. "It would be dishonest."

"Kills The Enemy is going to take a job."

"That is his business," the Medicine Man said.

Kills The Enemy was there promptly at 0-300, and so was the Seventh Cavalry. There were some professional Indians there, the kind that hang out on the plaza in Santa Fe and Taos, the kind you see in the movies. No Checkerboard Navajos were there excepting Kills The Enemy.

The Genius was not there. The Assistant Director was there to do all the small talking, all this in an orange and green tent in the park across the street from the Robert F. Kennedy Memorial Used Car Lot. "We try to help the Indian with an Edsel." The Assistant Director had been an assistant jockey at Santa Anita before The Genius spotted him as a comer. The Assistant Director talked quietly and gently, as he had talked to horses.

"When you come out of the gate," he said to the actors, "don't try for position till you've got a sound foot. Don't make your move in the backstretch unless you can take the lead. Don't get into the crowd at the turns, but lay back. We got into trouble with Gable and Monroe because they tried to push."

"Who are Gable and Monroe?"

"Indians from California," an Apache said.

"We never made a picture that didn't bring back its negative costs in Pennsylvania alone," the Assistant Director continued. "That's the yardstick. Are there any questions? One more thing, this is a clean picture. The Supreme Court said sex is illegal and we've always followed that principle, which is why we make Indian pictures. If there are no more questions, I'll start the interviews. Everybody on this side of the tent is hired and everybody on this side of the tent is fired. That's the way we did *Cleopatra*."

"It is?"

"Yes. You want to start a fight?"

"Yes."

"Were you hired or fired?"

"I was hired," Kills The Enemy said.

All the Checkerboard Navajo Indians went back to the Checkerboard excepting five, and McCandless and Senzaki went back to their book. The picture started okay, with Mr. Genovese showing the genius that made him the Dean of American Directors. But it was not enough for the picture to be okay. The Genius wanted everyone to be okay. The Genius figured—and that is the difference between people such as us and genius—that if everyone connected with film was not okay, then the film would bomb in Pennsylvania. Pennsylvania was the bellwether for the Dean of American Directors, and particularly Indiana, Pennsylvania, where to a simple hardware merchant an actor was born named James Stewart, which made the town a bellwether to The Genius. If you understood Jimmy, then you understood the artistic soul of America. It was Mr. Genovese's Peoria, Illinois, and his Winesburg, Ohio. It was the key to the American heart—and pocket-book.

"What did you say your name was?" Mr. Genovese said.

"I didn't say. I know."

"What do you know your name is?"

"Kills The Enemy," Kills The Enemy said.

"I don't know whether the vibes on you are okay or not. Okay," Mr. Genovese said, "I need someone here from Pennsylvania to stand close to this Indian."

"I'm from Philadelphia," a sound man said.

"No, that's too large for correct vibes. Any town smaller?"

"Aliquippa."

"Too small," Mr. Genovese said. "Is it asking too much if there is anyone here from Indiana, Pennsylvania?" It was asking too much. "Does Jimmy Stewart ring a bell?" It rang no bell. Mr. Genovese retreated back into the aloneness of his genius, but not before saying to Kills The Enemy, "I'm not picking up good vibes. Still, I never pick up good vibes from an Indian. Jimmy said he never met an Indian he didn't like. That's where we part company. I never met a straight arrow. I never met an Indian who wasn't drunk or dishonest or a combination of both. I hope you make me regret saying that."

"I promise you I will make you regret saying that," Kills The Enemy said.

"Roll it. This is a take!"

"There is no film yet in the camera, Mr. Genovese."

"Roll it anyway," Mr. Genovese said. "It's the only way I can think."

Mr. Genovese thought a great deal before the film was ended. He thought most about the penultimate scene. The penultimate scene, Mr. Genovese explained to the ignorant, was the scene before the last scene. The last scene cannot grab you if the proper device is not laid in the next-to-the-last scene. The last scene would be the scene where, after all the savages had been killed off, some good Indians would be discovered in a small buffalo-hide tepee who had saved a virgin white woman from a fate worse than death. Because of the new antisex ruling this scene cannot be shown, but you can trust the people of Pennsylvania to get the idea. This way the picture will end on a positive note and reinforce the idea of the native American Indian as the savior of white American womanhood, in a subtle way, and all that she stands for.

"What do you think, Kills The Enemy?"

Kills The Enemy said nothing.

Mr. Genovese had set up the penultimate movie scene this way. The savages have retreated to a rocky redoubt beneath a butte, pursued by the Seventh Cavalry. Each assault on the redskins is unavailing—bravery is shown on the part of the Indians as well as cunning. Just when it seems the Seventh Cavalry will fail completely, the script girl came up with the idea that McCandless and Senzaki should grab the Seventh banner, lead the charge, and carry the day. That way it is dramatically shown and not just talked about that the civilian as well as the Army contributed to the growth of America.

Mr. Genovese had to withdraw into himself and think about this, as was his custom. He finally bought the idea because it had been his stroke of creativity to hire McCandless and Senzaki away from their book, *Some Indians I Have Known,* to play the part of two lonely but hardship-loving trappers who stumble on the lost Seventh in a blizzard high in the Bozeman Pass and lead the soldiers down to the old Gerber ranch on the Yellowstone, where they live happily until the Indians learn from the radio where the soldiers are and attack the Seventh again.

"Back date that by changing radio to rumor, and you've got it," Mr. Genovese said.

The night before the big fight scene at the butte, Mr. Genovese was careful to have a final Transactional Analysis session with McCandless and Senzaki so that everything would be okay when they carried the Seventh colors to victory. But he did not have a TA session with an Indian who was defending the butte—Kills The Enemy.

According to McCandless and Senzaki, "It was a dark and stormy night when the fateful day arrived. A day that was to leave the field strewn with some dead white people I have known."

The day started quietly enough with everything going okay. The Seventh attacked the savages and were repulsed according to plan, then they retreated, leaving their Seventh Cavalry dead on the battlefield. No one seemed to notice that the dead were dead.

"A-okay," Mr. Genovese said over the megaphone. "Now we will send McCandless and Senzaki up for the victory charge."

"I don't think so," McCandless and Senzaki said. "There is something strange going on out there."

"It looks real, doesn't it?" Mr. Genovese said. "I believe the picture will be socko."

The trick was that as the Seventh advanced, the Indians would pretend to shoot arrows at them. The Indians were supposed to shoot over the soldiers' heads. Each soldier had had half an arrow stuck on the front of his chest and the other half stuck on his back by the Special Effects Department, so from the camera's point of view he seemed to have an arrow going through him. But it was a trick.

"But is it a trick?" McCandless and Senzaki said. "Some of the soldiers seem to have more arrows through them when they are dead than when they started out."

"The Special Effects Department never goofed yet," Mr. Genovese said. "I want you boys to go out there and storm that position."

"I think we should check first to see if anyone out there is dead," McCandless and Senzaki said.

"I've made nineteen Indian pictures and I've never had a white man killed yet," Mr. Genovese said.

"Have you ever had real Indians shooting at them before?"

"No."

"Senzaki is trying to tell you something," McCandless said.

"And I don't want to hear it," The Genius said. "I've always been a friend to the red man."

"Then lead the charge yourself," McCandless said.

"By God I will," The Genius said. "Senzaki, lend me your horse and sword." Senzaki handed The Genius his horse and sword, and Mr. Genovese pointed to what was left of the Seventh to follow him.

Kills The Enemy put another arrow in his bow.

It was not until three hours later that it was discovered that many in the Seventh Cavalry were dead. Nothing was done about it until the next of kin were notified. By that time the soldiers of the Seventh were turning bad. A Santa Fe coroner's jury blamed the Special Effects Department. Eugene Genovese's last words were influenced by his last picture, where the bankrupt once-millionaire miner Horace Tabor, on his deathbed with only one empty gold mine left, The Matchless, whispers to his love, Baby Doe, "Never sell the rights to The Matchless." Eugene Genovese whispered now on his deathbed to the head of the studio Script Department, "Never sell the rights to *Some Indians I Have Known.*"

Which, as McCandless and Senzaki observed, just goes to show you how Nature imitates Art.

The next day the FBI man Rhodes was again sitting in the bar. He had witnessed everything from the Robert F. Kennedy Memorial Used Car Lot. Now he was silent.

"Seen any good pictures lately?" McCandless asked.

"No."

"Any suspects in the killing?"

"No."

"Keep talking," Senzaki said.

"It's not the Indian Kills The Enemy I'm watching," Rhodes said.

"Who?"

"Thomas Charles."

"No, Tom Charlie can think like a white man," McCandless said.

"Those are the kind to watch," the FBI man said.

"A precocious Indian can be dangerous?"

"I believe the evidence will bear me out."

"But if you get caught in the reservation, who will carry you out?"

Rhodes, the FBI man, was silent again, thinking about this.

"No shit, how do you intend to get on the reservation?"

"Where there is a will," Stewart Montalban Rhodes said, "there is a way."

"That's an original thought. We'll use that in our book, *Some Indians I Have Known*," McCandless and Senzaki said.

11

While Stewart Montalban Rhodes was thinking about Thomas Charles, Tom Charlie was thinking about Thomas Charles, too. He was two people in one. He was what the Indians call an apple, red outside, white inside. One side of him wanted to blow things up, the other side wanted to put things together. One side wanted to get drunk, the other side to stay sober. One side decided to go to school, the other to make it the Indian way. It's enough to drive an Indian crazy. To drink. To school and become a nuclear physicist. Then go back to the reservation. Los Alamos was okay, a nice mountain setting. You could see all the Indian Country from there. But the people at Alamos were crazy. They could not stop making the bomb. They had enough bombs to blow up this world, but they continued to make bombs.

"It's enough to blow anyone's mind," Tzo said, "but all bull-shit aside, have you got the gift ready?"

Tom Charlie was still thinking about Thomas Charles. Now he tried to think about what Tzo asked. He had kept secrets for so long he could not even tell his other self. How could he tell Tzo?

"I do not know," he said.

"I suppose you will not know," Tzo said, "until you try to explode the creature."

"I do not know," he said.

"Well, that makes sense," Tzo said. "I guess we will have to wait and see."

"I do not know," he said.

"Well," Tzo said, "if you want to try it out on the British bus, you're welcome. It's the last trip before the flood. I saw them coming up the Chiwilly Draw, past the work on the Atlas Dam, in a double-decker London bus. It is an open-top old sightseeing bus, and they sit up there and shoot at everything that moves. They charter these buses in Albuquerque. It is called an Indian Country Safari. For a hundred and fifteen dollars you can shoot at anything that moves. Rumor has it that the person who gets the largest animal gets the Ernest Hemingway Medal—three balls rampant."

"I don't believe it."

"Would you believe four?"

"I do not know," Thomas Charles said.

This last safari was now below the Portales Mesa, moving along at full steam with hunters shooting at everything including the hills which did not look like elephants.

The British double-decker bus that was open on top still had the advertisements on its side for Cadbury Boiled Sweets and Players Cigarettes. Stewart Montalban Rhodes, disguised as the British conductor, walked among the clients on the top deck and told them in a British accent that soon they would see Indians and wild animals. He said because of the dam they would be the last safari to this part of Indian Country. He also warned them not to shoot the Indians. Half the safari consisted of a musical rock group called The Measles. The Measles were playing in Albuquerque at the Desert Inn and were from Manchester, England, and spoke with lower-class Midland accents and were married to Japanese girls with names like Yoko and Yum-Yum. The Measles were not on the safari to shoot but to see and photograph; they had come from a class in England that couldn't afford to shoot and a generation that did not believe in shooting. Stewart Rhodes noted that they all had Japanese cameras. The Measles all sat up front "where it could all hang out." Some of their telescopic camera lenses were two feet long and hung down with straps below their waists when not shooting, so that they all appeared to have plastic genitals with a glass eye—even Yoko and Yum-Yum. Everyone the Measles talked to was "mahn," including Yoyo and Yum-Yum, and everyone and everything they talked about was a mother and outta sight and neat and far out and cool and had good vibes, and Indian Country always had good karma.

A young lad Measle up front named Alice, who was their leader, with an enormous dangling lens, said to Yoko alongside, "Tell me, mahn, like will the Indian mothers surround us and shoot, like"—he paused—"flaming arrows?"

Yoko giggled.

Stewart Rhodes stared at Theodore Armbruster II, who sat in back of the open-deck bus with his wife and brood. His wife, Cripsie, was small and fragile and claimed to be a direct descendant of James Fenimore Cooper. She had large white ears and wore small dark Boy Scout pants and oversize Kenya mosquito boots. One of her children was dressed as an American cowboy, the other child as an American Indian. Teddy looked like an ad for an expensive gin. He wore a tan safari jacket beneath a floppy white hunter's hat, and despite the many-patched, once-blue Levi pants, came across as money.

They had all been outfitted in New York City at Abercrombie and Fitch for the Albuquerque safari. They had all sizes and sorts of guns, one of which could have been a small cannon. The purpose of this safari was to blood two of the youngest Armbrusters who had not yet been blooded on the last trip to Nairobi. Teddy Armbruster II wanted his children to kill something before it was too late—so they would not grow up to be homosexuals or get into politics.

"Show me a real man," Teddy said, "and I will show you a boy who was blooded early."

Teddy, who wore a reddish martini complexion, had himself been blooded early on an African lion shoot with a fashionable and famous American writer in the thirties, and Teddy had been very happy ever since and would be happy evermore if the stock market behaved itself. A cousin of Teddy's who had not been blooded early was running for President of the United States.

"Will he make it?"

"Not blooded early," Teddy said. "Who knows? He probably will."

"But seriously—"

"Damn it, Cripsie," he said to his wife, "I am being serious. Choate doesn't give it to them any more and Princeton is becoming a pansy school. Cripsie, I've reached the end of my rope." He paused and then said, "Look at The Measles up there."

"They're cute," she said.

"You can't tell the boys from the girls."

"The girls are Japanese."

"And all draped with cameras as though this were a pornographic safari," Teddy said.

"They're going to shoot the Indians."

"Well then, why didn't they bring a gun? Not one gun among the whole lot."

"Maybe they weren't blooded early," she said.

"Whose side are you on, Cripsie? My God, whose side are you on? Or do you want all of our tads to turn into fairies?"

"Our two eldest boys were blooded early in Kenya and then killed in Vietnam."

"I know, Cripsie," he said, touching her arm. "I know. But let's think of something pleasant for now. Let's try to make a day of it."

They had already shot two antelope when the English double-decker passed through the Ojo del Spirito Santo Grant. The conductor–FBI man had punched their tickets twice.

"I didn't even know," Cripsie said, "there were antelope in New Mexico."

"Yes," he said, looking over at the antelope where they were tied to the top railing and hid part of the Whitbread Ale sign. "Yes, and damn fine specimens, too, excellent trophies. But it's the coyotes I'm after and the conductor tells me we're in coyote country now. Good show."

The Measles were happy with Indian Country.

"We dig, mahn."

The Measles withdrew musical instruments from under the seats and at once and all together made loud noises. They called the song "The Night Miss Nancy Ann's Hotel for Single Girls Burned Down."

"They're cute," Cripsie said.

"It sounds like all the other songs they have been playing on the safari," Teddy Armbruster II said.

"It's 'The Night Miss Nancy Ann's Hotel for Single Girls Burned Down,'" Cripsie said.

The two Armbruster children said nothing because they were taught to say nothing. At pre-Choate they were taught Latin and Greek and probably spoke these languages very well.

"I don't want our young tads to be exposed to this sort of music," he said.

"Just killing," she said.

"I want them to learn important things."

"Like Greek," she said.

"Cripsie," he said, touching her again, "you knew I was an

Armbruster when you married me."

"But I didn't know what an Armbruster was."

"We believe in the code," he said.

"Listen to The Measles," she said, "and please please don't say you don't want your children exposed to The Measles."

"I really don't, Cripsie. That's part of the code."

Now The Measles began to dance, led by the English lad named Alice, who was dressed like a turkey. They hopped and flipped and jerked and sang and played loud noises, so that Indian Country shook.

The coyote named Eva Tanguay howled.

Everyone was gathered in the summer wickiup outside the Learning Hogan, which was why the coyotes were attending. The coyotes seldom went inside the Learning Hogan.

"I guess," Mary-Forge said to the coyote Sister Courage, "you can all go safely. It sounds like this safari is only The Measles again."

The coyotes were off in a cloud of sand, traveling through the greasewood and sage and yellow yucca bloom. The three-legged coyote, Sister Courage, set a good pace. Now Sister Courage could hear The Measles band and she paused, and all the coyotes bunched up midst a profusion of orange bloom of ocotillo that stood straight up and flew pennants of bright flower. Sister Courage could see from this ridge the double-decker bus making its way up the Puerco Draw. The huge bus looked small in the wide canyon, but it made a big noise. Now someone stood up with a gun in the rear of the bus. There was a loud explosion and Sister Courage went down.

"As I was saying," Mary-Forge said to the Indians in the Learning Wickiup, "the others are at it again."

"They have a game plan."

"Yes."

"And there is nothing we can do about it?" Nice Hands' Sister said.

"Nothing at this time," the Medicine Man said. "And how can we complain when our Tom Charlie is behaving like their Thomas Charles?"

"Yes yes yes," Mary-Forge said. And she looked at the Medicine Man and said, "Yes. Because there must be something we can do about it. Yes yes yes yes. We can stop the killing that's coming from the bus."

I do not know how to treat hysteria," the Medicine Man said, staring at Mary-Forge. There was a big silence in the wickiup with all the quiet Indians looking out into the infinity of Indian Country, then a shot sounded from the Puerco Arroyo.

Mary-Forge stood up so that the top of her head touched the ceiling of the wickiup.

"Who will help me stop the killing?" she said.

The Indians were absolutely silent, studying out into the quiet glory of perfect silence. Yes, Mary-Forge thought, yes, the Indians say no because saying yes has almost exterminated them.

"I will go alone," Mary-Forge said.

The Medicine Man rose, then did all the Indians.

"I do not know how to treat hysteria," the Medicine Man said, "but I do know how to treat decency. We will go with you."

The Indians were off and onto their horses quicker than darting hummingbirds, quicker than movement, so that they were here and then abruptly there, so that the Indians seemed not only incorporeal but phantom, and you wondered how the Indians lost to the whites.

When the Indians got to the Puerco, Sister Courage was down on two legs. The coyote named Hector was bleeding from a shoulder wound, and Shaw had taken a bullet in his left hip. Eva Tanguay wanted to get back to her young ones across the arroyo, but a steady line of fire was coming from the bus, so she circled confused in the melee of wounded and dying. It was the first time Shaw had been hit by a bullet and it did not feel real. There was a sharp sting in his hip that was turning to a dull pain, then a throb. The coyote Emily Dickinson had taken a bullet in the front foot as though it were a self-inflicted wound, but it hurt very much and she yip yip yipped.

"Don't you think," Cripsie said to Teddy between handing him clips of ammo, "don't you think other animals suffer, too? Do you think we are the only animal that suffers?"

"We don't think about that, Cripsie."

"Why don't we think about that?"

"Because it's morbid."

The two Armbruster children, Bimbi and Siegfried, were told to be silent and watch Papa hunt.

The Measles continued to play. They had ceased playing "The Night Miss Nancy Ann's Hotel for Single Girls Burned Down" and were playing one of their own pieces that had sold four million records last year and now was only remembered by Alice and The Measles. Whatever the song was, they played it very well. Neither Alice nor the other Measles remembered the title of the song, but they played it loud so that it almost hid the noise of the shooting. That's what they were trying to do, hide the noise of the shooting, which they found obscene.

"Notice that I've potted two of the coyotes," Teddy said. "I am happy that Siegfried and Bimbi could make it."

"I am very happy, too," Cripsie said and she ate a bullet.

"Did I see right?" Teddy said, lowering the gun. "Did I see you eat a bullet?"

"Yes."

"Why did you eat a bullet?" Teddy said carefully.

"Because that's what Bimbi and Siegfried will remember, that

I ate a bullet. When they think of hunting they will think of their mother eating a bullet while The Measles played something no one remembers."

"Well," Teddy said, "watch this, children," and he turned the rifle to automatic fire to blast the coyotes. Dust clouded up all down the ridge where the coyotes were, and bloom from the ocotillo and yucca were cut down.

"I saw her eat a bullet," Alice hollered to the other Measles.

"Is that the title of this song?"

"No, I saw her eat a bullet in front of the children."

"Cool, mahn."

"Why don't you," Cripsie said to Teddy, "why don't you kill —why don't you kill . . ."

"Myself?"

"No, no," and she held the ammo clip tentatively, not passing it to him.

The children Bimbi and Siegfried watched their mother in child wild-eyed amaze now, expecting her to swallow another bullet or perform some other strange magic. Bimbi, who was five, and Siegfried, who was four, saw her, saw Mother not passing the bullet to him, to Father, but saying, "No, not kill yourself but that thing in you that kills animals for a game."

"Why have you turned on me?"

"Siegfried and Bimbi."

"You don't want me to blood them."

"That's right."

"I heard you," he said, and he let loose a clip at the coyotes on the ridge. Then he said, "When we get back to Albuquerque away from the children we will have a talk."

"If we get back to Albuquerque alive," she said.

Cripsie was watching a stream of horse people coming down the side of the arroyo without benefit of path. They exploded down the side of the arroyo in a riot of dust, then swept in a giant circle around the bus.

Teddy put in another clip. "But I refuse," he said, "to become involved in a TV show. I am not going to shoot at Indians circling a bus."

"The Indians must be protecting the coyotes."

"Coyotes are fair game, and the coyotes will all be drowned anyway when the dam is dedicated. Maybe the Indians, too. I wonder if the buggers have a card up their sleeve," and he continued to shoot at the ridge.

Now the Indians were circling the bus in horse wildness and shouting for the white man to stop. Then the Indians all at once realized that they were behaving the way they did in the movies, the way they did in the films at the missionary's and the trader's, excepting that they were supposed to have bows and arrows and circle a wagon train. Instead they were empty-handed and circling an English bus that said "Cadbury," "Whitbread," and "Guinness is good for you." Now the Indians flew off to the ridge, excepting one, and the bus stopped and Teddy went down the outside circular stairs with his rifle to the lower deck to see what had happened. The driver pointed to a girl, Mary-Forge, who had planted her horse in front of the bus.

"Go around her," Teddy said.

"Cactus on either side," the driver said. "It will blow the tires."

Teddy rolled down the driver's window and hollered to Mary-Forge, "Will you please get out of the way?"

"When you stop shooting the coyotes."

"I understand your problem," Teddy said. "You don't want to lose face in front of your chaps, the Indians. Good show. But I can't lose face in front of the Missus or the tads. Why don't you let me get two coyotes for trophies, then we'll buzz off, the whole lot of us."

"Two coyotes for trophies? Wouldn't you like a couple of Indians for trophies, too? Say, Tom Yazzie and Hosteen Begay?"

"No."

"Where do you draw the line?"

"I have a code."

"I can't let you kill these coyotes."

"Why?"

"I have a code," Mary-Forge said.

"Then it's a Mexican stand-off."

"Yes," Mary-Forge said. "I am going up on the ridge with the Indians and the coyotes—don't shoot."

"I can't promise you anything," Teddy said. "I promised the tads first. I promised them a trophy. I can't destroy their father image."

"What about the death of my coyotes?" she said.

"Are you crazy? I suppose anyone living out here with the Indians and coyotes would have to be crazy," and Teddy fired a shot over Mary-Forge's head to clear the way. Her horse bolted and Teddy told the bus driver to proceed.

Upstairs on the top deck, The Measles band was throwing out Teddy's rifles to the Indians. Not because they thought it would be good sport, but because they thought it would be the decent thing to do. The Indians heard the latest shot coming from the lower deck and saw the rifles coming out from the upper deck. They came on like actors playing themselves, playing Indians, riding fast and swooping down to pick up the weapons. Some of the Indians failed. All of them had trouble. Some of them cheated and got off their horses and picked up a gun. Neither Mary-Forge nor the Medicine Man picked up a gun. Today Mary-Forge and the Medicine Man did not believe in guns.

Theodore Armbruster II, who all his life had believed in guns, now no longer believed in guns.

"This isn't fair, you know," Teddy told the fake conductor, the FBI man. "One doesn't go on a safari to be shot at by Indians. I never shot at an Indian in my life. I came here to shoot coyotes. Tell the Indians to go home."

The fake conductor, Stewart Montalban Rhodes, just sat there, quietly making out his manifest and bills of lading or whatever

British conductors made out when the Germans were bombing London.

"The raid will be over shortly," the conductor said in his best fake British accent. "Try to maintain your calm. According to American cinema, these things happen in the States."

"Not now—"

"Oh they do, old boy. Look outside."

Theodore Armbruster II went outside and up the circular stairs, circled by the Indians. At the top of the stairs he announced to Cripsie, "It's a bad show. Get the tads under the seats." He did not speak to the band; he hated the band. His code had proven correct. Never go on a safari with strangers, particularly a strange band. Never discuss anything to do with children with a woman. What's that got to do with being shot at by Indians?

"Cripsie, I'm losing my grip."

"Sit down," she said.

"I can't sit down while I'm being shot at by Indians."

"Make peace," she said.

"How?"

"Jump off the side of the bus; it's a gesture. It will save the tads."

"The Indians will rape you."

"I've considered that; sit down," she said.

"Seriously, Cripsie . . ."

"I want you to be serious for the first time in your life. Stop playing games. Stop killing things."

"I did it for the tads."

"The children don't want it."

"The children don't know what they want until we show them."

"That's what I mean. Sit down," she said.

The band filed by, carrying their instruments. They were going down to the lower deck. They would sit in the lower deck and join the Indians. They did not look at the Armbrusters as they filed past. The Armbrusters did not look at them. The tads looked at them from under the seats. The drummer caught his tambourine in Mr. Armbruster's elbow and could not get it untangled until Teddy crushed the tambourine and threw it overboard. It glinted in the sun and made a sweet sound when it hit. An Indian shot it on the second bounce. The drummer followed the second trombonist down the steps.

Teddy sat down and said, "Cripsie, it's a bad show. It's not true that I kill only defenseless things. I bombed Germany during the war."

"You bombed here, too," she said.

"Yes, it's turned into a bad show," he said.

The bus was going out of the arroyo, making its clumsy British accomplishment up the narrow trail close by the Cabazon, causing the Indians to fall behind.

"Give me your gun," Mary-Forge said to More Turquoise.

"There's a Navajo totem against giving your gun to a female," More Turquoise said.

"It's not a totem, it's a taboo," Tom Yazzie said.

"I didn't realize that," More Turquoise said, and he handed Mary-Forge one of Teddy's guns.

It was a thirty-ought-six Springfield with a Hitachi telescopic sight. She cocked the piece and fired quickly from her horse at the British bus, and a rear tire exploded, then another, then another.

"Now I'll get the gas tank," Mary-Forge said, sighting.

"The petrol tank," Bull Who Looks Up said.

"I'll get that, too," Mary-Forge said.

The double-decker bus with all advertisements flying accomplished the Cabazon slope without benefit of tires and made its waddling way toward the Cabazon Peak without seeming benefit of gasoline.

"Look at it piss its way across the desert," Kills The Enemy said. "Detroit couldn't do that."

"They don't make them like that anywhere any more," Hosteen Begay said.

"It's going back to London to die," Three Shoes said.

"It can't cross the Atlantic Ocean."

"A little water can't stop a determined bastard like that," Kills The Enemy said.

The British bus left a wet trail of gasoline in the desert all the way to the tailings of the Cabazon Peak and started up—then it stopped.

Kills The Enemy dropped off his horse and lit a match.

"You will notice, Cripsie," Teddy said, "the Indians have fled. Notice too," he said, pointing, "a fire back there."

"It's coming this way," Cripsie said.

"It will probably veer off before it gets to us," Teddy said.

But it did not veer off.

"Very peculiar," Teddy said.

"I'll get the children out," Cripsie said.

"Yes, rescue the tads," Teddy said, "in case the fire comes this way."

The Measles were already out and making their way up the Cabazon Peak, playing as they went. The peak is a volcano, actually a volcanic plug. It sticks up like a penis. Cabazon Peak was thought at one time to be holy, to be worshiped by the Indians, but this is not true.

"Now the Indian worships the buck," Hosteen Begay said, hoping to bait the Medicine Man.

The Medicine Man on his sorrel did not bait. He just sat solemnly on his horse and watched the fire running toward the bus and ignored the young Indian.

The young ignored Indian settled for watching the fire.

"Here comes the fire, Cripsie. Is everyone out?" Teddy said.

"Yes," she said.

"Where is my gun?"

"Which one?"

"The only one, the best, the thirty-ought-six Springfield with Hitachi scope."

"I don't know."

"It could still be up there," Teddy said, and he bounded up the circular stairs, followed by the fire. On top he looked under all the seats and found nothing, but coming out from under the seat he was hit by the fire. He went to the railing where the antelope hung, but hesitated to jump, and when he jumped he had already caught. When he hit the ground he was blazing. When he ran across the slope of the Cabazon that culminates in a phallic plug he was flaming. When the Indian on his big bay caught Mr. Armbruster II from his running horse and smothered the fire with his blanket, Teddy was medium-well-done.

The Indians were on the ridge where the coyotes had been.

"When the coyote-killer makes it out dead or alive," Mary-Forge said, "he will probably want to be buried in Africa with his trophies."

"Are there still animals in Africa?"

"Yes, there are some elephants left," Mary-Forge said.

"Well, we probably saved those."

"Yes," Mary-Forge said.

"What happened to the coyotes?"

"They went back to their den to lick their wounds."

"The whites will never kill off all the coyotes."

"Because the coyote is holy," the Medicine Man said.

"All animals are. All of us."

"That is correct," the Medicine Man said, and he looked around at all the water rising behind the dam.

Tzo rode up now with Tom Charlie.

"Where is the gift?" the Medicine Man asked.

Tom Charlie looked around as though he were looking for Thomas Charles. "I do not know," he said.

But Tom Charlie did know where Thomas Charles had the gift. All the Indians knew it was in his hogan. And all the Indians were afraid that it would work and all the Indians were afraid it would not work.

"What happened to the bus conductor?" Tzo said.

"He got off at the ashram."

"That was no conductor. That was Stewart Montalban Rhodes," Tom Charlie said.

"What is an ashram?"

"It's something they are building out of tin on our property and they call it an ashram."

"Before the next moon," Lucy-Lucy said in perfect Navajo, "we must get their ass out of here."

12

William William told Mary-Forge it was true that there was a chrome building going up, a building that had nothing to do with the project, with the gift.

"Thomas Charles is trying to kill us all," she said. "But we can all move a little further back into the reservation. The reservation of the mind."

"You can run out of reservations, including the reservation of the mind," William said. "Both of us can."

"Move over," she said.

"I am on the edge of the bed."

She gave William a quick touch and he fell off. Now all of her body was on top of him. "Now, whatever you were thinking, stop," she said. "Stop and enjoy, before the ashram gets here."

And so the Great Western Ashram was built in Navajo Indian Country by Maharishi Marakech, the Perfect Yogi and Zen Master from Delhi. The ashram was built in the Checkerboard between the Wild Horse Mesa and the Tinian Post. White people came from Albuquerque and Santa Fe to the ashram for meditation before the flood.

At the Great Western Ashram, the Perfect Zen Master Maharishi Marakech had just dismissed The Measles, who after fleeing the bus came to the ashram to learn to play Country Zen on the sitar.

"One moment," the Maharishi called to the leader of The Measles, the young man named Alice Dallas. "Your rear fly is open. Let me button it for you."

Like all The Measles, Alice wore long red woolen underwear with white pearl buttons all down the front and one button in the rear.

"That's better," the Maharishi said, fastening the button. "Now have you all said your mantras?"

They had.

"Have you done your yoga, your meditations, eaten your organic foods?"

They had.

"Cleaned the plate?"

They had.

"What are you?"

"Capricorn rising," the Yellow Tambourine said.

"Oh, that's a good sign," the Maharishi said.

"And you?"

"Leo quiescent," the Drummer said.

"That's a good sign, too," the Maharishi said.

"And you?"

"A Navajo Indian entering," Bill Who Looks Up said.

"That's a good sign, too," the Maharishi said.

"Thank you."

"You're not a Measle?"

"No, I'm an Indian."

"I'm an Indian, too," the Maharishi said.

If the Maharishi had looked over his stomach he could have seen that Bull Who Looks Up was not a Measle. Like most of the Navajos in the Checkerboard, Bull Who Looks Up wore roughout boots, Levis, and cowboy shirt, but The Measles all wore green-suede cavalier boots and long red underwear, which made them appear like some undiscovered insect of some unreported sex, some androgynous epiphyte, symbiotic to orchids or flame trees—flamboyant and freak.

Now all The Measles stood in their green boots and waited for the Maharishi to speak.

"Like, cool."

"Welcome," the Maharishi said. "We are just founding our Great Western Ashram in Indian Country. Happy mantras," he said to Bull Who Looks Up.

"The same to you," Bull Who Looks Up said. "But your ashram is showing." He paused, then said, "Your ashram is on Indian land."

"No, this is the Checkerboard," the Maharishi said. "Every other section of Indian land was given to the railroad in 1868 to build a railroad that was never built. My lawyers looked it up. Anyway, we are the Indians who have the bomb," the Indian from India said.

"Why?"

"Happy mantras. We are the Indians of the Bahaluni religion."

"I never heard of that Indian religion," Bull Who Looks Up said, "and I've been an Indian all my life."

"There are different kinds of Indians," the Perfect Master said. "We come from India. Columbus was looking for us when he found you, so to make a long voyage short Columbus called you Indians."

"Do we look like Indians from India?" Tzo said.

"No, not much."

"How did Columbus get away with this, then?"

"Columbus looked the part."

"Did he look like the fearless discoverer of us?" Tzo asked.

"Yes."

"Did he wear a velvet tricornered hat, silk stockings, and pointy turned-up red shoes?" Bull Who Looks Up said.

"Yes."

"And now you Indians from India have the bomb?"

"Yes."

"We Indians from here have it, too."

"Welcome to the Club," the man from India, the Maharishi Perfect Yogi and Zen Master, said.

The Maharishi was sixteen years old and had organized twenty-three ashrams and according to the London *Times,* Dun and Bradstreet, and BankAmericard was worth twelve million pounds, which did not count residuals from Mantras on Decca, which was a "biggie that could become a goldie."

"Does it bother you if I type?" Maharishi's male Sikh secretary said.

"No, it bothers me if you don't," the Maharishi said.

"I've got to go pee," the secretary said.

"That can wait," the Maharishi said. "I want you to take down in legalese what this young man says."

"What are you?" he said to Bull Who Looks Up.

"A Navajo."

"I mean, of course, what sign are you?"

"Coca-Cola."

"I don't mean those kinds of signs. What sign were you born under?"

"I was born under a Coca-Cola sign."

"That's interesting," the Maharishi said.

"Our hogan was on Route Forty-four," Bull Who Looks Up said.

"I don't have a chart on that," the Maharishi said.

"Maybe the Coca-Cola sign people have his chart," the secretary said.

"Did you take your pee?" the Maharishi said.

"No."

"Try to hold it off," the Maharishi said. "Tell yourself a couple of mantras. I think we've got something important going here, and I'd like to get it down in legalese. Have you heard," he said to the young man, "have you heard my latest Mantras on Decca? We've got a biggie that could turn into a goldie."

"You said that."

"It bears repeating," the Maharishi said. "It's good karma. Have you heard about my positive erection?"

"Is that a biggie that could become a goldie?"

"We don't know. I haven't looked at the chart. Have you taken that pee yet?" he said to his secretary.

"No."

"Then look at the chart," he said. "What have we here?"

"These are Checkerboard Navajos led by a Medicine Man, When Someone Dies He Is Remembered, and this is Mary-Forge, our teacher in the Learning Hogan," Bull Who Looks Up said.

"With that orange hair and scar over her right cheekbone I can spot she's not an Indian," the Maharishi said. "I'll check her out with a teleprint to Delhi."

"She's okay," his secretary said. "She's a bourgeois."

"My secretary," the Maharishi said, "has everyone near a new ashram classified as a bourgeois or freak for our file in case of trouble."

"Have you ever had trouble?"

"Only from a British bus conductor who busted in our ashram, destroyed everything, and left a note saying, 'How can I say I'm sorry? Your ashram looked like a physics laboratory. It really does. I was searching for something. I trust that this experience will not in any way affect, now or in the future, the opinion you may, or may not, have had, in terms of, or relationship to, the need for national security.'"

"I'm sorry," Mary-Forge said. "You're going to have to move your ashram. It's on Indian land."

"What is your sign?"

"It is not in our stars, dear Maharishi," Nice Hands' Sister said, "but in our ashrams that we are underlings."

"There you go again," the Maharishi said to Mary-Forge. "Why do you put the Indians up to saying things like that in my ashram in front of my students?"

"Are The Measles your students?"

"Yes."

"Are you the Perfect Master?"

"Yes."

"And only sixteen years old?"

"Yes."

"How could you get such a big belly in only sixteen years?" Kills The Enemy said.

"He's pregnant," Lucy-Lucy said.

"We are all pregnant with learning in the ashram," the Maharishi said.

"As one Indian to another," Hosteen Begay said to the Maharishi, "is business good?"

"This is not a business," the Maharishi said. "It is a search for God."

"What will it cost to find Him?"

"In Santa Fe we are lucky to break even," the Maharishi said.

The young Maharishi Marakech stroked his belly and dwelt on the injustice of this. And his sparkling black eyes turned dull and inward as he tried to think of an interesting platitude to get these Columbus Indians to support the Great Western Ashram. Like: Where you are is where you should be. An ashram in Indian Country would be excellent karma. No one would know what kind of an Indian he was. He could be any kind of an Indian anyone wanted him to be. Without lying. If the drift toward the Columbus Indians continued he would have a sheet to the wind. There is no law against mantras in Navajo. Another biggie that could become a goldie.

"Where were we?" the Maharishi said.

"On Indian land," Mary-Forge said. "You're going to have to move."

"Why don't we Indians stick together?" The Maharishi touched his gold record of mantras and tilted it toward the light.

"I want to find out," Lucy-Lucy said, "what is a biggie that could become a goldie."

"It is," Alice Dallas said, "a record that sells one million copies."

"Is that what he did?"

"Yes."

"Then he should be arrested," Lucy-Lucy said.

"I can't move the ashram," the Maharishi said. "You're going to have to live with it."

All the Navajos looked at Mary-Forge.

"Then we will move it for you," Mary-Forge said.

All the Navajo looked at Alice Dallas and the Maharishi.

"If you could do it safely, that would be worth a goldie," Alice Dallas said.

They all quitted the Great Western Ashram and went outside to have a look. It was a Buckminster Fuller mechanical-shaped hexagonal structure that did not fit in Indian Country—that did not fit anywhere on earth.

"We are all hallucinating well today," Alice Dallas said, standing alongside Mary-Forge.

"What does Buckminster mean?" Tzo said.

"It means," Alice Dallas said, "the latest. It means you are into space; it's neat. Don't you agree, Mary-Forge?"

"Yes, Alice, you are hallucinating well today," Mary-Forge said.

"Since you brought it up in the ashram," Alice Dallas said, "trying to move the ashram, I've given it quite a bit of hallucination, and I hallucinate that you can't get the ashram off Indian land without crossing that arroyo"—he pointed—"unless you circumnavigate the earth with the ashram and get it on the other side that way."

"As I said," Mary-Forge said, "you are hallucinating well today."

"Yes, if you believe," Lucy-Lucy said, "yes if you believe in shitolosis."

And so when Mary-Forge came into William's barn he knew it was for the horses—that there was no other way out because the ashram would not burn—she came here for the horses to move the damn thing.

"You saw it going up," Mary-Forge said. "Why didn't you stop them?"

"Because it was erected, thrown up, from numbers stamped in a factory before I, before anyone, could get to them to tell them they had the wrong land. I've been thinking," William said. "How are you going to get it across the arroyo?"

"I will build a bridge across the arroyo," Mary-Forge said.

"With what?"

"The Measles."

"The way I see it," Tzo said, "now that you have the house on the log skids, the bridge over the arroyo The Measles built is not going to hold. The bridge is made of straw."

"Jack pine."

"It will hold," the Maharishi said, "if we hold the right mantras." The Maharishi held his hand up as a visor against the other sun, the golden sun. The Maharishi was surrounded outside the ashram by his belly, his bags of gold, and The Measles. His bags of gold were actually bags of jewels given to him by God through the rich people of Tucson and Phoenix, Arizona. His belly was given to him by love of rich food. The Measles were his through their mutual need. The Measles needed the spiritual concern of the Maharishi, and the Maharishi needed The Measles' money. Not that the Maharishi worshiped money, but the money seemed to worship the Maharishi and always found its way into the ashram along with the jewels of Phoenix. There were still many ashrams to be built—but he still had time.

"He only being sixteen and all," Lucy-Lucy said.

Then there was his Sikh secretary, dark and dressed in a black silk suit with a crisp white towel around his head, who carried the orgone box. The orgone box gave potency to the impotent. Through cosmic vibrations it was able to channelize the energies of the life force.

"Gives you a hard-on," Hosteen Begay said.

The orgone box was an American invention that had been adopted by the Maharishi.

"Incorporated into the act," Lucy-Lucy said.

"I don't see why," Mary-Forge said, "you Navajos have to be so tough on other people's faith. Why don't you listen and learn something?"

"O orange-haired teacher of the savages," Bull Who Looks Up said. "We will build an orgone box of our own and live happily ever after."

"You do that," Mary-Forge said.

But even with the horses the ashram still did not move. It was important that the ashram walk the arroyo soon because of rain. You could see a rain falling on the foothills of the Sangre de Cristos, so that soon the arroyo would be at flood, so that soon the matchsticks of Jack pine would shatter when the lightning-moving mountain of flood hit the sticks they called a bridge, bearing the ashram they called a house.

"The ashram will not move without the Perfect Master inside," the Sikh secretary said.

"The Perfect Master will not travel across the arroyo without his secretary," the Maharishi said.

"Very well," the Sikh said, and he stepped into the ashram. The Perfect Master followed and the ashram moved. The water moved, too.

"Stop," Mary-Forge hollered, and the horses stopped. "Run," Mary-Forge hollered. "Here comes the flood."

"There is no need to run," the Perfect Master said quietly, and he sat down on the ashram balcony chaise longue, and the Sikh sat with him. The horses tried to get the ashram started again and failed. Tom Yazzie's Brother unhitched the horses and they all ran. You could see them finally zipping up the Largo Canyon.

And so the Perfect Master and the Sikh faced the flood until they saw it. Then it was too late. When you can see a flood on the Largo arroyo it is already too late. Flight is an attempt to escape lightning, to evade God's whim or seeming caprice, because the water that starts on the high slope is joined by thousands of rivulets which become hundreds of tributaries which on the Largo become one instant magic mountain of water that hurtles at you in one thunder. It is no longer even water but the seeming terrible hand of God—terrific and instant and awful, and it hit the bridge, and the bridge disappeared along with the ashram all commingled in a clap, so that palpable matter became a mere sharpness, a mere noise, and that which was there became not there.

It took a long time for everyone to recover, to understand. The Measles went back to their "gig," to their strange noise-making called music at the Desert Inn in Albuquerque, where Alice Dallas got into a new sound and the sound was neat. The Navajo Indians wanted more time to think. Mary-Forge was remote. She just sat there in the midst of all the Indians in the Learning Hogan and was subdued.

"They were two human beings," Mary-Forge said.

The Medicine Man was quiet. He had stayed out of the whole incident. Maybe because he felt that anything he did or said would be considered prejudiced because of the ashram competition. Now he said, "We do not know for certain the other Indians are dead. It was a great stream of water. Perhaps now the other Indians along with their ashram are safe in Texas."

"Where they belong," Kills The Enemy said.

"No, they will end up behind the Atlas Dam," Sinoginee said.

"All of us will," Tzo said.

And the rain hit them, the rain that would fill the dam and end a country.

"How many days before the dam dedication, Tom Charlie, before we give them the gift?"

"Three."

"How goes the project?"

"Perfect."

"How do you trigger it?"

"It can be set off remotely."

"No bullshit."

"The device can be triggered from a distance even by a TV channel selector."

"That simple?"

"It has got to be simple if the Indians from India have the bomb."

"Don't downgrade them."

"True, now that we are in the Club, all Indians must stick together." Now Thomas Charles drew on the hogan floor the design for splitting the atom and creating the bang and all the Indians were amazed at the simplicity of the project and wondered why no one had thought of this before—they had come a long way, in a short time, from the bow and arrow.

13

William remembered what Mary-Forge said about love when he handed her the horseshoe. She held the shoe up for the horse's inspection. The horse, Elegante, nodded his okay, and she proceeded to nail it on.

"You said before about the gift, the project," William said.

"Did I, Billy?" she said.

"You said, I think, when you were quoting the Medicine Man."

"I did."

"You said love is the biggest gift."

"I did."

She caught another hoof and proceeded with a kind of studied deliberateness and at-once fury to pry and wrench off the old worn nigh shoe and nail on the new. And William thought, it's not the part Indian she can't accept in me because she's more than proven that, nor the part rancher because she's proving that now, and I don't think it's even the part writer because that's only a mild form of insanity that she's big enough if not to forgive then to forget. So that it's not me, maybe, but herself, and it's not that scar on her cheekbone but a bigger one.

"Yes, you said love was a larger gift, that we—"

"Did I, William?"

She dropped the hoof. This time not in her lap but on the ground. Because she was finished. All done. She slapped the horse on the flank, and rising from her cramped and fetal position said, "Come on, Elegante, let's dance." She paused and said, "Dance before the Japanese tourists get here."

The Japanese tourists had come to America to see the American wild Indian and the biggest dam in the world. The Indians discussed this in the Learning Hogan. Thomas Charles was particularly interested. The Japanese had a guide, Hiroshi Hitachi. Hiroshi Hitachi carried a red and white flag and spoke some English. And so everywhere Hiroshi Hitachi the guide went with his red and white flag, the Japanese tourists were certain to follow.

"Even over a cliff?"

"Yes."

"Did the Japanese win the war with the United States?"

"Yes."

"How?"

"The Japanese stopped fighting, so they won. The Japanese decided that instead of fighting they would build things, so they won."

"What are the Japanese tourists doing here now?"

"They have come for the dam dedication."

"Do the Japanese actually follow the guide with the flag over a cliff?"

"Yes, and into rivers and into ladies' rest rooms, where they are swept away to their deaths."

"I don't follow you."

"But the Japanese tourists will," Hosteen Tzo said.

Here at the Learning Hogan and all over northern New Mexico everyone was on the lookout for the lost Japanese-tourist battalion. The Japanese had left the railroad station at Lamy, which is ten miles south of Santa Fe, the morning of October 7 and headed in a northwesterly direction searching for the dam. After crossing the Albuquerque–Santa Fe highway, the Japanese battalion passed the Santo Domingo Pueblo at noon the next day on a forced march. Still no Indians. Early in the morning of the twelfth, after having made a dry camp at the Piñasco Butte, the Japanese marched into a band of cowboys out of Espanola and were warned by the cowboys not to try to cross the Jemez Mountains this late in October because the passes would soon be blocked with the first heavy snow, but to go back to Tokyo and try again next year.

"Osaka."

"What does Osaka mean?"

"We are from Osaka, not Tokyo."

"Is it true?" John Clearboy, the leader of the cowboys, asked. "Is it true that the Japanese tourist will follow the guide with a red and white flag over a cliff?"

"No," the Japanese guide Hiroshi Hitachi said. "Sometimes into a rest room but never over a cliff. These stories are getting to be like Polish jokes. Because Japan won the war, it need not mean you people lost the war. It depends on what you do after a war is over. We are searching for knowledge. Last year we searched for the Loch Ness Monster in Scotland. Tomorrow it will be the Atlas, the biggest dam in the world. Right now we are searching for wild Indians and Thomas Charles."

"The Indians are on the other side of the Jemez Mountains."

"Then we will cross the Jemez," Hiroshi Hitachi said.

"I understand now how you won the war," John Clearboy said.

The Japanese passed Los Alamos on the twelfth and pushed on into the night of the thirteenth when a light snow was falling.

"They have not yet been reduced to eating their women and children."

"I don't like that remark," Hosteen Begay said. "Particularly coming from an Indian. You're saying that nonwhites will eat their women and children the first cat out of the bag."

"We had a case here that our deputy Mr. Breckenridge handled in Bernalillo. This white trapper ran into a blizzard on the Sangre de Cristos, was starving, and ate his partner."

"Mr. Breckenridge was very angry and told the white trapper, 'Do you realize what you done done?'

" 'What?'

" 'Listen to me. Stop picking your teeth and listen to me. Outside myself, you ate the last Republican in Sandoval County.' "

"But the case had to be dismissed?" Looks Important After A Rain said.

"Yes, lack of evidence."

"The hungry trapper cleaned the plate."

"Yes."

"How do you expect people to take us Indians seriously when you tell stories like that?"

"Some others have a sense of humor."

"No, they don't."

"They will take Tom Charlie seriously."

"Yes, they will."

The Japanese made camp that night on the edge of the Valle Grande. They were still a thousand feet from the summit and the snow was coming down very heavy. The next day Hiroshi Hitachi decided to stay put and allow the snow to abate. The Japanese tourists decided to follow Hiroshi and stay put, too. This was difficult because following always meant moving, so Hiroshi Hitachi marched with his flag in a big circle around the floor of the Valle Grande and the people followed him and they ended up where they started, "but they were happy."

"There you go again, you're making damn fools of the Japanese."

"No, this may have saved their lives. In the freeze it kept them moving."

It was discovered on the seventeenth that the Japanese group was immobilized on the Via Grande. Because of the deepening snow they could not retreat back to Los Alamos or advance over the mountains to Indian Country on the western slope. Los Alamos telephoned Santa Fe that the Japanese had advanced into the storm and by now all must be presumed dead. Because of the continuing storm, all the modern technical junk was useless. The helicopters could not see to fly; the snow was too soft for snowmobiles and too deep for tractors. A gloom settled over northern New Mexico. Except for the quiet smoke coming out the smoke hole, even the Learning Hogan was quiet.

"That Japanese fellow came from halfway around the world to see Tom Charlie. I understand the Japanese leader and Tom Charlie were buddies at Los Alamos."

"Yes."

"That Tom Charlie has a problem with the project and the Japanese fellow has the answer."

"They also came to see the dam and the wild Indians."

"Nevertheless the big deal," Tzo said, "was to consult with Tom Charlie."

"And to see the dam and the wild Indians."

"Yes."

"Does it make you feel like a wild Indian?"

"I feel," Tom Yazzie said, "like an actor that didn't show up."

"It was the Japanese that didn't show up."

"Nevertheless, if they can't get to us, then we should go to the Japanese."

"Rots of ruck," Lucy-Lucy said.

"What does Mary-Forge, the great white hope and teacher to the poor Indians, think?"

Mary-Forge said nothing.

"Come on."

"I came here," Mary-Forge said, "because you kicked the BIA out because they were telling you what to think."

"We didn't ask you to tell us what to think. We want to know what you think."

"Don't be rude to her," the Medicine Man said.

"Mary-Forge comes here," Lucy-Lucy said, "smokes our cigars, drinks our whiskey, sleeps with our husbands, and then won't tell us what she thinks."

"Quiet," the Medicine Man said.

Mary-Forge went to the blanket door, lifted it, and looked out and up at the Jemez with all the weather roiling down the big long western slope. There was a soft rain here and a big snow on the mountains. For only a flick of time the sun danced out, making it all diamond and scintillant, then it became sad-dark again here on the last wave of the Rocky Mountains. She remembered the Donner Party, the people a big time ago traveling west over the Sierras who got caught in the winter snows and the strong ate the weak. When a rescue party arrived, it was too late. Mary-Forge came to live with the Indian nation because on the big white reservation the strong were eating the weak. This is called competition. All of the walking wounded are piled in a city ghetto and told to behave themselves. This is called law and order. When a rescue party arrived it was too late. The Indians are placed in outdoor ghettos and told to behave themselves. This is called honoring our treaties. When a rescue party arrived it was too late. This is a speech, Mary-Forge thought. I came to Indian Country for personal reasons. All reasons are personal. I came then to find the part of myself that was missing, the part we killed in the Indian and in ourselves. When the rescue party arrived it was too late.

"How far is it to the summit?" Mary-Forge said.

"Twenty-eight miles."

"But the Japanese are not at the summit," the Medicine Man said. "They're on the Via Grande."

"Thirty-seven miles."

"Yes."

"If we can get them to the deputy Breckenridge's cabin on the Rio Las Vacas, we can revive them and get them back from there."

"How do we get to the Breckenridge cabin?"

"Fly."

"No," Mary-Forge said, "our horses can break through if we stick to the Telegraph Canyon ridge as far as Blue Lake, then circle south using the protection of the dolomite cliffs. That will bring us up in back of Breckenridge's cabin."

"That's okay except . . ."

"Except what?"

"I never take orders from a girl," More Turquoise said.

"That's fine except . . ."

"Except what?"

"Except you will now," Kills The Enemy said.

Hiroshi Hitachi, the Japanese leader, had survived Hiroshima. After the war he went into business and one of the businesses was to build nuclear-powered ships. He went to Los Alamos at the invitation of the U.S. Government to find out how this was done, and Thomas Charles had helped him to know how this was done, and now Thomas Charles wanted help.

While in the States last time, Hitachi had bought with some leftover yen most of California and all of the United States Steel Corporation, but this time the Arabs had all the Japanese money "in exchange for three quarts of oil." Americans had deceived the world for one hundred years now with the idea that business was exciting. Without oil, business was a bore. But the Indians are different. Indians are exotic. Indians are worth a foray into Indian Country even if you get lost. But I am not lost, Hiroshi Hitachi told himself. I am only fifteen miles from Los Alamos, where I learned to make the reactor. I am not lost; we are snowbound. I would rather be here than in Philadelphia, that is, here searching for Indians rather than making money. I plan to resell California, the southern part anyway. Cheap. Maybe I will give it to Thomas Charles.

"Will you stop that wild business talk and get us out of here?"

"I learned during the war," Hiroshi Hitachi said, "that the color of the pen is not the color of the ink. For example, when we go down the western slope of the Jemez, the first Navajo section will be the Checkerboard area, so named because every other section of Indian land was given by the United States to the railroad for a railroad the railroad never built. The part of the Navajo land that will not be buried under water by the new Atlas Dam is now being sold off by whites to other whites. The land is circled each day by an eagle named Star, and an Indian named Thomas Charles is building an atomic bomb to blow the dam."

"What does that mean?"

"You speak Japanese as well as I do. Listen," Hiroshi said carefully. "We have rations to last us two more days. There is a cabin four kilometers from here that belongs to a deputy named Breckenridge. If we can reach that, we are safe. I know about the cabin because I know all about this country because I studied at Los Alamos, and now a former colleague, Thomas Charles, has a problem and that's what I'm doing here."

"I thought you were leading us for Linblat."

"The color of the pen," Hiroshi said, "is never the color of the ink."

The snow continued to fall and the Japanese party did not move.

Breckenridge's cabin was perfectly buried in snow, so that even if the Japanese expedition had reached the cabin they would not have seen it. Now Breckenridge's radio came on and it was Tokyo. That is, the announcer spoke with a Japanese accent. He said, "Can you help us?"

"I don't know," Mr. Breckenridge said. "Do you have one of those Japanese two-way radios? Just stay where you are. If you're looking for the Indians, the Indians will find you."

"This is where the cabin should be," Mary-Forge said.

"It was here last month."

"Do you suppose Breckenridge repossessed it?"

"No, his cabin must be under the snow."

"Where?"

"We will never find it."

"I have a bank robber here in the balcony!" Tom Yazzie hollered. "I have a bank robber and no deputy to arrest him!"

There was still no answer.

Hiroshi Hitachi pocketed his Sony citizen-band radio and went back into the tunnel he had had his people dig into the snow. He shone his flashlight into each of their faces. "We will never find the Indians," he said.

"Why do you say that?"

"Because two hours ago I was told to stay put by Mr. Breckenridge, and the Navajos would find us."

"So the whole Navajo thing is a movie put-on."

"What do you mean, put-on?"

"You speak Japanese as well as I do."

"Then the Linblat Tour people are ripping us off."

"I don't think the Linblat Tour people know that kind of language."

"They're ripping us off," the young Japanese boy said. "They said they were going to provide real live Navajos. We've been ripped off."

"Linblat made a mistake. They meant another country."

"Not the United States?"

"That's right."

"What about your friend Thomas Charles?"

"He may have blown himself up."

"That's what I mean," the young girl from Osaka said. "There are no Navajos."

"That's right," a newcomer said, entering the Japanese snow tunnel. "The dam builders are seeing to that, but there are still a few of us Indians hiding in the woods."

"Well, you're not an Eskimo," a Japanese boy said.

"How can you tell?"

"It's not Eskimo country."

"It is cold enough," the newcomer said. "I'm heading a relief expedition from below. We came up here looking for a party of lost Japanese and my friend Hiroshi Hitachi."

Hiroshi Hitachi stood up in the snow tunnel and stepped forward in the semidark to greet the Indian rescuer and said, "Doctor Thomas Charles, I presume."

When everyone got down from everywhere to someplace which is Indian Country, specifically the Checkerboard area, the moral capital of the world, Tom Charlie and Hiroshi Hitachi had a lot to talk over.

"How can Indians call themselves the moral capital of the world when we talk the way those two are talking about the bomb?" Mary-Forge said.

"Indians don't call themselves anything."

"Who did, then?"

"Linblat."

"Because it's good for business?"

"It was until Hiroshi Hitachi bought Linblat."

"He showed you the receipt?"

"Yes."

Someone came into the dark Learning Hogan and the Medicine Man rose, stepped forward and stuck out his hand in greeting and said, "Doctor Hiroshi Hitachi, President of Linblat Tours, I presume?"

"No," Hiroshi Hitachi said. "Of the United States."

"So named because you bought the United States?"

"So named," Hiroshi Hitachi said, "because I was in the process before Arab oil."

"But the Arabs will never buy Indian Country. Indian Country was never, is never, FOR SALE," the Medicine Man said. "But the United States has never appreciated that fact."

"Will you tell the next person that asks about your land to go fly a kite, to get lost forever and ever?"

"Yes."

"Perfect. We will print that," the young lady from Osaka said.

"But I notice," Bull Who Looks Up said, "you Japanese still have the yen to travel."

"I thought I said no more one-liners," Mary-Forge said.

And the Japanese all followed the gentleman from Japan to Albuquerque, where they got on a plane that said Air Arabia; then they were content to watch down at the desert and at the Pacific and Hawaii and all the world the Japanese had conquered without a war, before Arab oil.

"Even without an unkind word," the gentleman from Japan said.

"But even when you were rich you couldn't buy Indian Country."

The gentleman from Japan, Hiroshi Hitachi, hunched down in his seat, lit a cigar, glanced out over the wing of the Air Arabia 747 to everything below, thought about Indian Country, and wondered aloud, "We will not see the dam. We will not go to the dam dedication because there will be trouble there. And even when we were rich we never bought Indian Country. So we lose a few. But we discovered the mystery, the wild beauty of the New Mexican Indians. We discovered that beauty, didn't we? As well as winning the war, didn't we?"

はい はい the young lady from Osaka said.

"What's that mean?"

"It means 'yes,'" everyone in the plane said. "Yes."

The gentleman from Japan leaned back in his seat, blew out a cloud of cigar smoke. "And so we also won a few," he said.

"Did Hiroshi Hitachi solve your problem?" everyone wanted to know of Tom Charlie.

"No."

"What did he say?"

"He said, 'After what happened at Hiroshima—don't.'"

"Does that mean the project is finished?"

"No," Tom Charlie said. "If there is one thing I learned from the whites, it's to get the job done."

"Success."

"Yes, their dam dedication will still get off the ground with a bang."

14

The war came as no surprise. The Vigilante Committee of Stake, New Mexico, had been warning the people of Gallup for some time now that Indians and blacks and Mexicans and women would no longer be tolerated after dark. The laws must be enforced even during the flood, particularly during the flood that brought a lot of new Indians to town.

"But there is no law that says that."

"You cannot have laws to enforce morals," the Chief of the Vigilante Committee, Adrian Fox, said. "People have got to do what they know is right in their hearts. The people of Gallup have been allowing the Indians and all to run around pretty much as they please without a thought for tomorrow. Somebody's got to put a stop to it."

The Vigilante Committee pulled into Gallup about eight and sealed off the town from the outside world by detouring the traffic around the town and cutting all telephone lines. The Vigilante Committee set up headquarters in the police station after they had convinced the police of the need for law and order. The police had received three million dollars from the federal government to stamp out crime for which they were able to purchase three Cadillacs, two Lincolns, one sailing yacht, two M60 tanks, and three 155-millimeter howitzers with which the Vigilantes proceeded to bombard the Indian section of Gallup.

"I like it when people know what to do and do it," the Police Captain said to the Vigilantes. "Every police department in the country has had to take it on the chin from the criminal. Those anarchists are out there someplace doing exactly what they please, and we police are stuck in here with a lot of antique laws that don't protect us, and being knocked off one by one. The Indians have been running around loose in Gallup for I don't know how long, and there is nothing the police can do about it. You Vigilante people have taken the bull by the balls and gotten me off the horns of the dilemma. I want to cry."

"Why did you buy a yacht?"

"Ask yourself," the Police Captain said, "why did we wait so long to buy a yacht?"

"Because the federal government refused to appropriate the money. They don't realize the problems unique to the frontier. They have given all the money for the war on the blacks. Meanwhile the Indians have seized the opportunity to occupy Gallup under the guise of protesting the dam. In the war on crime we should have equal money for the western front. What can you do with two M60 tanks and three 155 howitzers?"

You can continue to shell the northwestern Indian section of Gallup, and that's what the Vigilantes did, the shells arching over the railroad tracks and into the Bullet Proof Bar and Grill. The white residents turned up their TV sets to the Miss America Contest.

Adrian Fox, the leader of the Vigilantes, was a former sociology professor at Harvard University who believed that the Indians should be treated with benign neglect and discipline. American police departments tend to be politically controlled and soft on Indians, and Adrian Fox was just what the doctor ordered.

"We sure do appreciate the help you Vigilante folks are giving us," the Police Captain said as the cannon roared and Miss Alabama on the television set banged out a high-class rendition of "Stars and Stripes Forever" in her underwear.

The owners of McCandless and Senzaki's Bullet Proof Bar and Grill had completed the job of barricading the doors but could make no provision for an artillery shell coming through the roof. McCandless and Senzaki did not suspect that everything was not normal in their drinking until they saw Humphrey Bogart across from Tom Charlie sitting in the corner minding his own business.

"Hello, sweetheart, how goes the project?" Bogie said.

McCandless and Senzaki ignored a man they knew to have been dead lo these twenty years and realized that they, and the Indians, had gotten drunk on the hundredth anniversary of Custer's Last Stand and that the Miss America Contest was not real. It was conducted as though there were no blacks or Indians in America, and now Miss State of Alaska rendered a classic rendition of "The Boogie-Woogie Bugle Boy from Company B," and answered to the blind and deaf judges that her ambition in life was to do something about her sagging breasts which would not interefere with her goal of becoming a theoretical astrophysicist.

Which shows you cannot drink too much of the white man's booze, even though you are celebrating the Custer Centennial.

"That's right, sweetheart," Bogie said.

"This is my cup of tea," Jonathan Swift said. Joe Swift was an Irishman who never touched tea. He came to the Bullet Proof Bar with a girl named Stella to write about Indians and Stella and McCandless and Senzaki and the Indian flood.

"Indian flood?"

"Yes," Joe Swift said. "You notice that the Vigilantes picked the night of the Miss America Pageant, which coincided with the Custer Centennial, which coincided with the new moon.

Stella made a face.

"That's right, sweetheart," Bogie said.

"What's that got to do with our flood?"

"The government," McCandless said, "has only taken halfway measures to solve the Indian problem, like sending out Custer. Now the Vigilantes are going to do it right. The trouble with Custer was he left his cannon on the Rosebud with Reno."

"Another trouble with Custer was he did not spend enough time with his hair. I hear he went into the Little Big Horn looking like a Flora Dora girl," Senzaki said.

"Can an Indian say something?"

McCandless looked at the Medicine Man, who nodded yes to Hosteen Begay.

"Is that Greta Garbo sitting over there?" Hosteen Begay said.

"Yes."

"Is that Tom Charlie sitting over there?"

"The trouble with Custer was—"

"Look, is that The Lone Ranger sitting over there?" Hosteen Begay said.

"Which do you want, The Lone Ranger or Greta Garbo?"

"They are both sitting apart."

"That's their problem," Tom Yazzie's Brother said.

"I want to know," Hosteen Begay said, "whether I am hearing things or is that artillery?"

"Yes, that's the problem," Joe Swift said. "Whether we barricaded the door because we have been drinking too much or whether that Miss America Pageant is real."

A pretty young thing from Arizona came on the screen and announced to the horrified judges that she was going to dance Stravinsky's *Le Sacre du printemps* in the buff for openers. Then she wanted to devote her life to helping the little people.

An artillery shell burst across the street in front of the

Throw'em Out Inn, splattering the Bullet Proof Bar and Grill with shrapnel.

A commercial came on the television, advertising the Formosa Little League baseball team that had just beaten the American champions forty-four to zero.

"You realize why the Vigilante Committee has to take the bull by the horns," Hosteen Begay said.

An announcement on the television said that the American Air Force had wiped out a city in Hawaii by mistake.

"They're only Gooks," Hosteen Begay said.

"Let's get back to the Indian flood."

"We're only Gooks," Hosteen Begay said.

"Then let's get back to Bogart."

"And you better watch your language, sweetheart," Bogie said.

They all had a drink on that excepting McCandless, who was seeing the Vigilantes again in his vision.

Adrian Fox, the self-announced leader of the Vigilantes, had been in the preacher business, the used-car business, the political business, the academic business, and now he was in the business of solving the Indian problem. While solving all the white man's problems, he became a politician and built three palatial houses before he was caught. Now Adrian Fox decided to blow up a row of houses to save Gallup.

"From what?"

"Fire," Adrian Fox said.

The Police Captain thought about this. "You know, you might have an idea there. Where is the fire?"

"I haven't started it yet."

"You can't start a fire just to put it out."

"Why not?"

The Police Captain thought about this and then he said, "Why not? I don't know how else we are going to solve the Indian problem. When I was younger I used to have ideas like that. Now I've kind of gone to seed. In my grandfather's time, people were more religious. They'd think nothing of going out and killing a bunch of Indians. Now if you kill a few, they hit you with a writ of mandamus."

"Even a police captain?"

"Yes."

"There's no respect for law and order any more," Adrian Fox said.

"That's right," the Police Captain said. "I think you better start the fire and blow up a row of buildings."

"There's nothing else to do."

"I can't think of anything else to do," the Police Captain said.

"We'll be careful not to blow up any business buildings."

"No, blow them up," the Police Captain said. "We have to save the city. The business people are the worst kind anyway, any more. They are all hand in glove with the young people and the Indians. In my grandfather's time we never sold the Indians nothing. Now an Indian can walk right in and order a Hupmobile and nobody thinks anything of it. People aren't religious any more. I hate to burn the city down; then again if we don't, somebody else will."

"Do people know about these things?"

"They know, but they pretend not to," the Police Captain said. "People are not religious any more."

"And we were hesitating about burning this city down."

"Imagine that."

"I can't."

"You should—"

"You should never use the word 'should.'"

"I am the Police Captain," the Police Captain said. "You should not only burn this city down, but if it was up to me I wouldn't even blow up the buildings to save the city—if it was up to me. This city—"

"This Sodom and Gomorrah," Adrian Fox said.

"I could tell you things no one would believe," the Police Captain said.

"I know," Adrian Fox said.

"And do you know where the center of vice is?"

"The Vice Squad."

"Not only that."

"The McCandless and Senzaki Bullet Proof Bar and Grill is hiding Thomas Charles."

"How did you know that?"

"Everyone knows that."

"Then why doesn't someone do something?" the Police Captain said.

"We plan to," Adrian Fox said. "We are going to blow up the Bullet Proof before they blow us up. If we believe in law and order, the deed must follow the word."

"All right, blow her up," the Police Captain said.

"Just because," Adrian Fox's lieutenant said, "just because McCandless and Senzaki are hiding Thomas Charles is no reason we should blow them up, or is it?"

"There are other reasons," the Police Captain said.

"Like what?"

"National security."

"I'm sorry I asked."

"You don't have to be sorry you asked," the Police Captain said. "Just don't expect any answers."

"If you ever think," Adrian Fox's lieutenant, Marty Wampler, said to the Police Captain, "if you ever think I'm a threat to national security, if you ever think I know too much, you can kill me. I'll wait for you on any street corner you name."

"I appreciate that," the Police Captain said.

"Always remember that."

"I will always remember that," the Police Captain said.

"If you want to kill my mother, I'll throw her in, too."

"I don't think that will be necessary, Mr. Wampler."

"If it ever gets down to that, let me know."

"If it ever gets down to that, I will let you know, Mr. Wampler," the Police Captain said.

"Are you crying, Captain?" Adrian Fox, the leader of the Vigilantes, said.

"A bit."

"Would you like my handkerchief?"

"Yes, thank you," the Police Captain said, and he blew a big wad into it and said, "And now what are we going to blow up?" The Captain paused, remembered what they were going to blow up, and then got back to a more interesting subject. "I said before that people aren't religious any more. Well, it took Mr. Wampler here to turn me around. What did you say your first name was?"

"Marty."

"Thank you, Marty," the Police Captain said. "After our fire we will all try to meet here for a prayer breakfast."

McCandless and Senzaki at the Bullet Proof Bar had piled everything in their world against the door, against the Vigilantes.

"It does not pay to hide an Indian," Bull Who Looks Up said.

"You can say that again, sweetheart," Nice Hands' Sister said.

Bogie smiled, shifted his shoulder holster, and sucked his tooth.

Jonathan Swift, Stella, Greta Garbo, and The Lone Ranger mingled with all the Indians just like plain folks.

Through the whiskey haze, to McCandless Mary-Forge seemed the only reality in the Bullet Proof outside of the Medicine Man, When Someone Dies He Is Remembered. Mary-Forge and the Medicine Man sat together; they seemed withdrawn and distant as though they were not taking part in the Custer Centennial. So now and for the first time on this night of the big rain, McCandless turned sober. On the night of the big rain that filled the Atlas Dam, it was very cold and very quiet on the Navajo reservation in northern New Mexico. The wind and rain blended gently with the sounds of a dying coyote off the mesas of home, and the Indians were angry. Even here in Gallup, McCandless and Senzaki were doing no business. The fact that it was the Custer Centennial did not help. Mary-Forge and the Medicine Man had come in and that was all, so McCandless and Senzaki had decided to hang one on and serve the Medicine Man and Mary-Forge; then McCandless thought soberly—the Medicine Man's face is ravaged with the suffering, the nobility of time. Mary-Forge, too. They are both survivors. Both victims of the white man's wars: not the visible wars of slash and cut, although they had both seen that, too, but the slow and quiet destruction within, and this is the ultimate arrow that will accomplish what Custer failed to accomplish, because Custer was a Boy Scout, McCandless thought, a perfect and pretty vainglorious child who was brought up on the bauble victory; but now war has been repudiated and the whites have planted the flag of indifference and have won. We have seen that flag flying over Indian Country and it is red and white and sad, and when the wind blows it flutters red and white—and indifferent.

"That is true, but we must say it less pretentiously," Senzaki said.

Senzaki and McCandless, the proprietors of the Bullet Proof Bar and Grill, came up to their table and asked Mary-Forge and the Medicine Man why they were not taking part in the Indian celebration of Custer's Last Stand.

"We'll wait," the Medicine Man said.

McCandless and Senzaki said they were going out on a patrol to see whether they had been drinking too much or whether the Vigilantes existed. They said that the time had come to find out how much of their thinking had been governed by whiskey in the celebration of the Custer Centennial—to find out whether The Lone Ranger and Bogart were real, or how far the Vigilantes had penetrated. When McCandless and Senzaki got to the police station through a New Mexican rainstorm with the thunder cracking like artillery and told the Police Captain their story, the Police Captain pretended indifference. When they told the Police Captain that the Indians were being flooded out, the Police Captain showed boredom. Then the Police Captain said it had been a quiet night.

McCandless and Senzaki both laughed.

"Are you laughing," the Police Captain said, "because of joy or pain?"

They said they would try pain.

"For two cents I would lock you both up."

They came up with the two cents.

In the big cell drunk tank with twenty-three Indians, they flopped in a corner. It would be best to spend the Custer Centennial here. There had been only a few Indians at the bar and these had left early because they had no money. They said all the Indians were worried. Mary-Forge and the Medicine Man had come into the bar to order a coffee and confirmed that it was cold and the Indians were sad. That's when McCandless and Senzaki walked out into the rain and ended up in jail.

The Police Captain came in now to the drunk tank and said that three people had paid the fine. In the police orderly room they all nodded to each other, and then McCandless and Senzaki, the Medicine Man, Mary-Forge, and William walked out together and into the rain.

15

And the eagle Star from his godlike aerie was witness to Air Arabia taking off as he was witness to Hughes Air West arriving as he had been witness to, and monitor of, the high flame of the British bus. He had traced too the Japanese in the high Los Alamos snows and knew what white mound Mr. and Mrs. Breckenridge were buried beneath as with godlike soar and commanding sweep on this second day before the top gate was closed on the dam that would bury all his domain, the eagle Star swirled and swept the New Mexican sky in seeming afright at the skyjacking below. The Hughes Air West plane taxied back and forth back and forth in miniature and insect madness at the distant Albuquerque Airport afar and below.

The Indians were not in the summer wickiup but in the Learning Hogan because it was raining.

"Yes and yes," Lucy-Lucy said. "They have to scrape the ass

off Indian Country to get the coal, screw the Checkerboard full of holes to get the oil, cover it with water to make a dam?"

"Yes," Chee Sinoginee said.

"What else is new?"

"Tom Charlie's project is going well."

"And?"

"The radio says a white guy in Albuquerque has skyjacked a plane. The white guy is going to escape to Indian Country."

"That's not new," the Medicine Man said.

J. D. Cooper the bomber-skyjacker was wild about Indians. He was standing with a gun over the pilot in a plane filled with Elk at the Albuquerque Airport waiting for the Hughes Air West people to fetch two hundred thousand dollars so he could help the Indians, then he would not blow up Howard's nice new plane and ninety-eight Elk. The Elk had just finished their Elks Convention and were on their way to the dam dedication.

J. D. Cooper liked to think of himself descending on the Indians under a parachute with two hundred thousand dollars and a plan.

"What's the plan?" the pilot wanted to know.

"The plan is you follow my orders," J. D. Cooper said.

J. D. Cooper, the plane skyjacker, had never given orders before—he had always taken orders. The main problem in Jay Dee's life had been his psychiatrist. Another had been Stewart Montalban Rhodes. If the Indians had two hundred thousand dollars people would listen to them, and that would solve the dam problem. Money talks. J. D. Cooper thought, The pilot of this plane looks like Stewart Montalban Rhodes. Jay Dee Cooper had written three articles about his Indian theories, but the publishers are controlled by radicals and none of his theories were published. Now they would be forced to pay attention to him, and they would all regret they had not paid attention to him before. All over the world his name would be flashed. J. D. Cooper. J. D. Cooper. His name would appear on T-shirts. A doll would be named after him. The publishers would be after him to get his story. Why now? I am the same person I was before. When you turned me down. Before I gave the money to the Indians. Why did you turn me down? "Stand at attention, when I speak to you. I am J. D. Cooper. J. D. Cooper."

"Yes, sir," the pilot said.

"That's better," J. D. Cooper said. "I want to tell you now," J. D. Cooper said, "that I never have been in a mental institution. The skyjacker profiles are all wrong. I am a perfectly normal person. I am an average American. Did anyone ever tell you you look like Stewart Montalban Rhodes?"

"Who is that, sir?" the pilot said.

"Someone who follows me around. I tell you this while we are waiting for the money because the FBI will want a profile of me. They will try to make me out a nut."

"Yes, sir."

"I had a perfectly normal childhood. I had very strict parents. I went to Sunday School. I went to the Boy Scouts. I went to the Army. Where did this country go wrong? Why are they taking so long to bring the money? That's what's wrong with this country."

"What's that, sir?"

"You know what's wrong with this country?"

"No, sir."

"The aborigine in America has been neglected, and people here are victims of our own dialectic. We give people a lot of eclectic information, which leads to a devious behavior pattern without a center of power. Have you ever read Skinner, the psychologist?"

"No, sir."

"Chairman Mao?"

"No, sir."

"What do you read, comic books?"

"No."

"No, what?"

"No, sir."

"Is it okay, teacher, if Hosteen Begay turns on his Japanese radio?"

"Do you understand Japanese?" Tzo said.

"Not much," Tom Yazzie said.

"Then I don't see the point," Hosteen Begay said.

"It gives us a chance to practice."

"It's hard on the batteries," Hosteen Begay said.

"What are you saving the batteries for?"

"The dam dedication."

"Teacher, will you make Hosteen Begay turn on his radio so we can hear the skyjack?"

"You can't make anyone do anything," Mary-Forge said.

"I can," Kills The Enemy said.

Hosteen Begay turned on his Hitachi radio. A red light went on and a buzzer sounded but nothing happened.

"You forgot to fasten your seat belt," Tom Yazzie said.

Hosteen Begay turned the dial to KOB in Albuquerque. The radio announcer was selling used cars, but every once in a while he would throw in some news. The biggest news was the dam dedication, but now the announcer was excited about the skyjacking. He said the Hughes Air West 737 was full of Elk.

"Elks?" Sinoginee said.

"Elk," Mary-Forge said.

There had been an Elks Convention in Albuquerque and this was the portion of the Elks that were going to the dam dedication, the radio announcer said.

"Imagine that," Lucy-Lucy said.

"I don't think the announcer likes Elks."

"I think it's just that he wouldn't want his daughter to marry an Elk."

"Or an Indian," Tom Charlie said.

"Why," the bomber wanted to know from the pilot, "does everyone on the plane have on a badge?"

"They're Elk."

"All of them?"

"I think so," the pilot said.

"Where are they going?"

"To the dam dedication."

"I hope they get there," the bomber J. D. Cooper said. "I hope you don't make me blow us all up by being cute."

"That's what I hope, too," the pilot said.

The bomber J. D. Cooper had a short crew haircut so you could always see the gleam of all his scalp in the instrument lights on the control panel. He had a round good-natured face that looked like a small pig's rear end. His bomb was in a bowling-ball bag that was lettered in blue and white HAVE A GOOD TIME AT THE INDIAN ALLEYS BEER AND SOFT DRINKS. Every time he gave an order he would wave the dynamite bomb, which he usually carried straight down with his left arm. In his pudgy right hand he carried an automatic pistol which he steadily pressured into the head of the pilot whose cap said Hughes Air West.

"You do look like young Stewart Rhodes," J. D. Cooper said.

"Does that bother you?"

"I said not to be cute. What's your name?"

"Lyle Franklin."

"Do you mind if I call you Stewart Rhodes?"

"No."

"Where is the money and the parachute?"

"It's coming now. See."

"That's better," J. D. Cooper said. "The Elk might make it yet."

The two fat policemen, one carrying a canvas money bag and the other carrying a parachute, disappeared into the passenger gate instead of coming toward the plane.

"That's bad," J. D. Cooper said. "My friends call me Jay Dee." Then he said reflectively, "There is a rumor that was published in the *Albuquerque Journal* that the Indians have the nuclear bomb. Do you believe it?"

"No."

"That an Indian scientist who worked at Los Alamos saved up parts for a rainy day. Do you believe it?"

"No."

"They call him the nuclear Indian."

"Oh."

"That they are going to blow the Atlas Dam, but that everyone in Albuquerque is safe because Stewart Montalban Rhodes is on his trail."

"I believe that," the pilot said.

"Do you believe it's a threat to national security to say that Stewart Montalban Rhodes masturbates?"

"I can't say as I do."

"Do you know Masters and Johnson's *Human Sexual Inadequacy*?"

"I can't say as I do."

"I didn't think Masters and Johnson made a point. The behaviorists think they did, though."

"I bet they do."

"Do you know what Michael Beldorch said about the occult?"

"No. What did he say?"

"The occult's appeal, its dangerous widespread appeal, is to those with complaints about reality, for their solution is to overthrow reality itself."

"That's interesting," the pilot said.

"But it's an unfair criticism."

"It is? I guess it is."

"What do you think of Stewart Rhodes?"

"I don't think about him very often."

"He's a clever cookie."

"That could come in handy to know."

"It looks like I'm going to have to kill you."

J. D. Cooper turned his head to the copilot alongside the pilot. He could kill the copilot to let Howard Hughes know he meant business.

"Can you fly this thing all by yourself?" he said to the pilot.

"I can, but it would be very difficult."

"You won't have to," J. D. Cooper said. "Here comes the money and the chute. I'm as good as safe in Indian Country with two hundred thousand dollars."

The radio in the Learning Hogan said the plane was taking off from Albuquerque with all the Elk still okay. The announcer got so excited he forgot to sell used cars. He kept repeating that this would be the second jump for J. D. Cooper. That when you start jumping for money it's difficult to stop. J. D. Cooper's last jump had been over the Gila Wilderness area on a flight from Tucson to Silver City. He took two hundred thousand dollars of Frontier Airline's money with him that time. The announcer said that there were J. D. Cooper fans along the runway who had rushed down to the Albuquerque Airport as soon as the skyjacking went on the air. His fans waved white handkerchiefs toward J. D. Cooper as the Hughes Air West plane taxied for take-off.

"Why aren't you piloting the plane?" J. D. Cooper said.

"The copilot needs the practice."

J. D. Cooper was happy to be taking off; from here on it would be duck soup. The problem now would be to restore discipline—the pilot had not sir'd him for a long while. The slightest relaxation in discipline and the pilot could take over. The trick was to think what the pilot was thinking to keep one step ahead of him, to keep the pilot in a subservient role. It was probably a mistake to tell him he looked like Stewart Rhodes.

"You look like hell," J. D. Cooper said.

"Yes, sir."

"That's better," J. D. Cooper said. "What are you thinking?"

"Nothing."

"You are thinking that you are okay, that an Air Force plane has taken off from Sandia Base and will follow us and radio back my drop zone. Get on the radio and call them off."

The pilot did as he was told.

"Are you happy now?" the pilot said.

"I am happy," J. D. Cooper said.

"Can you take the pistol . . . can you take the pressure off the back of my head?"

"Then I wouldn't be happy," J. D. Cooper said.

The copilot watched the instrument panel and fed the jet engines more power.

"What are you thinking now?"

"I got a wife in Albuquerque," the pilot said.

"Good, then you won't get cute. What else?"

"I was thinking, what's an intelligent man like you doing . . ."

"Blowing up a plane?"

"Yes."

"It's for a cause."

"No, it isn't."

The pressure on the back of the pilot's head increased.

"I guess it is," the pilot said.

"Where is that long line of cars going down there?"

"The dam dedication."

"I want you to maintain your customary bearings to the dam. I don't want an overflight to Colorado Springs, to the Air Force Base at Colorado Springs. If your bearings are standard operational procedure, the beginning Atlas Lake will appear three degrees on our port side in six and one-half minutes."

"Okay."

"What?"

"Yes, sir."

"Get on the intercom and tell the Elk to close their eyes when I walk back to exit the plane. I want them to behave themselves. I don't want to have to thin out the Elk population of the Southwest."

The pilot did as he was told.

"Now, have the stewardess come up and help me in the chute. Is it true that the pilots sleep with the stewardesses?"

"No."

"No, what?"

"No, sir."

"Call her."

The pilot did as he was told.

While the chute was being put on J. D. Cooper, the pilot who was told he looked like Stewart Rhodes thought this: I must follow him out as quickly as possible. It will take me two minutes to put on the extra chute the police brought on board, but he will spend that much time below releasing the baggage-exit door. So I should be able to follow him out almost immediately. My chute has a homing bleep radio in it so the Air Force can keep track of us. My copilot can take the Elks on to the dam dedication.

"What are you thinking?"

"That the Elks will be okay," the pilot said.

"That's because you were a good boy. Think about the Elk and don't think about following me out of the plane with some chute you may have hidden on board the plane. If you do I will kill you. Do you have a chute?"

"No," the pilot said.

"No, what?"

"No, sir."

"Good. Good luck. Good-bye," and he quit the cockpit.

The pilot waited twenty long seconds before he moved, then jerked around and ran down the aisle, where the Elks were still holding their hands over their eyes as they had been told. He got on his chute and got out the open baggage exit in time, so that if he slipped air out of the chute, out of the huge canopy above that ballooned over him, if he collapsed part of the chute by pulling on the cords, he could catch up to J. D. Cooper on the way down. So he pulled on the cords. And there was J. D. Cooper dangling about sixty yards to his left, swaying and tiny under his big canopy, and shooting at him. But this was all like a movie. The only reality Stewart Montalban Rhodes could conjure up was the Elk on the plane still holding their hands over their eyes until the plane got to the dam dedication. But the dangling man kept shooting at him.

Tom Yazzie entered the Learning Hogan and said that everyone was dead.

"Everyone?"

"Everyone that jumped from the plane. There were two."

"What did they die from?"

"Water."

"Explain."

"They landed in the water."

"What happened to the two hundred thousand dollars?"

"I suppose that's important."

"Yes," Hosteen Begay said, "a white person can always have another life, he can become born again, but two hundred thousand dollars for the Indians doesn't grow on trees."

"Yes, it does," Tom Yazzie's Brother said. "Look at this." And Tom Yazzie's Brother placed two hundred thousand dollars on the teacher's lap. "The skyjacker dropped it before he went over the lake."

"What will we do with the money?" Mary-Forge said.

"What happened to the elk the radio man was talking about?"

"What happened to the skyjacker's dynamite bomb?"

"It was a bowling ball."

"What?"

The dripping pilot was standing in the Pendleton-blanket doorway. "That's what he had in the bowling bag, a bowling ball."

"Start from the beginning," Mary-Forge said.

"J. D. Cooper had this round thing he threatened us with. But on the way down and when he was shooting at me I figured that there was no such thing as a round bomb except in comic books. That he had his bowling ball and he wasn't going to let go. Then he let go of the money but not his ball. It cost him his life."

"Did anyone ever tell you you look like Stewart Montalban Rhodes?" Hosteen Tzo said.

"Yes," the pilot said.

"So let's get back to the dam," Hosteen Tzo said, "and the poor whites' need for electric power."

"To mow their wall-to-walls," Lucy-Lucy said. "The whites in Albuquerque tell me an Indian eats like a pig, dresses like a whore, and they won't let me in their restaurants. Well, the whites with their power problems give this little Indian a great big pain in the ass. It is nice of them, though, to allow Tom Charlie to go to their dam dedication with his gift."

The pilot, Stewart Montalban Rhodes, who still had on his soggy Air West cap, picked up the two hundred thousand dollars and made for the highway. When I left, Stewart Rhodes thought, the people in the Navajo hogan were still talking insane talk about dams and pains in the ass. And they had this big nice present in the middle of the hogan all wrapped up in nice gold and red paper. This gift was piled with flowers and it had a nice card on it. I wonder if the gift is for the dam dedication and I wonder, Rhodes thought, if on that card the Indians are going to tell us something nice.

Just on the other side of the Portales Mesa he could see the dirt road that led to the gravel road that led to the concrete road that led to the dam dedication.

The dam dedication will be an interesting ceremony, Rhodes thought. And I wonder who the Indians think they're fooling with this gift.

16

The parade to the dam dedication had begun.

On a naked bike, freaking through the high bright and empty glory of northern New Mexico and in the middle of the automotive cavalcade on the way to dedicate the Atlas Dam, hung a naked full professor of anthropology, Doctor Barnes. Doctor Barnes was the only person his girl student Didi Genovese knew who was constructed entirely of jelly beans and who had built his motorbike around high-rise handlebars and a V-8 Cadillac engine of four hundred horsepower. Doctor Big Bomb Barnes sat naked below the high-rise handlebars so that he had to stretch up to hold on. He mirrored a gymnast or a great ape hanging on to a branch or parallel bars. Sitting in back of Doctor Barnes or almost joined to him was his "Old Lady," Didi Genovese, a seventeen-year-old naked anthropology major at the University of New Mexico, the daughter of the late-lamented film genius, Eugene Genovese.

Four anthropologists on the naked bike were out on a spin

to get the bugs out of the new Caddy motor and see the wild Indians *in situ.* In back of the seventeen-year-old anthropology major were two more naked young ladies who minored in "anthro"—Pam McCandless and Bonnie Senzaki, the daughters of McCandless and Senzaki, the renowned writers of *Some Indians I Have Known,* soon to be made into a major motion picture that would make the girls' talented fathers richer than God. Four in a row naked astride a Cadillac engine. They were all naked because that is what the "in" people were into at the school that year. This is how they got it all together. You either lead in style, you either are in the forefront of the haute couture, or you are dead. Other youth, and later, would follow the naked style, but by then the haute couture might again be bib overalls and again the naked would be dead.

The Caddy bastard bike flying naked riders had smoked out of the University of New Mexico dormitory area past the fake pueblo architecture and onto the freeway, empty of cars except for the government limousines celebrating the fuel crisis, then between tall glass buildings in Texas Modern, accomplished by an architect with an edifice complex, then beneath and between the artificial trees with real birds coughing among the smoke-filled leaves, and across the Rio Grande at Bernalillo, where the road mounts up and up into the high and hushed and virgin plateau of Indian Country—primordial and bright.

Doctor Big Bomb Barnes had allowed the Caddy bike to freak terrifically through the perfect and absolute silence of Indian Country, the gaudy and awful stillness shattered in smoke now and exploded in bomb noises, ear-hurting, a quick-moving violence, and obscene. Now the naked bike was caught in the automotive dam traffic going to the dam site to dedicate and celebrate the dam.

Big Bomb Barnes was not in the dam cavalcade to go to the dam dedication. Doctor Barnes was in the cavalcade to kill himself and his three followers. Anyone who rides a high-rise Caddy bike bomb is insane or suicidal, and Doctor Barnes was some of both. Doctor Barnes had gotten into the auto stream going to the dam by accident. He did not believe in dams. Today he believed only in killing himself. He did not know this. Pam said Nietzsche suffered the same syndrome. "Friedrich Nietzsche relieved his depression by contemplating the option of suicide."

Her name was Pam McCandless and she was into philosophy as well as anthropology. All the naked riders wore yellow crash helmets with black wind visors. They all wore dangling Maharaj Ji Divine Light Mission peace medallions, and all of their breasts were misshapen in the wind blast. Doctor Barnes had tried to pass the dam traffic at White Sulfur Springs but had no luck and now found himself part of the cavalcade. Before he hit the cavalcade, Doctor Barnes had been traveling at two hundred and forty-three miles an hour, which is a land-speed record for the motorcycle. The record would probably not be allowed because it was done with three girls astride a Cadillac engine. It would not be allowed because Doctor Barnes was not interested in records; he was interested in sex at high speeds—what the girl on the end of the tandem bike called velocity sexual mitosis. "What?"

"It is a syndrome," Didi Genovese said, "whereby finally orgasm cannot be achieved at less than two hundred and ten."

"Two hundred and ten what?"

"Miles per hour," Didi Genovese said.

"Talk louder, I can't hear you up here," Doctor Barnes hollered.

"Are you achieving orgasm?"

"I haven't achieved orgasm since we ran into the dam traffic at White Sulfur Springs."

"Have you ever achieved orgasm on a bike under two hundred and ten?"

"Many times, many times," Doctor Barnes said, using his professorial tone. "I have achieved orgasm from a standing start in thirteen and a half seconds."

"Is that a record?"

"I don't think so," Doctor Barnes said.

"Do the Russians hold the record?"

"I believe so," Doctor Barnes said.

"But they cheated?"

"I believe so," Doctor Barnes said.

"What about the Chinese?"

"What about them?" Doctor Barnes said.

"Are the Chinese into science?" Pam said.

"They must be, there are so many of them," Doctor Barnes said.

"Who is that ahead?" Pam McCandless asked.

"A hitchhiker," Doctor Barnes said.

"He's dressed like a pilot," Didi Genovese said.

"Airplanes are suffering from the fuel shortage now," Doctor Barnes said, and he slowed down and stepped in front of the dripping Stewart Montalban Rhodes.

"I am afraid we are full up," Doctor Barnes said.

"I have a very important mission," Stewart Rhodes said. "I would appreciate one of the young ladies giving me her seat in the interest of national security."

None of the young ladies got up from her seat.

"Aren't you interested in national security?" Stewart Rhodes said.

"We are not interested in it this semester," Bonnie Senzaki said. "We're into anthro."

"It could mean saving the dam," Stewart Rhodes said.

"None of the young ladies is interested in saving the dam this semester. We will have to split," Doctor Barnes said, and he varoomed off on his Caddy bomb in such a varoom that he left all the girls behind, but they chased after him, and as he slowed down for them they jumped aboard the bike, leaving Stewart Rhodes still chasing after them and alone and losing ground back in the vast desert.

"Like, this is neat," Bonnie Senzaki said. "Holding our seminar on a high-rise bomb bike."

"It is possible," Doctor Barnes said, "to achieve orgasm at minus speeds. In temperatures you have minus zero. So it is with speed. You can go backward from zero as easily as you can go forward. Strangely enough, orgasm can be achieved at speed minus eighty-five."

"Why is that?" Pam said.

"We don't know," Doctor Barnes said.

"Like, that's what I like about Professor Barnes," Bonnie Senzaki said. "When he doesn't know something, he comes right out and says it."

"Like, but his not knowing anything has been happening quite a bit lately," Didi said.

"Like, it could still be a sign of genius. Doctor Barnes be the baddest person I ever knew."

"I know something," Doctor Barnes said.

"What's that?"

"We're into Indian Country."

"I didn't know a motorcycle could go in reverse, could go backward and achieve subzero speeds," Bonnie Senzaki said.

"Watch this," Doctor Barnes said. Doctor Barnes stuck out his foot, then flipped the high-rise handlebars, and they were traveling backward.

"This feels funny," Didi Genovese said. "Doctor Barnes be the baddest person I ever knew."

"How fast are we going?"

"Well under minus eighty-five."

"That's why I don't feel anything now," Bonnie Senzaki said. "Can you increase the speed down to eighty-five?"

"Not in this traffic," Doctor Barnes said.

"Who is that?" Didi Genovese said as they passed a pickup with their cycle still going backward. Mr. and Mrs. Breckenridge and eight children were packed into the front cab of a blue '48

Dodge pickup; all of the children were popping bubble gum and screaming. Mr. Breckenridge had a determined look on his face, and Mrs. Breckenridge was sorting out eviction papers and battling with the children and losing. The back of the pickup was laden down too with a pile of snow, so that the rear end dragged and sparks flew, so that the snow seemed combustible and afire.

"Is there money in snow, now?" Pam McCandless wanted to know.

"With inflation there's money in everything, now," Doctor Barnes said.

Then they went past an open green Army command car that went by to the dam with eight dam sheriffs all wearing identical green uniforms and identical blue-tinted glasses and carrying at port identical M16 rifles and all staring in different directions to monitor the entire scene.

"Does a genius like yourself get ideas while off his motorcycle, too, Doctor Barnes?"

"Rarely," Doctor Barnes said. "Charles Darwin never got an idea while off the *Beagle*. Darwin worked his ideas up later, but all his ideas were gotten on the *Beagle*."

"A dog?"

"No, it was a sailing vessel," Doctor Barnes said.

"This is cool," Pam McCandless said. "A rap trip on a bike bomb going backward. Like, it could drive you up a wall. It's something else. Doctor Barnes be the baddest person I ever knew."

The naked bike passed a jeep containing the renowned authors McCandless and Senzaki. They did not see their daughters on the naked bike, or they did not acknowledge their daughters on the naked bike. Anyway they were deep in thought concerning their next tome—about the late-lamented Eugene Genovese—*Some Geniuses We Have Known*.

"It's not everyone who can go backward on a motorbike," Doctor Barnes said.

"Like maybe it's because we're going downhill?"

"No, you will see when we get to the Portales, we will go up hill like a breeze."

Which they did, but going down the other side of the Portales, Doctor Barnes turned the bike around so that they were going forward. While going backward he had to drive the high-rise bike bomb by looking through the rearview mirror. Now he saw the road ahead in a straightforward manner without looking through a looking glass.

"I didn't feel anything when we were going backward," Bonnie said.

"Well, some women are frigid," Doctor Barnes said.

"*Ms.* magazine said there is no such thing as a frigid woman," Pam McCandless said.

"Or a bad boy?"

"Yes."

"Charlie Darwin thought—" Doctor Barnes said.

"Chuck."

"Yes. Darwin thought that he had got hold of a tenable theory in *On the Origin of Species*. Actually it was only some interesting data on the finches in the Galápagos. Now I propose . . ."

"What does our own Doctor Big Bomb Barnes propose?"

"That we recycle known hypotheses."

"Can you give us an example?"

"I can give you an extrapolation."

"In view of Doctor Spatz's work on the Navajo, I don't think we are prepared to accept extrapolation."

"You are referring to Maggie Mead's work on the Navajo?"

"No, our own Doctor Spatz."

"I know he did work on the Dalmatian."

"The dog or the people?"

"I believe both," Doctor Barnes said. "Doctor Kunstler is of the opinion—"

"But Kunstler is only a lawyer."

"I mean our own Doctor Kunstler."

"Is he still alive?"

"He lectured this morning."

"I know. I was there," Bonnie Senzaki said. "But is he alive?"

The naked bike passed a yellow Ford Pinto containing Spanky Talley and Rollo Nye. Doctor Rollo leaned out to inspect the riders on the naked bike. Here was gold. Here were, he thought, some potential customers for his looney bin. But at the dam dedication there would be bigger and better catches. On the speakers' platform there would be several Napoleons, one or two Hitlers, and a President who thought he was Abe Lincoln.

Doctor Barnes allowed the naked Caddy bike bomb to float in and out of the dam traffic. The dam celebrities who were to speak at the dam dedication were "blown out of their little minds" by the naked bike. At first the rich and the beautiful tried to ignore the naked bike; then they had their uniformed black Tom chauffeurs try to drive the naked bike off the cliffs of Indian Country before they—the rich and the beautiful—gave up trying to catch the wily Doctor Barnes and retreated back into what the Indian Thomas Charles called the quintessential absurdity of their monied lives and allowed Doctor Barnes to go back to his contemplation of Indian Country.

"What we have here," Doctor Barnes said, "is an interesting phenomenon that we had to go only fifty miles to discover. These Navajo people in this area are known as the Checkerboard Clan Indians. These Indians are about to become extinct. We may be the last scientific group to work with them. The problem is that they will soon be under water."

"Like, what caused that?"

"Water."

"What caused that?"

"The dam."

"What caused that?" Didi Genovese said.

"We don't know. It seems to be a phenomenon among white groupings to build dams."

"Power?"

"No, they have sufficient power, then they invent other useless gadgets to consume more power. White groupings in the United States have electric toothbrushes and electric women. It's a phenomenon for which we have no explanation. We call it the power or dam syndrome. But giving it a name doesn't help."

"When are we going to see the last Indians?"

"Soon," Doctor Barnes said.

"And the neat part is the seminar has nothing to do with anthropology." Bonnie was talking with Pam in the back of the classroom in the back of the bike. The teacher was still dangling from the branch handlebars in the attitude of an ape. Pam made a bubble with her bubble gum and shot an elastic band at the teacher.

"Child behavior patterns," Professor Barnes said from below the high-rise handlebars.

"But what about your behaving like an orangutan?" Didi said.

"Apes are part of anthropology. Apes are anthropoids."

"Then you've done a paper on this?"

"No, it just occurred to me," Doctor Barnes said. The Doctor waved to the Governor of Texas, who had his Cadillac engine under the hood of his automobile; the Governor waved back, recognizing a kindred spirit in Doctor Barnes. The rear Texas license plate said "Governor," and then there was a big Texas star and then there was a big-assed Texas lady.

"What is Texas going to get out of this dam?" Pam said.

"All the water."

"California?"

"All the power."

"New Mexico?"

"All the grief."

"The Indians?"

"Burial."

"Who is that?"

"The President of the United States."

He passed illegally on a curve, staring out unimpeachably like a pig poisoned alongside his Barbie Doll wife and row of Barbie Doll children. The wife appeared immolated, and nailed to the seat. The bland children seemed worked by strings hidden in the car roof. Under the car floor were the alert Secret Service people, there in case the party was attacked by Indians. In case of an Indian attack, in order to maintain national security, the President's wife and children were to be handed over to the Indians, then the remaining Presidential party was to continue to the dam site, where the President would deliver his speech as though nothing had happened. In a sweet, quiet voice, as though a great burden had been lifted.

A Lincoln Continental Mark IV went by.

"Who is that?"

"Minority groups."

The minority groups' Lincoln going to the dam dedication contained one black and one woman and one Mexican and one Puerto Rican and one Indian and another woman.

"How come there will be *two* women at the dedication?"

"If you notice at the next curve," Doctor Barnes said, "they are all women."

"How come?"

"Women," Doctor Barnes said, passing the minority groups' Lincoln on the curve, "women are into a feminist revolution. Women believe that women have been taking men's abuse for too long, beginning with Martha Washington. Now with the opportunities of the energy crisis, they have decided to kick men in the balls."

"Does it hurt?"

"Not when it happens but later," Doctor Barnes said. Doctor Barnes barreled his bike bomb through the San Gregorio Pass and observed the perfect buttes. "Until recently," Doctor Barnes said, "the feminist revolution had not gotten out of New York City. Until last month it was difficult for a man to walk alone on the streets of New York without being horsewhipped."

"What happened after last month?"

"The revolution is spreading out of New York, now. You recall that George Washington's army was buttoned up in Manhattan, too."

"The revolution hasn't reached New Mexico yet."

"I would not say that," Doctor Barnes said, gunning around the female minority groups on the down side of the San Gregorio Pass.

"Is there some way, Doctor Barnes," Pam said, "that we could contact the Indians *in situ*?"

"In what?"

"Where they live."

"If you want to contact them where they live," Bonnie Senzaki said, "I don't think the Supreme Court will go along with it."

A four-wheel-drive Jeep went by.

"Who's that?"

"A Supreme Court Justice."

"Which one?"

"The one that married a sixteen-year-old girl."

"I will go along with that," Bonnie Senzaki said.

"Who is that?" Didi Genovese said.

A helicopter went by very low, a part of the dam traffic. It was the Secretary of State flanked on either side by two Egyptian belly dancers. He waved to the naked bike—the belly dancers waved too. The naked bike-riders waved back, almost causing the naked bike to careen into an arroyo.

"What about the Indians *in situ*?"

"I have a surprise for you," Doctor Barnes said. "We are going to visit the Indians *in situ*."

Doctor Barnes hung down from his tree of high-rise motorbike handlebars *in nudo,* Didi Genovese observed, with all the hairiness of the greater ape found in the Lesser Antilles. Doctor Barnes's hairiness started out scattered around the chest with slight red but became a heavy black forest around his private parts. "Private parts?"

"A man has no private parts," Didi Genovese said. "His private parts are exposed to public view. A woman's private parts are private."

"In what sense?"

A Rolls Royce went by.

"Who is that?"

"The Chairman of the Board of Everything."

"Of what?"

"Everything."

"They built the dam?"

"Yes."

"In what sense are a man's public parts private?"

"Didi is doing a paper on it," Doctor Barnes said. "I can get it printed in *Science Today*."

"That's a break for Didi," Bonnie said.

"I rather think of it as a break for *Science Today*," Doctor Barnes said.

"We're getting away from anthro," Bonnie Senzaki said.

"No," Doctor Barnes said, "we are getting out into the country where anthropology happens. Indians. There is a young white girl living out here with the Indians—Mary-Forge Telluride. She could tell us a snootful. Mary-Forge could blow the minds of *Science Today*."

"Will she talk?"

"No," Doctor Barnes said.

"Why not?"

"I believe she believes anthropologists to be crazy."

"Any evidence?"

"None at all," Doctor Barnes said.

The cavalcade slowed down now and Doctor Barnes took the opportunity to glide the bike bomb out into the desert and listen to the girls squeal as he chased a jack rabbit between the cholla and paloverde. Then he crossed a deep rock-strewn arroyo dense with creosote bush, the girls screaming, then up the steep side of the arroyo, where he lost Pam. Near the top, Pam got back on before he allowed the bike bomb to drift back on the highway between the Governor of Texas and the Governor of California.

Doctor Barnes, still hanging from the high-rise handlebars, pulled over to the side of the highway beneath a paloverde and allowed the dam people to pass. "I told you, didn't I," Doctor Barnes said, "that I was going to show you the Indians *in situ*."

"Yes, you did."

"Well, over there," Doctor Barnes said, "that's a Navajo Learning Hogan we will visit."

They all stood up on the bike to get a better look. A covey of antelope and a pride of cowboys came up to watch all the girls standing on the bike. Cowboys are a modest folk, not like the wild characters that follow the rodeo circuit. Real cowboys are not used to naked bike-riders. The "Howdy, Ma'am" attitude in the slick movies is not far from the truth. Puerile, vapid, and unreal, but not far from the lie.

"What do you think?" the cowboy named Clearboy said to the cowboy named Cipriano de Godoy.

"Now having seen everything, I can die," Cipriano de Godoy said.

"They must be going to see Mary-Forge," Clearboy said.

"Why?"

"Naked. Those are the kind she attracts."

The horses, too, seemed perturbed by the naked people. The

horses had never seen naked people before and did not know how to behave. They had seen many naked horses and decided finally that a naked person is the same as a naked horse. Only different. Smaller. Funnier. Verbose and prolix. The horses swung their huge horse heads in disbelief, trying to work the steel bits between their teeth to become masters of their fate. Captains of their soul.

"Do you reckon?" Clearboy said.

"Yes, I believe those people are going to visit Mary-Forge."

"About the flood?"

"They are dressed for the flood," Cipriano de Godoy said.

The antelope, unable to talk, said nothing, but simply bounded away, leaving the Great Plain to the pride of timid cowboys and the naked bike.

The pride of timid cowboys walked, then trotted, then cantered, then ran their horses off in a quick racket of hoofs against the hard desert floor to put as much distance as possible before nightfall between themselves and the naked bike.

"I am Doctor Barnes," Doctor Barnes said, stepping into the Learning Hogan, followed by his fans. "These are my students. They have encountered many Indians before. Didi Genovese here speaks some Winnebago Sioux. Pam McCandless speaks some Hebrew she picked up in her junior year on a kibbutz. Bonnie Senzaki knows some black phrases she picked up in New York City in the Youth Corps. None of us speaks Navajo, but there's plenty of time to learn unless the water rises fast."

"Yes."

"But we all speak body language," Professor Barnes said. "Why don't we begin by all holding hands."

"What?"

"Holds hands. Make contact. We do that in class all the time."

"You do?"

"Yes."

"What do you do about the dam?"

"We could have a letter write-in to our Congressman. Let's all hold hands."

"We don't have a Congressman."

"Everyone has a Congressman," Doctor Barnes said. "Why doesn't everyone touch the person on his left. It's called feel therapy, widely practiced among the Eskimos."

"Touch the person on your left," Doctor Barnes said. "We know that affection is a developmental quality; that among the Diné, the People, among all primitive groupings there is no affection for the spouse or among the sibs. Love in our sense of the word is unknown among the North American Indians. Love, then, according to Briffault and Malinowski is an acquired characteristic. Will you smile at the person on your right?"

"No."

"Can I make a comment?" Tom Yazzie said.

"Smile," the anthropologist said.

"The water."

"Many primitive groups," the Doctor said, "perished through lack of water. You are endangered through surplus of same, namely water." Doctor Barnes paused to allow them to take notes.

"We thought perhaps," Tom Yazzie's Sister said, "you might organize a protest demonstration at the university."

"Outta sight," Bonnie Senzaki said.

"That's all well and good," Doctor Barnes said, "but I'd rather think along *con* rather than *de*structive techniques. *Af*fection rather than *de*fection. If instead of thinking of the white man as a builder of dams to destroy the Navajo, if we think of the white man as a builder of dams to irrigate the land and feed the poor —we are moving in the direction of *af*fection. If we conceive of the eagle-killer as a protector of lambs, of the coyote-killer as a protector of calves, then we are seeing the light at the end of the tunnel." He paused again for note-taking.

"Listen," Mary-Forge said. "You are not helping."

"Smile," Doctor Barnes said. "Give us a big smile. Can I tell you what Franz Boas has to say about the smile and the sexual contact?"

"No."

"Well, I have a plan," the good Doctor Barnes said.

"I am going to have to ask you to leave," the Medicine Man said.

"I have an idea," Doctor Barnes said.

"What is that?"

"Human sacrifice."

"Who?"

"Three white virgins."

Pam, Bonnie, and Didi looked at each other.

"I believe," Doctor Barnes said, "that the death of three white virgins in an attempt at white consciousness-raising to save Indian homes will awaken the American people to the plight of the Indians. It's a viable consciousness-raising activity."

"What makes you feel that three white virgins could be found?"

"They exist."

"Who would be willing to sacrifice themselves for the Indians?"

"They exist," Doctor Barnes said, looking at Pam, Bonnie, and Didi.

"Like, if it's pretend," Pam McCandless said, "like in the TV or the movies. We would be happy to do it if it's pretend."

"All we have to do," Doctor Barnes said, "is report that these three virgins jumped off the dam. To protest the flooding of the Indian homes. The whites would send divers down to look for the girls' bodies. Of course the girls would be here in your Learning Hogan all the time. It would give your Indian cause a great deal of publicity before the whites gave up the rescue operations. You could hire a public-relations firm to handle the whole thing for you. What do you think?"

"I think you better leave," the Medicine Man said.

"Where is the flaw in my plan? Shoot it full of holes," Doctor Barnes said.

"You have already done that," Mary-Forge said. "You were born full of holes. There is nothing to shoot at."

"You have got to understand," Doctor Barnes said, "that this is the way the world works. If the Indians are going to save themselves from what my colleague Toffler calls 'future shock,' you have got to learn to adapt. There is nothing wrong, according to Toffler, with having a public-relations firm cut the mustard for you."

"Lying."

"We don't call it lying any more. We call it . . ."

"Public relations?"

"Yes."

"Advertising?"

"Yes. All we're asking is for you to defend yourselves with modern weapons. Along with the tomahawk, war is obsolete. Public relations—"

"Are in."

"Yes, that's how the next war will be fought," Doctor Barnes said. "All we're asking you to do is let these three virgins jump off the dam."

Going back home with the three "virgins," Doctor Barnes was puzzled.

"Like, when you are perplexed," Bonnie said, "don't bottle it up. Let it all hang out."

"I don't understand," Professor Barnes said, "how all the work of Toffler, Marcuse, Malinowski, Mead, Darwin, and myself—how all this understanding can go by the board. We in the discipline are more and more coming around to the value of Malinowski's paper 'The Savage as the Child.' And I don't understand," Doctor Barnes said. "I don't understand how the Indians can be so generous. Did you notice the huge thing in the middle of the hogan —a present. It was almost buried in a pyramid of flowers. Apparently they are getting ready to carry the gift to the dam dedication. There was a card in the flowers which said, "For the people of the United States for all they have done for the American Indian."

"That's sweet of them," Pam said.

"It shows they have no hard feelings."

"Should we go to the dam dedication?"

"Yes," Doctor Barnes said, "I want to see how the white groupings react to the Indian's gift."

The three virgins got on the bike.

"Repeat after me," Doctor Barnes said before he touched the bike starter. "To the sun god I wish the dam away."

They repeated that.

"To the wind god I wish the dam away."

They repeated that.

"Some Indian has let all the air out of the tires."

Silence.

"Some Indian has released all the gasoline on the ground."

Silence.

"We white folks," Bonnie said, "are going to have to walk to the dam dedication."

They all repeated the silence.

"Why did you do that?" Mary-Forge said as Kills The Enemy came back in the Learning Hogan.

"Why did I let them live?"

"They were only trying to help."

"Gods save us," the Medicine Man said, sitting down behind the huge gift on the yellow and gray Two Gray Hills Blanket in the middle of the Learning Hogan and speaking up to all through his mauve and dull glow of necklace and headband and bright rings of silver and turquoise. "Gods save us from the whites who want to save us."

"Amen."

"We are off," Thomas Charles said. "With the gift."

"How are you going to explode the gift without exploding yourself?"

"I have adapted a remote TV channel selector. I can explode the gift from a safe distance."

"You mean you select *I Love Lucy* and that's the end?"

"Or *All in the Family?*"

"Or the *Mary Tyler Moore* show?"

"Oddly enough it's *Truth or Consequences,*" Thomas Charles said.

"Where is the channel selector?"

"It's not in my hogan," Tom Charlie said, "where Stewart Montalban Rhodes would search. I hid the channel selector in the Scalp House."

17

"What's that thing?" Mary-Forge said.

"A TV channel selector."

"What will I do with it?"

"Put it on the mantelpiece," William said. "It will make people think we're civilized."

This day, the day of the dam dedication, Mr. Breckenridge waded through the water and knocked on the door of the Scalp House and told them that they should have moved two months ago. He said he was surprised that they had ignored the order to move. He said he had read an item in *Newsweek* or *Time*—he could not remember which—or it could have been the *Albuquerque Tribune*—about a family behind a dam who would not move in Oklahoma or Texas—he could not remember which—on TV, he remembered now, it was on TV, and they, the home defenders, had a gun.

"We have no gun," Mary-Forge said.

"Will your dogs bite?"

"They are coyotes."

"Coyotes? Would you believe it?"

"We can't ask you in."

"Because you're naked?"

"Because you represent the dam."

The man turned to his Dodge pickup and hollered to a woman and a gang of children that filled the Dodge pickup cab to the roof. "Would you believe it, these dogs is coyotes."

"Land's sake, Breckenridge," she said.

"I have," the deputy said to Mary-Forge, "a responsibility to get you off the land. I expected you to have a gun. That's why I brought the wife and kids. I have a crowd, a right smart passel of kids, and I am not even a Catholic. I am between religions."

"Yes."

"I have a gun in the pickup."

Mary-Forge said nothing.

Mr. Breckenridge wore a tattered, once tan, cowboy hat above a squashed and serious dedicated tight face. His belly that was once tight, too, now spilled over his Levis, hiding the big rodeo belt.

"The government hired me," Mr. Breckenridge said, "deputized me because I am a local, a native from Placitas. They don't want deputies in store-bought suits and a badge ordering people off the land. You're not even an Indian."

"No."

"And them is coyotes," he said.

"Yes."

"I brought the wife and kids to avoid a shoot out. Is he an Indian?" he said, looking past Mary-Forge.

"Yes."

"I never seen a naked Indian before. Does he speak something we understand?"

"I believe so," Mary-Forge said.

"Some of my best friends is Indians," the deputy said, and then the man waited and then he said, "My name is Breckenridge. I used to speak some Apache."

"I must—"

"I know," Mr. Breckenridge said, "but is you going to quit the land?"

"No."

"Maybe I can help you," Mr. Breckenridge said, "if you would pop into something. Have you got a wrapper?"

"Yes."

"Well, if you could pop into something I might could help you."

"All right," she said, and she closed the door and said, "Get into something, Billy. There's a deputy here says he can help."

Mr. Breckenridge entered with his wife, he showed them his badge and papers of authorization, then he showed them his wife. "We been married nigh to fifteen years and we got that many kids," he said.

"Nine," she said.

She hugged a briefcase to a cowboy vest above white boots and new Levis. She could not have weighed more than ninety pounds and walked with a skip as though trying to catch step with Mr. Breckenridge.

"She can write," he said. "We might want to take something down and/or make it legal," he said.

Mary-Forge motioned them to sit down.

"Where?" the man said, staring at the no furniture.

Mary-Forge motioned to the Navajo rugs.

"We'll stand for a bit," he said.

Mary-Forge introduced William.

"What does he do?"

"He writes."

"Mrs. Breckenridge writes, too," Mr. Breckenridge said, and then he paced the floor.

"You said you were going to help," Mary-Forge said to the deputy.

"I can't help without thinking," he said.

"You've got to give Mr. Breckenridge a bit of time to think," his wife said.

"But he said—"

"It's not money," the deputy said, arresting his pacing. "They told me at the bureau that offering money wouldn't do no good, that it had all been sent back."

"That's my understanding," Mary-Forge said.

"Then we're in a real bind," he said, "because it's money that makes the world go round."

"That's my understanding," Mary-Forge said.

"What about religion?"

"What *about* religion?"

"I've got my thinking cap on," the man said, "and the thought just hit me if you had a religion or something in which you deeply and seriously and unconsciously believed, then you might could claim exemption."

"Conscientiously believed," his wife said.

"Do you have a religion?" he said to Mary-Forge.

"People and place. That which can abide," she said.

"I am in between religions," Mr. Breckenridge said. "But if you could select some religion like being a Quaker whereby you could object to flooding—"

"Drowning."

"You said your religion was people and place. I don't know what that means, but if you could have a real religion that's against something, then that might could not be a problem. If you could give your religion a name. An old-timey religion would be best."

"Pentecostal is good," Mrs. Breckenridge said. She looked into her briefcase as though looking for religions but evidently found none because she replaced the briefcase again on her tight lap.

"There are many fine religions," Breckenridge said. "Why don't you pick an old-timey religion and claim that."

"Pentecostal is a fine religion," his wife said.

"We have a religion," Mary-Forge said.

"It's best," the man said, "to have a religion that owns a building. It's best that it be incorporated and that way back someone was killed. If you say you believe in people and place they will probably lock you up. I can't go back to the office and say those people won't get off the land because they believe in people and place."

"You can't ask Mr. Breckenridge to do that," his wife said.

"They would de-deputize me," the man said.

"They would think Mr. Breckenridge was cuckoo," his wife said.

There was a quiet in the big room, and then Mrs. Breckenridge began sorting through the legal papers in the briefcase, and then she asked whether the property was free and clear and whether it was held in fee simple or deed of trust.

"She knows all them words," Mr. Breckenridge said.

The woman held up a legal writ of paper against the light so you could see the flourishes and fine print.

"When she was a little tyke she was smart as a whip, so smart no boy would have nothing to do with her. And that was before television. With television, any more, I don't suppose anyone can write. I can't write a lick, and I was before television."

"That's true," the woman said. "Mr. Breckenridge couldn't spell even long before they had television, and now they've done deputized him. They say that if he continues to come along— 'upward bound' is the words they used—there might be a place for him in the CI and A. A local boy from Socorro, Stew Rhodes, done made the FB and I, and so there might be room for Mr. Breckenridge in the CI and A.

"The Central Intelligence Agency," the man said.

"Did you ever hear tell of that?" the woman said.

"Yes."

"Can you see Mr. Breckenridge in the CI and A?" the woman said.

"Yes."

"Thank you," the woman said. "I never could. You seem right smart. And you don't even have a television, do you? Out here in nowhere, I mean. I see you got part of one, though."

"Yes."

"Well, you seem right smart. What do you do with your time?"

"Live."

"Well, you seem right smart anyway, don't she, Mr. Breckenridge? A person don't need television necessarily. Mr. Breckenridge came along before television was even heard of, and now the CI and A isn't saying him nay—if he comes along. If you sign here," she said.

"No."

"If *he* will sign here," she said, pointing to William.

"No," Mary-Forge said.

"What's the matter, has the cat got his tongue?"

"Yes," Mary-Forge said.

"You mean he don't speak English so good."

"No, the cat's got his tongue."

"The quiet type."

"Yes."

"That's the kind to watch out for," Mrs. Breckenridge said. "Them that knows don't say and them that says don't know."

"Listen," the man said.

"Listen to what Mr. Breckenridge has to say," the woman said. She folded her legal paper and then unfolded it, but quietly so that all could hear real good.

"Listen," the man said. "If you was to sign that paper and take your money and run, I would be much obliged."

"Listen to Mr. Breckenridge," the woman said.

Mr. Breckenridge was striding the floor again between the Navajo rugs and alongside the pictures of the heroes of the Indian nations. But he gave them all seated on the floor a sideways glance between strides to show them that he had not forgotten them, that he would always remember them, that he was thinking of them just now, that he would always think of them, dwell on them, cherish them, and nurture them if they would only sign the goddamn paper and let him go home in peace and remain upward bound.

"Mr. Breckenridge ain't often denied," the woman said.

"The last mission I was at," the man said, stopping on a Navajo blanket, "my last investigation, this alleged suspect was sayin' right in the open park in Albuquerque and standin' on a box, she said without as much as a by your leave, she said that the bourgeois sentimentality and the fake humanitarianism of the middle class needed to be faced at once if the feminist revolution is to be meaningful."

"She sure did," the woman said. "Mr. Breckenridge is not much for writin' and readin', but he has a powerful memory. I reckon that's why the CI and A cottons to him. Don't you reckon?"

"Yes."

"That was real good, Mr. Breckenridge," Mrs. Breckenridge said. "That's what the alleged suspect said. I declare. Say it again, Mr. Breckenridge."

"I done said it enough," he said. "We had best get to the matter at hand. I have eight deputies staked out over the ridge. Does that mean anything to you?"

"No."

"I don't want no shoot out," the man said. He stood under the picture of Red Cloud. "No one can stand against the United States Government, do you reckon?"

"We don't know," Mary-Forge said.

"I don't reckon you can," the man said.

"Mr. Breckenridge couldn't," the woman said.

"What!" the man said.

"When they built the Joseph R. Montoya Dam in seventy-one, we had to skedaddle."

"They paid us," he said.

"We had to take what they offered and skedaddle," the woman said.

"We went willing."

"We had to skedaddle. I believe that's why they gave Mr. Breckenridge little jobs, deputized him and such, don't you reckon?"

The man hit her.

"Did I see clearly?" Mary-Forge said.

The man had struck his wife abruptly with the hard back of his hand. Between Cochise and Red Cloud the arm had flashed out with the heavy whip-silent flashing of a bull snake, and now he repeated it again when she repeated again, "We had to ske-daddle," and then again. . . .

"Wait," Mary-Forge said. "You have got to go."

Mr. Breckenridge turned in his high boots as though he himself had been struck. "It's nothin'," he said.

"You have got to," Mary-Forge said, rising.

The man turned to William, continuing the motion on his high cowboy heels until he stopped at William, silent and questioning.

"Yes, you best get out," William said.

"Well, I never."

"Out," he said.

"The coyotes," Mr. Breckenridge said, "is they wild?"

"Yes."

"Bite?"

"Yes."

"Then we cain't—"

"Out," William said.

They both stumbled out and made for the pickup, he striding ahead and she behind and giving that little quick skip to get in step, and they made the pickup safe, she squeezing in her side and slamming the door, he squeezing in his side and almost making it but not quite, not quite slamming the door before a coyote got a piece, one piece of him, a long rip, gash down the thigh, taking Levis and underwear, flesh and all, and then he slammed the door, rolled down a slit of window, and fired two quick shots in signal, and eight men rose from over the ridge and started toward the Scalp House with rifles at the port.

"If they want a shoot out," Mary-Forge said, "they will have to shoot at themselves. We should not humor them by playing their games. We should let them know that some human beings are out of season."

The eight deputies came down the slope through the ocotillo and cholla. Mr. Breckenridge was screaming from inside the pickup truck from the big hurt he had only now discovered.

"You're bleeding, Mr. Breckenridge," she said.

"I am bleeding someplace else worse," he said.

"What do you suppose they're up to in there now?" she said, pointing at the Scalp House.

"Don't change the subject!" he hollered.

"I didn't say anything in there that wasn't true, that wasn't Pentecostal. We did have to skedaddle."

"Never use that word."

"Pentecostal?"

"Skedaddle!" he hollered.

"We had to skedaddle from our flood," she said.

"We went voluntary."

"I wanted to make them two feel that we are all in the same boat after they have their flood here," she said.

"Except their boat leaks," he said.

"Why?"

"Because, because they, any Indian or Indian-lover, is wed to the land. Take that land away or bury it in water and you got a collection of wandering bums. There is no need to kill them. Take the land and they will destroy themselves. Whites can pick up and leave without a fare-thee-well because we have forsook the earth."

"Is that Pentecostal?"

"Have forsook the earth," he said, "for Heaven or somesuch and don't give a damn, have forsook the land and attacked it with plows and want to leave it first cat out of the bag for a city and then a damn rocket to the moon or Pluto and will spend one hundred billion dollars to go there, some place we ain't never even seen, let alone touched or met the people there, and will destroy that Pluto or Mars, too, in the same manner and custom we done this one and tell those Pluto people cut ass or drown."

"You're bloodying up the floor boards, Mr. Breckenridge," she said.

"The Indians, no," he said. "They is wed to the earth."

"I don't believe that's Pentecostal, Mr. Breckenridge."

"It's the truth," he said.

"What are you going to do about the eight deputies?"

"Shoot them," he said.

They all watched out of the pickup front windshield at the deputies coming down the slope with their rifles still at port.

"I don't believe that," he said.

"What don't you believe, Mr. Breckenridge?"

"I don't believe that I can forgive myself if I don't take a shot at them deputies who disappeared when they was trouble. What did that lady say?"

"About the sentimentality of the bourgeoisie or was it the middle class? You remembered that real pretty, Mr. Breckenridge."

"No, the lady inside who ordered me out after you insulted me."

"And you hit me."

"And the coyotes took a piece out of me. Where was they all then, them deputies? I saw hide nor hair of them till we was all safe in the pickup and the war hadda quietened down."

"Shoot them," she said. "Is that what you want me to say? Shoot them real good because they did not show up on time. Is that what you want me to say?"

He rolled down the window and rested the rifle he took from under the dashboard on the top of the window glass.

"They tell me," he said, "I could get into the CI and A if I remain upward bound. "Well, I don't think I want to be in the CI and A if they behave like that."

"They is not in the CI and A," she said.

"They aspires to it."

"All right, shoot them. Is that what you want me to say, shoot them?"

"I'm just going to give them a fright," he said, cocking the gun and waiting.

"What do you suppose they're doing inside?" She again pointed.

"Screwing."

"I mean seriously."

"Screwing."

"And they looked like such nice young people. They could have been Pentecostal. I don't like their losing their land, being cast adrift. Especially if their boat leaks."

"It does."

"You mean there is no place for their kind in the outside world?"

"Yes."

"They look like such nice people. I hate to lose them."

"You've lost them. When I first seen them I knew they was losers. Or we was losers—you figure which."

"I thought they was nice. I could have taken them for Pentecostal, they was so nice."

"Not nice. Decent."

"Is there a difference?"

"Yes," he said.

"Then you forgive them for throwing us out?"

"They was not brought up with our advantages."

"Pentecostal?"

"Yes."

"Trash?"

He hit the woman and then he hit her again, and the tykes screamed and the balloons of bubble gum went off with grenade explosions inside the cab and the man fired a shot at the first of the advancing deputies and they took cover back into the greasewood and sage and the man hollered at the woman, "Again, you done done it again."

"And you hit me again," she hollered.

"Just to give you a fright," he said with an even coolness while his limber eye searched the greasewood and sage for the deputies. "Like as not I give them a fright, too," he said.

"Mr. Breckenridge, you done ruined your chances with the CI and A."

"I hope so," he said, "and with the damn dam, too."

"Mr. Breckenridge, I'm right proud of you," the woman said.

"I think," Mr. Breckenridge said, "I see one of them move in that motte of greasewood." He leveled the gun, petted the gunsight with his thumb as he had seen the hero do in film, and fired.

"Right proud," she said.

Inside the Scalp House it was the quiet becoming a northern church along with the silent stiff ambience.

"Goddamn it, William,"—there were two more shots—"they won't stop, will they?"

The coyotes Mary-Forge had allowed in the house when the shooting started all whimpered at the windows, their forepaws on the adobe ledge, whimpering, positing, and then the whimper as though orchestrated rose to a howl, then a bay, and then finally and still orchestrated, the high high mellifluous baying was chased into eternity by their short and furious yap yap yapping; their bay chased to the moon and back.

Standing above the coyotes at the window Mary-Forge and William watched the pickup smoke off through the water and watched the deputies march up to the front door through the patio. And then one of the deputies knocked, the one with a red-checked shirt knocked, and Mary-Forge went to the door and opened it a crack and the man, the deputy in the red-checked shirt, apologized for the shooting and asked if they had been served a paper, a legal paper of eviction, he said, and Mary-Forge said no and the man, the deputy, said that that was all our visitor was supposed to do, but he had a proclivity—"proclivity" was the word he used—to act, and that his behavior would now be investigated and he wanted to know from Mary-Forge whether she wanted to file a complaint against Breckenridge—was the man's name he said—or whether they was satisfied to take no action; on the other hand did they want to recommend him—he meant Breckenridge—for promotion and for Policeman of the Year.

"Policeman of the Year?" Mary-Forge said.

"Well, I was not privy to what happened in your house. We was just surrounding the house. We was not privy"—"privy" was the word he used—"to what taken place inside the house."

"Policeman of the Year?" Mary-Forge said.

"It will just help us make out the official report if we knowed what your reaction was to the fracas, if there was a fracas or misunderstanding or some such."

"Policeman of the Year?" Mary-Forge said.

The man, the deputy, wiped his wide face with the back of the hand that held the rifle. "Is there some question, ma'am?"

"Policeman of the Year? He shot at you."

"I wouldn't pay that much heed, ma'am," the deputy said.

"Mr. Breckenridge might could have had just a bad day traveling with his wife and such. You know how women can get some days, ma'am. Remember, we all, all the deputies, have to take a course in psychology now. Doctor Rollo comes over the third Thursday of each month and—"

"Policeman of the Year?" Mary-Forge said.

"And helps us to understand our problems."

"He shot at you."

"That might could be one of our problems. That's what we want to find out, whether Mr. Breckenridge was just lettin' off steam, which is healthy, or whether contrarywise he has a problem and/or we have a problem."

"Policeman of the Year," Mary-Forge thought outloud. "Why don't you just leave."

"The county will pay for any damage," the deputy said. "I might add the county pays for Doctor Rollo. It's all part of the new police. I tell you all this as part of our Operation Candor, which is part of Upward Bound, the new police image we work at. You are a taxpayer and entitled to know. I want to add personal that we are sorry about your eviction. You wouldn't be interested in two tickets to the Deputies' Ball?"

"No."

"I understand," he said. "Is them wolves?"

"Coyotes."

"Much obliged," he said, and he handed her an eviction notice and quit. "Much obliged," he said, and he stepped out into the shallow rising water.

Mary-Forge closed the door and said, "William, you will be pleased to learn, William, that our first gentleman caller was the Policeman of the Year."

And the coyotes wailed again that long shrieking bay, the howl without end, because when one coyote finished, another had recommenced, so that the liquid tremulous bay was continuous, became recapitulant; and whether it was an atavistic howl at the awful New Mexican ambience and terror of sundown, the coyotes answering that final silent color shriek in the sky, or some primordial coyote knowledge and complaint at the water that rose as the sun fell—none knew. None knew again, none whether the yip yip yip that followed, that chased and devoured the wail, the bay, was a precursor of a new era following and chasing the old, devouring the old, or some mere complaint against timeless injustice, a caterwaul against time and the whole damn universe, the chaos of ordained order as the coyote sees, feels, and sings it to the last explosion of a dying day. The dying night and day of the emissary of peace and justice in our time—any time—the Policeman of the Year. The coyotes quit.

"Let's not be ironic," Mary-Forge said. "Let's just stand at the window with the coyotes and feast the last sunset. We'll celebrate the last sunset within," she said. And then she said, "Some Indian must have come in while we were talking and took the TV part. It must have been an Indian because I sensed no one."

"The stealthy savage?"

"Oh yes."

18

As the land of the Indians disappeared, the city-yellow-stucco apartment high rise for the Indians rose. The city-yellow-stucco-Indian building. The whites called it The Residence of the Chiefs. The Indians called it The Prison. When the Chiefs' Residence for the displaced Indians was dedicated with all solemn panoply and decorum with everyone watching, some on distant hills with binoculars, the Governor pulled the switch, the audience leaned forward, and the building collapsed, fell down. The Chiefs' Residence dissolved in rubble and dust. "Now if everyone will lean back again," the Governor said. The audience leaned backward, expecting the building to rise, but it didn't. "You cain't win 'em all," the Governor said.

Bull Who Looks Up had finished his myth.

"I don't think your vision is funny," the Medicine Man said. "Must an Indian make a joke of everything?"

"It is our only protection."

"Today we have no protection," the Medicine Man said. "The Indian humor, the last weapon against the white man's disease, no longer works. The problem is even worse than you imagine. I have seen the apartment house they have for us in the city in the slum, a place the black man will accept from the white man but the red man will not.

"Then where do we go?"

"There is no place to go."

"Then we—"

"Stay," the Medicine Man said.

"Under water?"

"Who knows?" the Medicine Man said. "Bring me Tom Charlie."

At the dam site, everyone in the United States who was anyone in New Mexico was present. All the very important people were here for the grand opening of the dam. The Governor was here in tails. The President of the United States was here. The Governor of Texas was here. The Governor of California was here. The Governor of California was carrying a small sign advertising Disneyland, which is a parlor of entertainment in California. The wife of the President of the United States was carrying a large sign of fat around her belly, which is not an entertainment parlor in Washington. She carried a dog, too. The dog with its charm had helped win the last election and listened carefully and bit people.

The Governor of California, who had played bit parts in film and vaudeville and was planning to run for President of the United States, asked his wife if she wanted to put his speech in an envelope and mail it off to posterity or read it first.

"Just give the speech," she said.

The Governor of California began by thanking everyone, particularly the Indians. He said that we tend to forget the Indians, but that the Indian never forgets us in his heart of hearts. And he stared at the huge flower-piled gift in front of him. Then the Governor of California set aside the manuscript and said, "Thank you." There was some applause. The Governor of California had discovered in his film career that people enjoyed a cliff-hanger. No one was listening, anyway, excepting the President's dog, who barked and bit someone. The Vice-President got up and thanked all the contractors on the dam for contributing to his golf course.

"Is that what they're really saying?" an Apache from the Jicarilla said.

"Not exactly, but it must be close," his Apache-translator friend said.

The Secretary of State helicoptered in, embraced the President, and helicoptered out.

The President of the United States—his flat and plastic face spattered with the sweat of fear but unvexed by the troublings of principle and unmarked by the pettiness of morality—limped up and stood in back of the flower-piled gift and read this from his notes: "4 score and 7 years ago are 4 fathers floundered upon this continent a new nashion conseeved and deadikated to the proposition of exterminating the Indians. We now meat upon the battelground of this dam to decide weather this dam or any dam is worth a—"

The good pastor Billy Graham stood up, said "God bless," and then the President continued, "My Secretary of Labor—Mr. If— has informed me that there is cheap labor here. My Secretary of the Interior—Mr. And—has informed me that there is oil here. And Mr. Butz—my Secretary of Agriculture—has informed me that there is corn here. I want to make it perfectly clear I do not intend to ignore If, And, and Butz. But we shall not press down upon the brow of the red man the 👑 of thorns. We shall not crucify mankind on the ☩ of gold, and so forth."

"Is that what they're really saying?" an Apache from the Jicarilla said.

"Not exactly, but it must be close," his Apache-translator friend said.

"When are they going to give out the free beer?"

"There will be no free beer. This is a solemn occasion "

"Exclusively for the people in California?"

"Yes."

"How do you no?"

"It's not 'no,' it's 'know,' " the Apache translator said.

"How do you no I can't spell?"

"Because you haven't understood a word that's gone on here today."

No one had, but for the Indian to make the dam dedication a tragi-comedy was an attempt to survive this obscene disaster.

Actually, the potentates of government behaved with very proper decorum and gave proper speeches, then they pulled the switch which sent the past of New Mexico to the future of California.

"Do you know," the Apache translator said, "you don't even know what a coffer dam is."

"What is a coffer dam?"

"It is an enclosure you build around a ship that has sunk so you can try to fix it."

"What has that got to do with anything?"

"Nothing," the Apache translator said. "Nothing has anything to do with anything. That is the message for today. That is the end of the Checkerboard. Don't you realize the whites just buried the Checkerboard?"

"But there is nothing I can do."

"Nothing anyone, any Indian, can do, excepting Tom Charlie."

19

Thomas Charles was seated in his hogan listening to the dam-dedication ceremonies on a battery radio and in his mind's eye watching his gift on the speakers' platform, which was all cocked and ready to go. He had the remote channel selector on his lap that would select a program that would astonish the earth. Everything was all cocked and ready to go. About halfway through the speech by the Governor of Texas, Kills The Enemy had come up to him, stuck a concealed gun in his back, and said, "We must go."

Kills The Enemy brought Thomas Charles into the Learning Hogan, and the Medicine Man was there. Everyone was there. The Medicine Man sat at the table in front of everyone. Tom Charlie and Kills The Enemy sat down between everyone and the Medicine Man. Their seats were separated from the group of Indians.

"We have decided," the Medicine Man said, "that Thomas Charles is the enemy. Do you understand that, Tom Charlie?"

"No."

"Everyone was hoping that you would," the Medicine Man said quietly.

"Everyone was wrong," Tom Charlie said in a voice even lower than the Medicine Man's.

In the Checkerboard Clan no one had ever been told this before—that everyone was wrong. A low wave of shock traveled through the crowd of Indians.

"We have nothing against you, Tom Charlie," the Medicine Man said. "It is Thomas Charles we want to bury."

"How are you going to do that?" Tom Charlie said

"We do not know this yet," the Medicine Man said, "but what we do know is that your gift would kill many Tom Charlies as well as many Thomas Charleses. This we cannot allow. There is no hope or purpose in life by imitating the others' way."

"I put a lifetime of work on the gift."

"You have wasted your life," the Medicine Man said.

"But why did you take so long—"

"Because we did not think the gift would work," Lucy-Lucy said.

"No, because we thought it would make you happy," Hosteen Tzo said.

"Because we were fascinated by the gift," Hosteen Begay said.

"And we believed that if it leaked out that we had the gift, the whites would quit and go home and behave themselves and never take the land in vain again. But we did not know the others well enough."

"We thought one side or the other could win a war," Three Shoes said.

"We were wrong," the Medicine Man said.

"When I went to the University of New Mexico to study nuclear physics," Tom Charlie said, "you said that was all right."

"We were wrong."

"When I took the job at Los Alamos you said that was all right."

"We were wrong."

"And now when you will not allow me to explode the gift—"

"We are right," the Medicine Man said.

"But it took you so long."

"It takes a long time to be right," the Medicine Man said. There was a pause and then the Medicine Man said, "No one told you to go to the university."

"No one stopped me either," Tom Charlie said.

"We are stopping you now," the Medicine Man said.

"No one is stopping me," Thomas Charles said, standing up and looking at everyone everywhere in the hogan. The hogan smelled of all the high, sharp perfume of Indian Country, the greasewood and sage, the sheep hides and Levis mixed with piñon smoke and the dim light coming through the smoke hole mixed, all mixed, with confusion and chaos between Tom Charlie and Thomas Charles.

"No one is stopping me," he said. Then he started to quit the hogan, stumbling through the mix of Indian and smell and slanting light and then he was at the Pendleton-blanket door and out and then the Medicine Man nodded to Kills The Enemy with the gun and Kills The Enemy with the gun got up and followed him out and when he got out he saw the man ahead thirty yards away and he raised the gun and fired and the man ahead continued to walk resolute. And Kills The Enemy ran now until he caught the man ahead and gave him the gun and said, "It was only a warning shot. I fired over your head. Here, take the gun," and Tom Charlie took the gun and stared at the channel selector and then stared at the gun and went into his own hogan and waited and waited for something to happen and then he thought, No one is going to stop me without killing me, and then he thought, It would be so easy to kill Thomas Charles. We are all alone. There would be no witnesses, no one would even know, it would be so easy. I could blow everyone up, or like Sings In Pretty Places, blow myself up. No you couldn't. Yes I could. No you—

And thinking, An Indian is Siamese twins and an Indian is an apple, red outside white inside, and when there is no hope or purpose to life, when even the tribe has turned against me— and then he raised the gun to his head and pulled the trigger easy. And it went off. It was so easy. And this is what was heard in the Learning Hogan and that is what was heard in the Scalp House as the water rose until soon most would be standing on islands in the sea.

20

The eagle Star with less and lesser places to light, to land, who searched wide and wider far over the no earth, over the fast-disappearing land, for some signal of life, some message from the grave of earth, but saw nothing. The now glaring sun mounted up and searched the Checkerboard, too, the estancia, the home of Star, searched the one hundred square miles of static and awful New Mexican shock of home, the wild light that had once lit up the layer-caked-in-purple-and-green-and-iron-red mesas—the big sun searched with Star for some place to light.

"You cannot," the Medicine Man said to Mary-Forge, "you cannot return to the Scalp House. The Checkerboard is finished. It is all over. This is the end of our country."

"What now?"

"We will go to another country."

"What about William?"

"All of us will go."

Now Chee Sinoginee glided up to the Learning Hogan in a red canoe. The Sings In Pretty Places rose garden was already under water excepting some blue and white roses sticking above the black water as a bouquet on the grave. All of the hogan people were standing on a rise around the summer wickiup, still debating with themselves silently their no choice whether to quit their home and save their lives or quit their home and lose what their lives were all about. Physical death can be short and without pain. Spiritual death is hurting and abides.

Hosteen Begay helped pull in the canoe through the roses.

"We are all going to another country," the Medicine Man said.

Then the people got in the big red canoe, which made the canoe ride dangerously low in the water. The overladen canoe made its way over Sings In Pretty Places, around the fast-disappearing Learning Hogan and beneath the high-tilting shadow of the wide eagle Star, with the Medicine Man paddling in the stern; funereal and stately the catafalque moved silent and awesome, so that it slid into a dream, the absence of sound almost melodramatic and loud—deathless.

The great eagle Star was gliding above black water as far as it could see. Star could see a light go on below on an island in the sea. A fire was burning on an island in the sea. The Scalp House was burning. The flames wept upward, crying into the very deep dark blue of the sky and refracting against the black water. The black water was caused by the coal seams the whites had exposed. The blue sky was caused by God and New Mexico. The fire that wept up was caused by William setting fire to the Scalp House. He did not want the Scalp House to go unremarked into that black grave. William was standing in the water now, the flames climbing around him, when he saw the red canoe coming toward him in the black water. It was laden to the gunwales with everyone. When they came up, he was standing on a petrified wood log. The log that would not burn.

"Step in, my love," Mary-Forge said.

"If I do, the canoe will sink."

"Step in, Billy. I told you love was the only gift because it's the only . . ." and she paused and touched him.

He looked at the Medicine Man, When Someone Dies He Is Remembered. The Medicine Man and all the Indians nodded yes. He stepped into the red canoe on the dark sea. The canoe began to take water. Mary-Forge was paddling now in the bow, the Medicine Man in the stern, with all the Indians in between. Mary-Forge paddled with gentle, feckless strokes because there was no direction to go. "Because it's the only gift that abides," she said from the bow. The sun was locked at noon so it gave no bearings. The great shadow of Star accompanied them. Shaded by Star, the canoe journeyed to an undiscovered country.

The red canoe had taken so much water she listed to port badly. Now the great wings above them tilted with the loaded canoe, so that the pair—the canoe and the bird—were going earthward in a sympathetic and symbiotic downward motion, the canoe sinking beneath the new ocean sea gently but firmly as a blade might enter sand, entering something not insubstantial such as the water, but something palpable such as a grave, and the great bird Star encircled on and up in a last upward glide, its wide shadow encompassing all of the nothing. Below there was only the sunken empty upturned red canoe against the black water. The wide shadow of Star leveled off; catching no updrafts from the no earth, it glided swift and steady along the surface of black water—then the bird hit.

And now we shall see and feel and must reckon to the country lost down within the dark water, down among that liquid green light, and harken too, to lost earth to lost love to mesa to butte to arroyo to barranca lost, to the hushed desert lost beneath the waves and the dancers in the Scalp House and the laughter lost, all lost now down among the roses, the garden of Sings In Pretty Places.

The dam dedicators were going home from the dam-dedication ceremonies.

"I expected some trouble, but nothing happened," the Governor of California said.

"Nothing, it was very quiet," the Governor of Texas said. "What do you suppose happened to the Indians—dead?"

But the Indians of the Checkerboard Clan, led by the Medicine Man, When Someone Dies He Is Remembered, do not believe that there is a death up there with streets of gold and angels in the big space. The Indian believes that all of everything is continuous on earth—a continuum through nature—so now again it was the time of the cactus-fruit harvest, when the Indians gather tunas, those red-ripe berries, and fruit from the cow's-tongue cactus and the beaver tail. It was the time again, too, when they would gather again the pitahaya fruit from the saguaro and the organ pipe. It was also the time again when they would gather wild piñon nuts from the high country. The Indian belief completes a circle, and life comes back on itself, so that there is a continuity in time and place and person. The Indian belief is a circle that recontinues all the rhythms and the poetry of life—so abruptly and alone and together the red canoe rode up the deep and blue river of the undiscovered country, guided by the eagle Star.

The undiscovered country is a perfect wilderness before civilization, before death—around them now a virgin continent abloom with the glory of nature, alive with quick flashing streams, a smogless sky, all the world a dance of light where all was beginning, nothing ever ended, because the undiscovered country is the delight of cold morning sunrise; it is truly the ecstasy and somber fulfillment of the human spirit in watching the sun come down red red redding all in magnificent effulgent blaze from in back of the Sangre de Cristo Mountains. The red snow-drenched mountains. The undiscovered country is the gamboling of the sheep. It is the myriad dancings of the yebechais of Blessing Way, of Healing Way.

The undiscovered country is the crisp mornings and the piñon smoke and the brother sister and peoplehood of all Indians on a July day; it is all the sweetness of infant Navajo babes in cradle boards and the way a coyote looks at you when you talk at him.

The undiscovered country is love and compassion and an inkling into the sufferings of others and the smack of lightning and the tintinnabulation of a small rain on the hogan roof and the joy in the feeling for life. The undiscovered country is not the complications of and dismay at life's problems but the ease and wonderment at life's mysteries. It is the only country that abides.

DATE DUE

PRINTED IN U.S.A.